"If Tomson Highway is a benchmark from which we can look backwards at the native contribution to literature, then Thomas King ... is, even more properly, a point from which we can look ahead. From that vantage point, the future for native literature looks bright."

The Whig-Standard (Kingston)

"A lovely book. Thomas King is off to a wonderful start."

Tony Hillerman

"Thomas King has a deft narrative touch ... Characters come to life with quick strokes, the plot flows with a variety of rhythms and everything occurs within a clever structure."

The Toronto Star

"Comical, touching and sometimes painfully realistic."

The Chronicle-Herald (Halifax)

"A light-hearted — sometimes hilarious — view from within a native community by a writer with a gift of limning personality and a sense of dialogue which can illuminate character even while demolishing syntax."

The Leader Post (Regina)

"[King] has made an impressive debut with his first novel."

The Vancouver Sun

PENGUIN BOOKS

MEDICINE RIVER

Thomas King is a native writer of Cherokee, Greek and German descent. He is currently teaching English literature at the University of Guelph in Ontario. His short stories and poems have appeared in journals in Canada and the U.S. He is the author of the children's book, *A Coyote Columbus Story*, as well as *All My Relations: An Anthology of Contemporary Canadian Native Fiction*. He has also written the film script for the CBC TV co-production of *Medicine River*. Thomas King's most recent books are *Green Grass, Running Water* and *One Good Story, That One*.

MEDICINE RIVER

THOMAS KING

Penguin Books

PENGUIN BOOKS
Published by the Penguin Group
Penguin Books Canada Ltd, 10 Alcorn Avenue, Toronto,
Ontario, Canada M4V 3B2
Penguin Books Ltd, 27 Wrights Lane, W8 5TZ, England
Penguin Books USA Inc., 375 Hudson Street, New York,
New York 10014, U.S.A.
Penguin Books Australia Ltd, Ringwood, Victoria, Australia
Penguin Books (NZ) Ltd, 182-190 Wairau Road, Auckland 10,
New Zealand

Penguin Books Ltd, Registered Offices:
Harmondsworth, Middlesex, England

First published in Viking by Penguin Books Canada Limited, 1989

Published in Penguin Books, 1991
Published in this edition, 1995

1 3 5 7 9 10 8 6 4 2

Publisher's note: This book is a work of fiction. Names, characters, places and incidents either are the product of the author's imagination or are used fictitiously, and any resemblance to actual persons living or dead, events, or locales is entirely coincidental.

Manufactured in Canada

Canadian Cataloguing in Publication Data

King, Thomas, 1943-
Medicine River

ISBN 0-14-025474-9 (trade format)

I. Title.

PS8571.I5298M44 1991   C813'.54   C90-095505-8
PR9199.3.K56M44 1991

American Library of Congress Cataloguing in Publication Data Available

For Helen, Christian and Benjamin.
Just in case.

My thanks to the Ucross Foundation, Ucross, Wyoming for the writer's residency which allowed me to complete the final draft of *Medicine River*.

MEDICINE RIVER

chapter

one

Dear Rose,
  I'll bet you never thought you'd hear from me
again. I've thought about calling or writing, but you
know how it is. How are you and the boys? Bet
they're getting big. Bet you're probably mad at me,
and I don't blame you. I'm going to be in Calgary for
a rodeo. Thought I might drop in and see you. . . .

Medicine River sat on the broad back of the prairies.
It was an unpretentious community of buildings
banked low against the weather that slid off the east-
ern face of the Rockies. Summer was hot in Medicine
River and filled with grasshoppers and mosquitoes.
Winter was cold and long. Autumn was the best season. It wasn't good, just better than the other three.
Then there was the wind. I generally tried to keep my
mouth shut about the wind in Medicine River.

   Harlen Bigbear was like the prairie wind. You
never knew when he was coming or when he was
going to leave. Most times I was happy to see him.

Today I wasn't. I had other things to do. There were photographs in the wash and three strips of negatives that had to be printed. But that didn't stop the wind from blowing, and it didn't stop Harlen.

"Hey-uh," said Harlen, which is not the way Harlen normally says hello.

"What?"

"Hey-uh . . . what do you think, Will?"

"Real busy, Harlen. Somebody in trouble?"

Harlen had a strong sense of survival, not just for himself but for other people as well. He took on a lot of weight, and the one thing he enjoyed more than helping someone out with their burden was sharing it with others. "If you pass misery around and get everyone to take a piece," Harlen liked to say, "you won't throw up from the taste of too much grief." It wasn't something I went around repeating.

"Nobody's in trouble, Will. Hey-uh . . . time I took you out to lunch. Thought we could go on over to that new place with all the posters and plants."

"Harlen, it's ten o'clock."

"Beat the crowd. Give us a chance to talk. Hey-uh, good friends should do that, you know."

Dear Rose,
Boy, you should see the weather around here. Snowed like the blazes last night. How's the weather down south? Sorry I didn't stop in. I called a couple of times, but you must have stepped out. I want to come down and see you and the boys, maybe take you out to dinner and a show. Write if you can, chick. If you have someone else, you should let me know. . . .

There was no one else in Casey's. The woman at the

counter told us that lunch hadn't started and that all
we could get was coffee or tea.

"Tea's fine. Just had breakfast. How about you,
Will? Not hungry yet, are you?"

She put us at a window table. Casey's was on the
third floor of the old Merchants' Bank Building. You
could see the Medicine River Fire Station across the
street. The fire-engines had moved to the new fire
house on Sixth Avenue, leaving the station with its
turn-of-the-century round bell tower to the pigeons
and the seagulls.

"Say," said Harlen, "what a great view. What do
you think? If we stood on the table, we could probably see the river. Reserve is just over there."

It was going to take Harlen until noon just to get to
what he wanted to tell me. The tea arrived, and
Harlen dipped the bag up and down in the pot, long
easy strokes, like he figured on staying through until
supper.

"Will, you remember Wilma Whiteman? Hey-uh,
she passed away last week."

I nodded.

"Wilma used to look after Granny Pete all those
years. You know, everybody used to leave their stuff
at Granny's house, whenever they went somewhere.
Reserve storage. Should have seen the folks come by
when Granny died. Those who were still around
picked their stuff up, and Wilma took and stored the
things that were left over."

"I remember."

"Lots of memories. Louie Frank's wife went over to
help Wilma's family. One of her girls found them, in a
cardboard box. Edith gave them to Bertha over at the
centre, and Bertha gave them to Big John, and Big
John gave them to me."

Harlen reached into a coat pocket and pulled out a package. It was a thick rectangle wrapped round with blue velvet and tied with yellow yarn.

"Letters," said Harlen, "hey-uh . . . from your father."

> *Dear Rose,*
>
> *I'm going to stop by and see you and the boys soon. Sorry you had to leave the reserve, but Calgary's a better place for a swell girl like you. Stupid rule, anyway. I'd send some money, but I'm short right now. Got to save up for a new saddle. Man's got to work, you know. Hey, could you send me a picture of the boys. Yourself, too. . . .*

I had seen the letters before. My mother used to keep them in a wooden chest in her closet. The chest was always locked, but that's what bobby pins were for. James and me had listened to countless detectives pick countless locks with bobby pins. I found the key and the bobby pins in the same drawer.

There was a box of photographs in the chest. Most of the photographs were of groups of men and women standing against the prairie and the sky. The men were tall and dark in white shirts and cowboy hats. The women wore long dresses. There were several pictures of George Harley on a horse. I recognized him. There was one of an old man with braids sitting in a straight-backed chair on the edge of a coulee. Years later, Granny Pete showed me a picture of the same man and said he was my grandfather.

My mother was in most of the pictures, and while I didn't know who the rest of the people were, I supposed they were family. There was one picture of my

mother. She had on a pleated skirt that was fanned
out like a blanket on the ground in front of her.
Kneeling behind her with his hand on her shoulder
was a man in a uniform.

> *Dear Rose,*
>
> *I got a new job with a real-estate company.*
> *Nothing to it. Beats the hell out of rodeo, and it pays*
> *better, too. Figured I'd try it for a while till my leg*
> *heals. If I like it, I may just give up the circuit and*
> *settle down. You know, my boss drives one of those*
> *big Chevrolets. You got to have money to buy one of*
> *those things.*
>
> *Thanks for the pictures of the boys. Good-looking*
> *boys. I didn't know I had such good-looking boys.*
> *Well, you had something to do with it, too, chick.*
> *Maybe you could send me one of our wedding pic-*
> *tures. . . .*

The letters were in the trunk under the photographs. I was reading them when my mother came
home.

"I didn't do anything wrong," I said. "I was just
reading."

She stood there, and I could see her hands clench
and tremble. "Those are my letters," she said.

"I was just reading."

"I don't want you in my things."

"They're from . . . my father . . . the letters."

"Just put them down. Damn! You keep out of my
things."

And she slapped me. Hard. "Stop reading those
letters! You hear me!" And she began to cry. "They're
private. You never heard of private?"

Then she slapped me again. I tried to jerk out of the way, and I scattered the letters on the floor. I lay beside the bed, my tongue clamped between my teeth to keep my lips from shaking. I remember her on her knees, crying and trying to gather up the letters and the blue velvet cloth and the yarn.

I ran past her and down the stairs.

"Will!"

I spent the rest of the day at the river. She had never hit me. Never. James found me that evening.

"You better come home. Mom's real upset. She's been crying, Will."

"Let her cry. I'll come home when I feel like it."

"She said I was supposed to bring you home."

"Tell her you couldn't find me."

"What'd you do to get her so mad?"

"I just read some of her dumb old letters."

We ate dinner in silence that night, my mother, my brother and me. Afterwards, she took me into her bedroom. "I don't want you ever to go in my chest again. Those things in there are mine. Do you understand?"

I didn't say anything. I kept my eyes on the yellow throw rug beside the bed.

"I don't want you reading those things."

I could feel my lip begin to shake. "I don't see what's so wrong," I said. "The letters were to me and James, too. They're not just yours!"

My mother sat on the edge of the bed for a long time. I knew I was to sit there, not move. And I did. I thought she was going to hit me again for talking back like that, but she didn't.

"Do I have to burn them?" she said very quietly, almost a whisper. Her eyes were hard, and her face didn't move. "Do I have to burn them before you'll leave my things alone? Is that what I have to do?"

"Those are my letters, too."

"Go to bed," she said, in that same quiet voice. "Just go to bed."

I ran home from school the next day. The letters were still there. I opened the blue velvet wrap just to make sure. Then I got some tape from the kitchen and taped them to the bottom of the chest.

Dear Rose,

Merry Christmas. I would have sent a cheque, but real estate sort of drops off round Christmas. The leg is one hundred percent. Soon as the season comes around, I may do a little rodeo on the weekends just to keep in shape.

How old are the boys now? Maybe I could come on down and visit. I could take the boys out for the day and give you a break. I bought one of those musical tops at Zellers. You think the boys would like it? I think about you and the boys. They've probably forgotten me by now. . . .

"You ever see your father rodeo, Will?"

"No, he took off when I was about four."

"He and George Harley were good friends. George says your father was a real good bronc rider." Harlen looked out the window towards the river. "You know, it was Harley introduced your mother to your father. Caught hell for it too, from Granny Pete."

"Harlen, I don't even remember what my father looked like."

"George says he was real good."

I must have seen my father, heard his voice. But there was nothing. No vague recollections, no stories, no impressions, nothing. He was from Edmonton. I knew that. Granny Pete blamed George for the marriage, because he got them together and stood up as best man at the wedding. "Damn bottle Indian," she said. "Just got to show off his relations to whites. No more sense than a horseshoe."

But George was only trying to be polite. Years later he told me, "Your mother was real pretty, and Bob just wanted to meet her, so I said okay. Granny was awful mad with me, especially when they got married. I didn't know they'd do that. Your mother had a mind of her own."

We grew up in Calgary, James and me. Granny Pete came over by bus every month or so, but none of my mother's brothers ever came by. Granny talked about the rest of the family, so James and me knew we had relations. We knew about Uncle Tony and Uncle Rupert and Uncle Frank, but I never met them until the day my mother came home from work and began packing. "Get your things together," she said. "We're going home."

My uncles all showed up the next day in their trucks to help us move. They shook hands with James and me and talked like we had never been away. "You're the man of the house, Will," Uncle Frank said, and he offered me a cigarette. "Look after your mother and brother. You got to do that now."

"I can look after Mom, too," said James.

"Bet you can," said Uncle Frank.

We didn't have much, and Uncle Tony's pick-up went back empty, except for me and James and Uncle Tony's boy, Maxwell. The three of us rode in the back wrapped up in a tarp.

"We going back to the reserve?" James asked.

"Maybe," I said.

"No," said Maxwell, "you can't. You guys have to live in town cause you're not Indian any more."

"Sure we are," I said. "Same as you."

"Your mother married a white."

"Our father's dead."

"Doesn't matter."

I could feel my face get hot. "We can go to the reserve whenever we want. We can get in a car and go right out to Standoff."

"Sure," said Maxwell. "You can do that. But you can't stay. It's the law."

I pulled the tarp around me and told myself that we *were* going back to the reserve. But I guess I wasn't surprised when we stopped at Medicine River. It wasn't so much the law as it was pride, I think, that let my mother go as far as the town and no farther.

Dear Rose,

Things are going swell up here. How about you? I called the post office, and they've put a trace on that top I sent. Boy, doesn't the mail drive you nuts. They're always losing things. If they can't find it, I'll try to buy another one. It was a red one with those cute animals along the side. It had a real nice sound, too. I've got some bills to pay off first, so it may have to wait a bit. Hope the boys had a good Christmas. I sure miss you all. . . .

"Hey-uh, Will. Your mother must have loved him. Keeping all those letters."

"The guy was a jerk, Harlen. I don't know why she kept the letters."

"Hey-uh. Maybe you should go see him," said Harlen. "Maybe take him out to dinner."

"He's dead. He died in a car accident. He was drunk."

Harlen poured some more hot water in his cup. "Too bad that. He wrote a good letter. Bertha said they made her cry."

"Bertha read these?"

"You know Bertha."

"Shit."

"She didn't mean any harm, Will. She says your father loved your mother a lot."

"Had a damn funny way of showing it."

"Hey-uh. Maybe he was just young. Hey-uh. What do you think, Will?"

"About what?"

"*Hey-uh*. Saw Will Sampson on television. It was a movie about him being a sheriff. That's what he said all the time. *Hey-uh*. He's a real Indian, too. What do you think?"

I couldn't help it. I started to laugh. "Harlen," I said, "it sounds dumb as hell."

"Hey-uh," said Harlen, loud enough for the cooks in the kitchen to hear, and he began to laugh, too. The two of us sat there laughing.

As we walked out of Casey's, Harlen handed me the letters. "You should read them, Will. Your mother must have kept them for you and James."

Harlen stood there with the packet of letters in his hand. The velvet had cracked at the edges, and the yellow yarn had lost most of its colour. And I remembered the picture of the two of them. My mother with her dark hair and dark eyes, the pleated skirt spread all around her. She was looking back, not turned quite far enough to see the man behind her. His hand lay on her shoulder lightly, the fingers in sunlight, his eyes in shadows.

chapter

two

Harlen Bigbear was my friend, and being Harlen's friend was hard. I can tell you that.

Just before Christmas, Harlen came by my studio wearing a basketball jersey pulled tight over his plaid jacket and carrying a brown grocery bag. "Morning, Will," he said. "Wind's coming up. Good thing, too. Cold as hell. You remember Wilton Joe?"

"At the Friendship Centre?"

"That's right. He used to coach the team."

The jersey was bright blue and there was an orange number seven on the front. "So," I said, "what's in the bag?"

"Wilton left. Martha Bruised Head called around to find another coach, but nobody wanted to do it. So I said I would."

"So, what's in the bag?"

"Your uniform, Will." And Harlen opened the bag and took out a blue jersey just like the one he was wearing, orange shorts, and a pair of white socks with two yellow stripes around the top. "Medicine

River Friendship Centre Warriors," he said. "All-Native team, Will, and we need a centre. You know Clyde Whiteman?"

I shook my head.

"Great player, Will. He can jump. Slam-dunk the ball. Quick as a Cree. Boy, you ought to see him play. Probably the best centre in all of Alberta."

"Then you don't need me."

"Clyde can't play right now. We need a centre. Someone big, like you. Be a lot of fun. You got a talent for it. I can tell."

Every person born has a talent. My mother used to tell me that. Some people have three or four, but everybody has at least one. Sometimes a talent is hidden, and other times you can just look at someone and see it as if it were stuck up there on their forehead. Granny Pete liked to say that my father had a talent for lying and drinking, but that wasn't what my mother meant when she was talking talents. Talents were good, things you did well, things you could be proud of.

My brother James had all the talent in our family. He could draw any animal you wanted: moose, bears, tigers, giraffes. Sometimes I'd watch him to see how he did it. He'd draw a line and then another. It never looked like much, and then there was the lion, just like magic. James kept the drawings in a shirt box under his bed, and whenever Granny Pete would come over, he would bring them out and show them to her one by one.

"Them beavers look like they're alive.

"Look at that antelope!

"Not even your Uncle Tony draws elk this good."

I tried drawing too, but it was useless. My lines were stiff and crude. James tried to help me, but I just couldn't see what he saw.

"Will's the athlete in the family," my mother said. "James is the artist."

I played basketball. Mr. Bobniak, who taught math and coached basketball, told me he could see that I had a talent for the game, that I owed it to the school to come out for the team. I told my mother what Bobniak had said, and she went out the next Sunday and came back with a pair of black canvas high-tops she had found at a yard sale. They were almost brand new. And they fit. Damn, they were good shoes. I put them on, tied them down tight and jumped up and down on my bed. Shoes like that helped you jump higher, run faster. And you never got tired.

I wasn't very good, but Bobniak promised me that I'd get better. A little more time, a little more practice. Fact is, I got worse. By my fourth year, the guards and the forwards stopped trying to feed me the ball inside and took their shots from the perimeter. I was left to grab rebounds and block shots. The last four games of the season, we played a three-guard, two-forward offence, and I spent most of that final year watching the games from the bench. I was big and I was tall, and that was it.

"Harlen," I said, "I can't play basketball worth shit."

Harlen laid the jersey on the table and smoothed the shorts out next to it. "Number four, Will. That's a sacred number. Lucky, too. Person always looks better in a basketball uniform. Team needs you. You don't have to be real good, Will. You can get those rebounds, you know. Use your weight. Intimidate those little guards. Block some shots. You must have played ball in Calgary."

I said no. No time. No interest. No energy. No shoes. I said my knees were gone. I said I was too old.

"Hey, Will, forty's not too old. A few work-outs, and you'll be fine. I can get you a discount on shoes at Bill's Sports. Women love basketball players, Will. You know Louise Heavyman comes to most of our games. So does Thelma Simpson and her cousin Rosemary. You know Rosemary?"

It wasn't the flattery as much as it was the memories and the guilt.

"Make a comeback, Will. Be a star," said Harlen, holding the jersey against his chest. "You know what they say about basketball players."

So I said yes and somehow I managed to compound the original injury, adding the embarrassments of middle age to those of adolescence. But Harlen was good to me. I missed easy shots, fumbled rebounds, dribbled the ball out of bounds, and Harlen sat on the bench, twisted his towel and yelled encouragement.

"Next time, Will.

"Way to move the ball.

"Nice try.

"No sweat, we'll get it back."

We had a good team. Elwood and Floyd had played a little college ball, and Frankie and Leroy had been starters up in Edmonton. Most weekends during the fall, we'd travel around to the money tournaments. We'd drive out to Gladstone Hall on the reserve or up to Siksika or Gleichen or Hobbema. Sometimes we'd drop across the line and play some of the reserve teams around Great Falls or Browning or Missoula. Friday nights, we generally won. Floyd would put in those jump shots of his, and Elwood would muscle in on the boards. But after the game, the boys would go out to a bar and drink until closing. We generally lost our early game on Saturday, and the afternoon game wasn't much

better. The championship game was played on the
Sunday, and by then, most of the time, we were driving home.

One Sunday, as we were coming back from a tournament in Browning, Harlen pulled the van to the
side of the road.

"Come on, boys, hop out. I want you to see something."

There wasn't much to see, just the river and the
prairies stretched out gold and rolling. Harlen stood
with his back to the wind. It blew his hair out into a
spiked fan. He looked like a thistle.

"You boys don't try hard enough," Harlen began,
which was the way he always began when he was
going to give us one of his coach's talks.

"Christ, Harlen," said Floyd, "it's cold and blowing
like hell."

"You boys look around you," Harlen shouted,
ignoring Floyd and the wind. "What do you see? Go
on, look around. Where are you? What are you standing on?"

Elwood and Floyd looked down. "Looks like a
road to me," said Floyd. "What about you, Elwood?"

"That's why you miss them jump shots. That's why
you get drunk on Friday night and can hardly get
your shoes tied on Saturday. That's why we lose
those games when we should be winning . . .
cause you don't know where you are."

"Couldn't we do this next week?" Floyd and
Elwood and Leroy jammed their hands in their pockets and began to walk around to stay warm.

"You're standing on Mother Earth." Harlen looked
at Floyd hard. "That's right, go ahead and smile."
Harlen gestured with his chin. "You see what's over
there?"

"Give us a hint," Floyd said, under his breath.

"Ninastiko."

You could see Chief Mountain clearly, its top chiselled back at a slant, its sides rising straight off the prairie floor. There were no clouds, just the Rockies, and above them, the sky. The wind was gusting, strong. Harlen rocked back and forth as he talked. We stood there, our heads pulled down, our eyes closed to slits, and we slowly turned away from the wind and Harlen and the mountain.

James's best drawing was an eagle, its wings spread, riding the wind. It was my favourite. Henry Goodrider who lived on the floor below us figured he could draw as well as James. "Anybody can do that stuff. Nothing to it," he said.

"You ought to see the rhino James did."

"Nothing to it."

"I'll bet you've never seen an eagle like the one James drew."

"Bet you can't draw at all."

"I'm not an artist. I'm an athlete."

"Hear all you play is the end of the bench."

"Hear all you can draw is flies."

Henry and me were always talking like that. Just fun. And to tell the truth, Henry was a pretty good artist. He didn't draw pictures like James. His were more cartoon characters with big noses, bushy eyebrows and huge bellies. Most of them had cigars sticking out of their mouths and stuff dripping out of their noses. Henry drew them in chalk on the basement floor and the walls by the washers and dryer.

"Who cares about drawing eagles?" Henry would say.

Henry was up in our apartment one day, and he

saw one of James's drawings on the refrigerator.
"Hey," said Henry, "what's this one supposed to be?"

"It's an elephant. Anyone can see that."

"Looks like a big, grey turd."

"You must be blind."

"Know a turd when I see one."

I knew where James kept his drawings. I got the
box and put it on the kitchen table.

"You want to see some real art?" I said.

Henry looked at all the drawings, and when he
was done, he said, "Your brother draws okay, draws
better than you play basketball. But you know, there's
still something missing." And then he grinned at me
and pulled out his pen.

I was in the darkroom on Monday when Harlen came
by. I could hear him prowling about just outside the
door. "Will, I got to talk to you."

We had had these talks before. I put the prints in
the wash, turned on the lights and opened the door.
Harlen was leaning against the frame. "What am I
going to do with those boys, Will?"

"They're just young."

"We could have a good team, you know. We've got
talent. You know what we need?"

At the first of the season, we needed new uniforms,
something to give us pride. After the first three losses, we needed to be in better shape. The last time
Harlen had dropped by to talk to me, we needed dis-
cipline.

"What we need, Will, is a leader. Someone the boys
respect. Someone with maturity."

"You got someone in mind?" I don't know why I
thought Harlen was talking about me.

"Me," said Harlen. "I'm going to have to play. Used to be a good athlete. Need the exercise anyway. Set a good example for the boys. Team drinks too much."

"I don't drink."

"Course you don't, Will. You're too old for that. You know better. It's those young boys I'm worried about."

"I'm not old."

When Harlen came to practice that night, he had on a red T-shirt that said Indian Power. He looked taller in shorts.

"Where'd you get the shoes?" asked Elwood.

"Antique store," said Floyd. "Must of had a sale."

"Ten laps around the gym," said Harlen. "Come on, we got to get in shape."

Harlen took off, and the rest of us hung on his tail. Most of the boys could have passed him at any time, but the pace was comfortable, and all of us were content to let him lead. By the eighth lap, he was struggling. The back of his shirt was dark with sweat, and the old black canvas high-tops were smacking the floor, all the spring gone out of his legs.

Floyd ran alongside me and motioned towards Harlen. "A beer says he doesn't last the night."

Harlen was horrible. His jump shot was a brick. His hook shot, which he liked to shoot from twenty-five feet out, reminded me of John Wayne throwing hand grenades. He had a set shot from half-court that occasionally went in. But he ran and he jumped and he sweated with the rest of us, and Floyd bought the beer.

"He's just trying to compensate." Floyd signalled to the waitress for another beer. "He can't dance any more, so he figures to make his name in basketball."

"Harlen doesn't dance."

"Used to. Harlen was one hell of a dancer. Won all sorts of prizes at the powwows. Used to hoop dance, too . . . exhibition. Elwood's auntie says that there was no one could work those hoops like Harlen."

"Hoop dancer, huh?"

"Back when he was young. But he don't do it any more. One night at Gladstone, he was giving an exhibition. He'd had a little to drink, and half-way through, he fell. Hard."

"Did he get hurt?"

"Hurt his foot, but mostly it was his pride. That's why he's always trying to compensate."

"Harlen's not trying to compensate."

"All you old guys are trying to recapture the past. You knew Pete Johnson, didn't you?"

"Rodeo?"

"Yeah. Got busted up by a bull in Calgary. Couldn't rodeo any more, so he took up stock-car driving."

"So?"

"So, he killed himself. Couldn't rodeo, wasn't much of a stock-car driver. One night he just drove his truck off Snake Coulee."

"Floyd, I saw Pete last week."

"What? . . . Oh, yeah . . . I remember now, it wasn't Pete, it was Jimmy Bruised Head."

"Jimmy's in law school."

"Well, you get the picture. Harlen's trying to compensate, make up for that mistake with the hoops. He made a fool of himself that night, and he's going to make a fool of himself again. First game we play, you watch."

That Friday, we drove out to Siksika. We had the six-o'clock game.

"Will, need to talk to you for a minute." Harlen

walked over to the bench. "I been thinking, and I figure I won't start you tonight. Save your legs the first
game. Keep you fresh for Saturday."

"I don't mind. I feel good."

"It's nothing like that, Will. You'll get to play. Just
want to try a few new things."

Harlen started in my place. I got to play the last
two minutes of the first half, and that was it. We won.
Floyd put in thirty-two points. Harlen didn't make a
fool of himself. He played well and even scored six
points—two half-court set shots and one John Wayne
hook. I generally scored eight points. But there it
was—my past. The same solicitous tone, the same
concern. Mr. Bobniak had said much the same thing
in much the same way when he put me on the bench.

We showered, talked about the game as we
dressed. Harlen reminded the boys not to get drunk,
that we had a big game tomorrow. I was standing at a
locker when Harlen came by and swatted me with a
towel. "Good game, Will. Hell of a move on the base
line."

I had brought my own car. I finished dressing,
threw my uniform in the team bag and left. It was a
two-hour drive back to Medicine River. I turned the
radio on and rolled back the sun roof to let the night
in. The moon was out, and you could see Ninastiko
standing alone against the Rockies.

James found the drawings right away and showed
Mom.

"Henry did that," I said. "I tried to stop him, but I
couldn't."

My mother shook her head. "You're the oldest,
Will. You should look after James."

"I can look after myself," said James.

The next day, James went down to Mr. Pugh's butcher shop and got a long piece of brown paper. He drew another eagle on that paper and hung it out our bedroom window. I helped him tape it to the ledge.

"I can make them as big as I want," he said. "And I can draw eagles over and over again."

"This will show Henry, all right," I said.

The eagle hung on the side of the building until the rain and the wind tore it apart, and there was nothing left but the tape and shreds of brown paper.

I figured that Harlen would come by on Monday. I had all my lines rehearsed. Harlen came by on Tuesday. He looked shorter draped over the crutches.

"What happened?"

"Twisted my ankle pretty bad, Will. Went after a rebound and landed on someone's foot. Hurts like hell. Elwood had to drive the van home."

"How'd the team do?"

"Lost Saturday's games. Close scores though. Could have used you, Will."

I tried smiling. "Had to come back . . . forgot about it, the photographs. Couldn't stay if I wanted. You'd already gone. I left a message with Buster . . . you know . . . at the registration desk. Didn't you get it?" Lies are hard things to smile through.

Harlen smiled back and shifted his weight. "Figured it was something like that. Floyd said you left because you were mad I didn't play you more."

I shook my head.

"You know, after the game, Louise Heavyman came over and asked where you were. Good-looking woman, Louise."

"Sure."

"I must be getting old, Will." Harlen leaned over the crutches. "I haven't hurt this ankle since high school."

"Dancing?"

"What?"

Harlen's face was a blank. I was still angry. Playing dumb wasn't going to help. I wanted a piece of him.

"You know, that night at Gladstone Hall, hoop dancing, wasn't it? You fell and hurt your foot."

Harlen's face tensed up, and he shifted around on the crutches. It was a cheap shot.

"Dancing? Hell, I'm a horrible dancer, Will. Hurt the ankle playing basketball. My cousin Billy, he's the dancer in the family."

"Billy?"

"Yeah, real good, too. Funny you know about that. Happened . . . damn, happened years ago. Just bad luck. Billy stepped on a hoop and went down hard. Real embarrassing. Hurt his arm, but that wasn't the worst of it. You know Thelma Simpson? Billy drove her out to Snake Coulee that night . . . a little romancing. Well, Thelma got mad, pushed him out of the truck and drove off. And it was February. Billy almost froze to death."

"Damn it, Floyd . . ." I caught myself saying it out loud.

"Floyd's okay," said Harlen. "He's got a great jump shot."

It served me right, it damn well served me right. I wanted to laugh.

Harlen laughed instead. "Floyd bet me a beer you were quitting the team. How I love those easy beers."

I looked at him, standing there on his crutches. "Look, I appreciate your coming by to talk me into staying with the team."

Harlen raised his hand and shook his head. "Serious now, Will. I came to talk to you about the team. Team gives the boys something to belong to, something they can be proud of. The boys look up to you, Will. Like a brother. Floyd said it wasn't the same, driving into the key and not seeing you standing there under the basket."

"That's about all I do."

"You give the boys confidence, Will. They got respect for you, and we got a good team. We can win the league championship. You know what the team needs?"

What the team needed, Harlen said, was a better grasp of the basics. He was going to bring some folding chairs down to the gym, so we could practise dribbling around them. He'd also bought some record on how to be a successful coach. It came with a book of plays and a poster of Bobby Knight.

I knew what the team really needed. A new centre. Someone young, fast, good hands, strong jumper. But I wasn't going to tell Harlen that. Not yet, anyway.

I had expected James to be angry about his drawings, but all he talked about was the eagle and how he was going to do a whale next. The eagle looked great hanging out the window. You could see it all the way down the block. Even Henry said it looked good.

"James say anything to you?"

"Nope."

"Figured he'd be angry."

"He didn't mind. He thought it was funny."

"If my brother did that to me, I'd stuff his face in the trash."

"I didn't do anything. You did."

"Hey, you helped, Will. You drew the cigar on the

eagle and that stupid hat on the buffalo, too."

"It was just a joke."

The rain came first and soaked the butcher's paper and plastered it to the side of the building. The wind came a few days later and tore the drawing loose. Some of the ink bled through, and for a long time after, you could see a faint outline of the eagle in the brick. James could draw. He really could.

I caught up with Floyd at the American Hotel a couple of days later. He was having a beer with Elwood.

"Hey, Will," said Floyd, and he pulled out a chair for me, "don't see you in here much. Sit down. You seen Harlen? Really twisted that ankle. Christ, it looked like a purple grapefruit."

I was still looking for a piece of someone. "Great hoop dancer, huh? Trying to compensate, huh?" Chewing on Floyd was going to make me feel better. "Why don't we talk about Harlen's cousin Billy?"

"Billy?" Floyd looked at Elwood and then back at me. "Harlen doesn't have a cousin Billy."

chapter

three

"You know," said Harlen, "they got people who get paid for figuring out ways of breaking things down into little pieces."

Harlen always talked like this around tax time.

"Categories, that's what they call them."

Harlen would spend a good month musing about the wonders of taxes, and then he would take his T4s over to Louise Heavyman.

"They got names for those categories that I can't even pronounce. You know why they do that, Will?"

I took my tax forms to Louise too. Neither of us could be trusted with the mysteries of simple addition.

"Bank called me up, Will. Said I was overdrawn again. You know, they must have made a mistake."

Before Louise opened her own office in Medicine River, Harlen and I took our tax business to Jerry Peterson. Jerry ran a finance company, but he did taxes on the side, when the loan business slowed down just after Christmas.

"You ever read any of those brochures Jerry used to give us, Will? One of them said I should be making a thousand dollars for every year I've been alive."

Jerry gave out free pens in plastic wrappers.

"You know, I really liked those pens. I told Louise she should give out pens too."

"What did she say?"

"You know Louise."

Jerry liked to get paid at the same time he did your taxes. "Not good business giving out credit," Jerry told Harlen once. "It'll just lower your self-esteem." And then he'd give you a pen.

Louise wanted to be paid at the same time she did our taxes, too. But she wasn't worried about our self-esteem.

"I've got rent to pay. I can't be spending my time chasing out to the reserve or tracking you guys down."

Harlen, who sees the good in everyone and is always trying to help, told her that he really didn't mind her not giving out pens, but that now that she was a successful businesswoman, she should think about getting married.

"What did she say to that?"

"She said she'd consider it."

Which wasn't exactly what Louise had said. Elwood had been there with Harlen.

"Should have heard her laugh," Elwood told me. "Big tears in her eyes. Had to blow her nose six or seven times."

Louise had never been married.

"Real smart though, Will," said Harlen. "Even in boarding school, she was real smart. Has a great sense of humour. Good personality, too. What do you think?"

I liked Louise, and I told Harlen I liked her, but that wasn't what Harlen meant.

"Good-looking woman, Will. Strong hips. You know, for children. Tall, too. Always good to have a tall woman."

Harlen and I had had this conversation before. "You must be forty or so, Will. Don't look it, though. You're a handsome man, good job. Good teeth. Good personality, too. You ever think about getting married?" Then he would drop hints about the way a life should be lived.

"A man's not complete until he has a woman by his side.

"Nothing more important than the family.

"A son of yours would probably be a sports star of some sort.

"Beats the hell out of eating your own cooking."

I didn't mind. Harlen meant well.

"Seeing a man live alone is sad, Will. You get all drawn out and grey and wrinkled. Look at Sam Belly."

"Sam's over ninety."

"And he's not married."

"Sam was married for over fifty years, Harlen."

"Course he was. Wouldn't have lived this long without a good woman. But do you think he'll live another ten years?"

Every so often, to keep these conversations from being one-sided, I'd throw out a few statistics of my own.

"You know, Harlen, I was reading an article on marriages, and it said that at least fifty percent of marriages end in divorce."

"Hell, Will. If you could get odds like that in Vegas, you'd be rich."

That was Harlen.

Harlen kept up on all the gossip. Nothing happened on the reserve or in town that Harlen didn't know about. When he stopped by the studio on Wednesday, I could see he had something big on his mind. He was smiling inside, and it was leaking out the sides of his mouth and his ears.

"Morning, Will." And he helped himself to a chair.

I had a stack of order forms in front of me, and with any luck, I figured I could get through them before Harlen got around to what he wanted to say.

"Morning, Harlen."

"Nice day outside, Will. You remember Louise Heavyman?"

"She did our taxes last month."

"That's the one."

The corners of Harlen's mouth started bending up, and his head began bobbing up and down like a turkey's.

"You know, Will, I don't really mind that Louise doesn't give out free pens."

"Hmmmmmmm."

"Those pens Jerry gave out never did work too well, you know."

"Hmmmmmmm."

"A couple of them leaked all over my shirt. Skipped a lot, too."

"Hmmmmmmm."

"And the colours . . . black and yellow . . . looked like you had a shiny bumblebee stuck in your pocket."

"Hmmmmmmm."

"The next time I see Louise, I should tell her that."

"Hmmmmmmm."

"What do you think, Will? You think she'll invite

us to her wedding?"

"Who?"

"Louise."

"What wedding?"

Harlen looked all around the room. "Louise is probably getting married."

You never knew just how far Harlen's *probables* were from *actuals*, and most of the time, neither did Harlen.

"That was pretty sudden."

"Fellow from Edmonton. Leroy and Floyd saw them at Casey's. Leroy says that they both sat on the same side of the table."

"When's the wedding?"

"Leroy says he thinks the guy is Cree."

"When's the wedding?"

"Probably soon. You don't sit on the same side of the table unless it's serious."

For the next month, Harlen brought me all the new information about Louise and her boyfriend.

"Should have seen them, Will. Walking hand in hand. Daylight, too.

"Rita Blackplume saw them at the movies . . . off in a corner by themselves.

"His name is Harold. Drives a Buick. Comes down from Edmonton every weekend. Floyd saw his car in front of Louise's place . . . all night."

After the second month or so, Louise and her boyfriend slipped into third place behind Mary Rabbit's divorce and Elgin and Billy Turnbull's driving their father's truck off the Minor Street Bridge into the river. Elgin broke his arm. Billy put his head into the windshield and broke his big toe. Louise and her boyfriend were interesting, but Harlen was intrigued by Billy's toe.

"Can't figure how he did that, Will. Broke his toe. Can you figure that? Hit his head and broke his toe."

Billy's toe healed, and Elgin's arm was out of the cast in two months. And Louise didn't get married. Harlen called me at two in the morning to tell me that.

"Will, you awake?"

"Harlen?"

"Will, wake up. It's important."

"Harlen, it's the middle of the night."

"Louise isn't getting married, Will. Betty over at the hospital told Doreen that Louise and her boyfriend broke up about three weeks ago, and Doreen called me. You awake?"

"I'm in bed."

"Will, Louise is pregnant. I'll be by in ten minutes."

"Harlen . . ."

"Okay, twenty."

I was in the bathroom brushing my teeth, when Harlen let himself in.

"Coffee on, Will?"

Louise was pregnant all right. Betty at the hospital had seen the results of the tests. About two months along.

"Louise told Betty she had planned it this way. Said she wanted a baby, but didn't want to get married. That's Louise, isn't it?"

"She's a strong woman."

"No, I mean the front. You know, Will, lying like that, so everyone will think you're okay."

"You think . . ."

"Sure. She's all alone. Made a mistake. Scared to death. Family will probably disown her. Probably lose all her friends."

"What about the boyfriend?"

"He's Cree, Will." And Harlen held his arms out and shook his head. "We got to do something. What do you think?"

Helping was Harlen's specialty. He was like a spider on a web. Every so often, someone would come along and tear off a piece of the web or poke a hole in it, and Harlen would come scuttling along and throw out filament after filament until the damage was repaired. Bertha over at the Friendship Centre called it meddling. Harlen would have thought of it as general maintenance.

"People are fragile. Doesn't take much to break something. Starfish are lucky, you know. You break off one of their arms, and it grows back. I saw it on television."

Harlen poured himself another cup of coffee.

"Most women would just fall apart, you know. You got to admire Louise. Betty says you could never tell she was on the edge of a mental breakdown."

I couldn't imagine Louise on the edge of anything.

"We got to help her, Will. Somebody's got to look after her. Be with her. Take her out, so she's not ashamed to be seen in public. You know what I mean?"

I was afraid I did.

"Harlen, you're not suggesting I should start seeing Louise just because she's pregnant?"

"No, I wasn't thinking that. Course you are single, so your wife wouldn't get upset, and you're not doing anything anyway. And you are good friends with Louise."

"I like being single."

Harlen smiled. "You know, Will, your mother and Louise's mother used to be good friends."

"I don't want to get married."

"Who said anything about getting married? Louise is going through a bad time. Some Cree gets her pregnant and then runs away. All her friends and family desert her. She's afraid to be seen in public. She's your friend, Will. Couldn't hurt to help out. Take her out to lunch."

"I've got a lot of work to do."

"You know what they say, Will. Lunch is the most important meal of the day."

I felt like a real ass walking into Louise's office the next day. I probably wouldn't have gone, but Harlen knew me too well. He picked me up and drove me over.

"You can go now, Harlen," I said. "I can get across the street by myself."

"I'll just wait here, Will, in case you need to ask any questions."

Louise was in. She didn't look pregnant, but she caught me looking. "Yes, Will, I am pregnant. God, you guys are the biggest bunch of goats."

"I didn't come here about that."

"And Harlen didn't send you."

"Harlen? No. Just thought I'd come by and say hello. See if you wanted to go out for lunch."

"The same Harlen who just happens to be parked across the street. Will, Harlen's already sent over Floyd and Jimmy and Jack Powless."

"Jack Powless?"

"All three hundred pounds of him. They all wanted to say hello and take me out to lunch."

Sometimes you get into situations where you can do nothing but lie. It's the fear that does it, I think. "Really, just came by to say hello."

Louise smiled at me the way you smile at a two-year-old. "Thanks, Will," she said, and she went back into her office.

"Is it okay if I use your bathroom?"

"Help yourself, Will."

I let myself out the back door and walked home. I unplugged the phone and lay down on the bed. When I woke up, I felt better. I was still angry with Harlen, but I felt better. So I called Louise. What the hell. "Louise," I said, "it's Will. About the lunch date . . ."

There was one of those long pauses when you think you might have lost the connection.

"Will . . ."

"This has nothing to do with Harlen or your being pregnant. How about tomorrow? We can go to Casey's."

There was another pause.

"How about I pay for my own meal?" she said.

"You eat that much?"

I was sweating when I got off the phone, and my heart was racing. And I didn't call Harlen.

Casey's was crowded. The hostess jammed us into a corner, and between the lunch crowd, the music, the dishes clacking in the kitchen and the waitress dropping by every two minutes to ask us if everything was okay, we could hardly hear one another. We were reduced to either yelling across the table or just smiling and nodding.

The food made me brave. We passed the Paramount Theatre on the way back to Louise's office. *Revenge of the Nerds* was playing.

"You got plans for Saturday night?"

"This about a date?"

"Good movie, that one," I said.

Louise laughed.

I got braver. "How about it? See the early show

and grab some burgers at Baggy's after."

"Not supposed to be eating things like that. Not good for the baby."

She caught me flat-footed.

"I better eat at home," Louise said. "But the movie sounds fine. What say I pick you up around six-thirty?"

"Where am I going to eat?"

Louise was a pretty good cook. I'm not big on vegetables, but I suppose they were better for the baby. Her car was more comfortable than my truck, and it still had most of its paint. I'd been on dates where the woman used her own car. Normally, though, they always asked me if I wanted to drive.

The movie was awful. But about half-way through, I realized that, while the audience was snorting and laughing, Louise was crying. She caught me looking and laughed and wiped her eyes and said, "It's all right, Will. It's just hormones. Watch the movie."

I had a good time. I called Louise the next week, and we began to go out regular. She told me about Harold.

"He was real nice. But I didn't want to get married. I think he thought when I got pregnant that I'd change my mind."

But most of our conversations were about babies.

"You got to watch what you eat, get a lot of exercise. You can't drink coffee or take any aspirin. I don't smoke, so that's okay. Babies are sensitive."

I wasn't able to avoid Harlen for long. He came into the studio with his mouth all bent around his nose.

"Haven't seen you around, Will. Some of the boys on the team were asking about you."

"Been busy."

"You got to get out every so often, you know." Harlen shifted around in the chair. "You doing anything for lunch today?"

"No."

"How about tomorrow?"

"No, nothing then either."

"Thursday?"

"I'm busy Thursday."

Harlen shifted back. "Business?"

"Not exactly."

"Anyone I know?"

"Yes."

Harlen stood up and smiled and shook his head.

"You know, we're friends, Will. If you have any questions, you just call, even in the middle of the night."

"Thanks, Harlen."

"That's what friends do, Will. Even in the middle of the night."

When I saw Louise later, I told her about Harlen.

"God, yes," said Louise. "Betty and Doreen and Shirley are convinced we're going to get married."

Louise got bigger and bigger, and I guess I began getting protective. I started opening car doors. I held her arm when we had to cross an icy street. After dinner one night, Louise took my hand and put it on her belly. "Here, Will," she said, "you can feel her kick."

I was just helping, like Harlen said. I helped her watch what she ate. I even gave her a little help with some names.

"What about Wilma?" Louise said. "I had a granny named Wilma."

"God, no."

"Jamie?"

"No."

"Elizabeth?"

"Maybe."

"Sarah?"

"It's okay."

"Will, you're a big help."

We never got around to being lovers. There didn't seem to be the time for that. We were friends. Louise was good to be with, but there was a distance and Louise kept it. I figured it had to do with Harold.

I was dead asleep the night Louise called.

"Will, I need to go to the hospital. Don't know if I can drive myself. Can you give me a ride?"

It took the hospital over an hour to get Louise admitted. Every so often, she'd have to stop and bend over and take a deep breath. They finally got her into a room, and a doctor looked at her while I waited outside.

"I'm only dilated four centimetres, Will. Probably won't have the baby until morning. Thanks for the ride and all the attention. I'll have them call you when she's born."

"I got nothing better to do. Don't mind waiting. Maybe it's a boy, and you'll need some more help with names."

"No sense, Will. It'll be a long wait. You've got things to do."

"Maybe I'll wait for a little while. Just in case."

"I'll be okay."

The waiting-room was small, and it didn't have any windows. There was a big No Smoking sign stuck on the wall, and a fellow in a suit sitting on the couch smoking a cigarette. I walked over to the other couch, waved my arm around, coughed a couple of times, and stared at the sign.

"It sure takes a long time for women to have

babies," he said. "I've been here three hours already."

"I think this is a no smoking area," I said.

"They just leave you sit here. The nurse came by once to say that my wife was okay. They want you to be in the delivery-room these days, but, hey, what do they expect me to do? Catch the kid, right?" The guy laughed and put the cigarette out on the floor and shook another one out of the pack. "You don't mind, do you?"

I said that I did, and he put the cigarette back. We sat across the room from each other and looked at the walls. Finally, he stood up and said, "Our doctor said it might be better if Karen had the baby Caesarean, but she got all upset. What's your wife's name?"

"I'm not married."

"Oh . . . right. Well, look, I'm going to walk around. Maybe grab some coffee. If the nurse comes by, tell her I'll be back in a while. And if they want to do a Caesarean . . . hell . . . they can page me, right? Sometimes they don't have a choice, right? I mean, they do those things all the time. I told her it would be okay."

The first four hours weren't bad. Someone had left an old Nero Wolfe novel under the magazines. I had read it before, but I had forgotten who the murderer was. The guy with the cigarette never came back. After six hours, I caught one of the nurses who was coming out of the maternity area, and I asked her about Louise.

"What are you doing out here?"

"I thought I'd wait."

"I'll bet your wife would love to have you with her. There's lots you could do."

"Right."

"Sitting in a waiting-room is a little old fashioned.

Most men like to be there when their wives deliver. Is this your first?"

"Ah . . . yes."

"She's just down the hall, first door on the right."

Maternity was in the south wing of the hospital. South Wing was printed in large letters above the double doors. I stood in the hall for several minutes and thought about wandering down to say hello. One of the doors was slightly open, and I leaned against it and slid into the corridor just as another nurse came out of a room.

"Can I help you?"

I didn't have time to get the lie right. "She's just down there . . . Ms. Heavyman . . . Louise."

"You her husband?"

"Sure . . . I'm her . . . a . . . I'm a friend . . . in a way. . . ."

"Friends of the family have to wait outside."

I finished the novel, sat on the couch and watched the doctors and nurses going back and forth through the doors. I don't know what time it was when the nurse woke me.

"Mr. Heavyman, Mr. Heavyman. Your wife has gone to delivery. Shouldn't be too long now." She smiled at me and shook her head and left before I had any chance to explain.

The cafeteria was closed. I had to get my coffee from a machine. I took two sips and threw the rest away. I went back to the room and sat and waited. I began thinking about Louise, and for the first time since I had come back to Medicine River, I felt good. Clean and strong. Maybe we could give it a try with the baby and all.

I was thinking these thoughts when Harlen and Floyd and Elwood and Jack Powless came in.

"I told you he'd be here, Floyd," said Harlen. "You owe me a beer."

Harlen and Floyd and Elwood sat down on the couch across from me. Jack took up the rest of the couch I was on.

"What are you guys doing here?" And I tried to sound pleasant.

"Just checking up on Louise. How's she doing?"

"She's doing fine. Nurse said it would probably be eight, nine hours, yet. No sense in you guys waiting around. I'm probably going to go myself in a bit."

Harlen settled into the couch. None of them looked like they were going anywhere.

"Hell, Will," said Floyd. "How's it feel to be a father?"

Elwood roared and pounded on Floyd's shoulder. Jack leaned over and patted my knee. Harlen settled deeper into the couch.

We were all sitting there in the room pretending to read, when the nurse returned.

"Mr. Heavyman?"

"That's him," says Elwood, and he dropped the magazine and put his face in his hands so the nurse couldn't see how hard he was laughing.

"Your wife just had a baby girl. We'll get her cleaned up and weighed, and you can come in the nursery and see her. Your wife had a few minor complications, but she's all right, just tired. You'll be able to see her soon. Don't worry, she's fine."

All hell broke loose as soon as the nurse was gone. Floyd and Elwood got up and started dancing around and slapping each other on the back and coming over and shaking my hand and saying things like, "It's a girl, Mr. Heavyman," and "Your wife is just fine, Mr. Heavyman," and "You can see your daughter in a little while, Mr. Heavyman."

Even Jack Powless, who seldom says anything, shook my hand and said that children were a wonderful blessing. For the next twenty minutes, I had to sit with four grinning assholes. I was rescued by the nurse.

"You can see your daughter now, Mr. Heavyman."

Whereupon Elwood and Floyd collapsed into one another.

"She's a big girl," the nurse said, "eight pounds, seven ounces."

They made me put on a gown before they would let me hold her. She was wrapped up in a blanket, and all you could see was her face and eyes. I thought they would be closed like puppies' or kittens', but they weren't. They were open, and she was looking at me.

"I'll bet you have a name all picked out for her."

All I could see was the big sign outside the maternity ward. "Yeah," I said, feeling really good with the baby in my arms, "we'll probably call her South Wing." I guess I expected the nurse to laugh, but she didn't.

"Is that a traditional Indian name?"

"I was just joking."

"No, I think it's a beautiful name."

That little girl kept looking at me, and I just sat in the rocking-chair in the nursery. I would have sat there longer, but the nurse came in to tell me that my wife was awake and wanted to see the baby.

"Give us a second," said the nurse, "and we'll put her in a bassinet, and you can take her down."

I'd forgotten about Floyd and Elwood and Jack Powless and Harlen. As I pushed the bassinet down the hall, I looked into the waiting-room, but it was empty. South Wing was still awake and staring. I thought about Louise and her not having anyone, family angry with her, all her friends gone. Maybe it wouldn't be so bad, I thought. Maybe it could work out.

There are times when I don't know why I bother to listen to Harlen. Louise was in 325C. So were her mother and father, two of her brothers and all of her sisters, three of her aunts, a couple of people I didn't know, and Harlen, Floyd, Elwood, and Jack Powless, who was squeezed up against the radiator.

"Hey, Will," said Louise's father, "what you doing here? Hey, you got my little granddaughter. Boy, she sure is small."

Louise was sitting up in bed, but she wasn't comfortable, and she wasn't trying to fool anyone, either.

"Here," said Louise's mother, "let Louise hold the baby, and we'll get a picture. You be fast, Carter, cause that baby needs a lot of quiet and a lot to eat. Here, Will, give her to me."

Carter Heavyman got his Instamatic. "Hey, Will. You should have brought one of your cameras." He looked over at me and smiled. "Where'd you get that gown?"

Carter took the picture, and everyone crowded around to see the baby. On the card on the bassinet, the nurse had written "South Wing Heavyman". No one noticed me leave.

I left the hospital, and thought I would just walk in the dark and look at the stars, but it turned out to be ten in the morning. The sun was up and hot.

I stopped off at Woodward's and bought a stuffed penguin for the baby. I slept the rest of the day. I took the penguin to the hospital that night.

"Will, I'm glad you came by. That was a madhouse

this morning. Mom had to drag Dad away, so I could get some rest."

"I got this for the baby."

"Her name's Wilma, Will. She's down at the nursery, but you can see her if you want. The nurses think you're my husband. Where'd you get the name South Wing?"

"It was supposed to be a joke."

"Dad really liked it."

"Wilma's better."

"She's beautiful, isn't she, Will? As soon as we get settled, I'll make dinner. Maybe we can go to a show, too."

"Sure."

"You understand, don't you, Will?"

"Sure."

The nursery was bright and alive with light. Some of the babies were awake and crying. A mother sat in the rocking-chair in the corner nursing her child. The plate-glass window was hard and cool, and I lay my face against it and watched South Wing sleep.

The nurse at the desk smiled at me and came over to where I was standing. "This must be your first," she said. "Which one is yours?"

Harlen and the boys were at basketball practice, and Mr. and Mrs. Heavyman had probably gone back to the reserve. Louise was in her room. South Wing lay in her bassinet wrapped in a pink blanket.

I looked down the corridor. It was clear.

"That one," I said.

four

I drove January Pretty Weasel out to the reserve for the funeral. Her arm was still in the sling, and Doc Calavano said the medication might make her drowsy. I didn't want to go, but January was kin, and it was her husband's funeral.

Jake had shot himself. January found him in bed with his shotgun. Harlen gave me all the details.

"Harlen, I don't need to know everything."

"Sorry, Will, hard to tell half a story. RCMP wouldn't let anyone touch a thing for two days. Made the clean-up even harder. Everything had dried, you know. Why would they do that, Will? Make it real hard for Thelma and Bertha."

"Evidence, I guess."

"You think January shot him?"

Jake Pretty Weasel used to come out every so often and scrimmage with the team. He even went to some of the tournaments with us. He was a good player, one of those natural athletes they tell you about on television.

"You know about these things, Will," Harlen said. "Why'd you suppose Jake did that? Such a good friend to you and me and the rest of the boys. You know, he'd always buy the boys a beer or loan them a few dollars if they were short. Always telling a joke and laughing."

"That was Jake."

"You know, maybe he drank a little too much sometimes, but he wasn't no drunk. Good worker, too. Had that job at Exchange Lumber for what . . . eight, nine years? What do you think?"

"That was Jake."

"You think January shot him?"

James and me grew up in an apartment on Bentham Street in Calgary. Mom worked at the Bay cleaning up, and I guess we had enough money. There were other Indian families in the building, mostly mothers and children. We all spent a lot of time playing in the basement, and Henry Goodrider, who was a few years older than me and who was always doing something funny, made up a big cardboard sign that said Bentham Reserve, Indians Only. Henry didn't mean that the white kids couldn't play in the basement. It was just a joke, but Lena Oswald told her mother, and Mrs. Oswald came downstairs carrying a blue can with little animals painted on the sides. She put the can on the bench and took the sign off the door.

She gathered us all together and asked us our names. Then she shook hands with us and said we should all be friends. "White people do not live on reserves," she said. "And no matter what your colour, all of us here are Canadians."

Then she opened the can and gave each of us two big chocolate chip cookies.

It didn't make much sense, and after Mrs. Oswald and Lena left, Henry explained that Mrs. Oswald was really very nice, that she just seemed strange because of her illness.

Jake beat up on January. It was no secret. We played a tournament out at Gladstone Hall one year, and January and the kids came out to watch us. Jake hadn't had a good game, had fouled out, and afterwards, January had come over to the bench and sat down beside Jake and put her arm around him to make him feel better, I guess. Jake took hold of her arm real slow and started to twist it. January, you could see that she was trying not to cry, trying to make everything look normal, like the two of them were playing. Then Jake let go the arm and hit her—right in the face with his fist. And then he got up and walked away. January's mouth was bleeding pretty bad, and she was starting to shake. The rest of us just stood there, Harlen, and Floyd, and Leroy, and me. January tried to smile, and she waved her hand as if everything was okay.

"Jake was always good to us."

"That was Jake."

It was the only time I ever saw Jake hit January, but Betty down at the hospital said that January was a regular in the emergency ward. Betty told January to file charges, but she never did.

Mrs. Oswald was a tall woman with long blond hair. From behind she looked like a young girl, all slim and fragile. But when she turned, you could see her face. My mother said that the long dresses she wore were rich people's clothes and that Mrs. Oswald probably had had lots of money, but didn't now. People who were born rich could never learn to be poor, my mother said. It was too hard on them. They just shrivelled up from bad luck and bad times.

When Mrs. Oswald and Lena first moved into the apartment building, Mrs. Oswald told everyone that her husband had recently passed away and that she wouldn't be staying long, just until the estate was settled. To watch her in her long dresses, moving around the neighbourhood, perched on her toes, gesturing and calling out in her singsong voice as if she was in a movie, you'd think that she was filled up with herself. She was always laughing about something, her hands and arms constantly in motion, like a bird trying to fly.

James and me were on the roof one day, and Mrs. Oswald came up and walked to the edge and lifted her arms over her head as though she thought they were wings. When she saw us, it startled her. She smiled and waved at us and yoo-hooed the way she did, standing on her toes and leaning forward. Wasn't it a beautiful view, she said. Wasn't it a fine, manly wind, too, and how it blew and made your eyes water.

"You hear about the letter, Will?"

"What letter?"

RCMP found it on the bed. Jake still had the pen in his hand."

"What'd it say?"

"It was a long letter, Will. Seven or eight pages. Written on some fancy stationery. Thelma said it was neat with nice handwriting, all the lines straight."

"What'd it say?"

"Must have taken Jake an hour to write that letter. Thelma said it made her cry, Jake saying all those nice things about January and the kids, just before he shot himself. You know why he'd do that, Will?"

"Probably depressed. People kill themselves when they're depressed."

"No, I mean the letter. Why'd he write a letter like that. You know, those suicide notes you see on television just say 'I can't go on, please forgive me,' you know, like that . . . short."

Everybody was at the funeral. All of Jake's brothers and sisters came, and all the boys from the team were there. Jake was popular. Most of January's family stayed away, except for her sister, Irene. January had left the kids with her mother. Louise would have come, but South Wing had run a fever the night before. I was there because of January, and Harlen was there because there was a funeral. It was Harlen's way of keeping track. And seeing him at funerals and weddings, bad times and good, was somehow reassuring.

The service was short. The priest wouldn't come because it was a suicide, so January got this fellow she knew from the Mormon Church. Harlen made a little speech about how life was like basketball and how Jake had just fouled out of the game. The Mormon guy came over after and told January how sorry he was about her husband's death, and he told Harlen how much he enjoyed his life-is-like-basketball talk and would it be okay if he used it some time.

It was Lena who told us that her father hadn't really died, that her mother was hiding from him because he beat her. The last time, Lena told us, he had hurt her mother so bad, she almost died. My mother just nodded when I told her about Mrs. Oswald, and she told me I should leave such things be, that it was best to let white people work out their own problems.

One day, after school, Lena came downstairs to our apartment and asked my mother if we could help her.

Mrs. Oswald was sitting in a chair by the window. She had a towel pressed against her face, and it was covered with blood. There was blood all down her dress, and her face was bruised and swollen. Her left arm lay on the arm of the chair at a funny angle. My mother looked at Mrs. Oswald for a long time, and then she called the ambulance.

I drove January back to town. She leaned against the door. The clouds were beginning to pile up against the Rockies. In the distance, you could see the rain squalls moving out on the prairies.

"You okay?"

"I'm okay, Will."

We drove along in silence. January was crying. People have ways of doing that—crying without making a sound. I could see the tears staining her lap, but she wasn't shaking and she wasn't making any noise.

"I guess you'll miss him." I was just saying that to myself. "At least you've got a good job. Good kids, too. Things will get better. Give them a chance. Everything looks bad now, but they'll get better."

January turned to look at me. She had on dark glasses, so I couldn't see her eyes. Her lips were drawn tight against her teeth. "Will, you think they'll arrest me?"

"They don't arrest people for suicide," I said. I was glad she had the dark glasses on.

"You think they'll arrest me for writing the letter?"

I dropped January off at her mother's. When she got out of the car, she took off her dark glasses, and I could see the yellow and purple bruises around her eyes and the deep, black cuts across her nose.

"I'll be okay, Will. Things are better already."

Harlen wasn't surprised when I told him about the letter.

"Jake wasn't much of a writer. Thelma said the handwriting was too nice for a man. Woman's hand is what she figured. January said that, huh?"

I didn't tell Harlen everything January had said on the ride back from the funeral. I don't know that I understood it all.

"I found him like that, Will. Lying on the bed with that shotgun. I don't know what happened. Maybe he was just fooling around. There wasn't a note. So, maybe it wasn't suicide. Maybe it was a mistake.

"You know he beat me. Broke my arm the last time. I was coming home from the hospital when I found him. Everybody else he was good to. He hit the kids sometimes, but not like he hit me. I don't know why he did that. Sometimes he'd apologize.

"Last few years, he stopped apologizing and just beat me. I had to wear these glasses at work. Then . . . he's dead. He should have apologized before he died. It must have been an accident.

"So I did it for him. Wrote that letter. Pretty silly, huh? He says some real sweet things. You think the RCMP will give it back? I want it for the kids . . . when they're older."

Mrs. Oswald stayed in the hospital for about four days. Mrs. Wright, who lived two floors up and who had two girls of her own, looked after Lena. The police came around a couple of times, and they asked about Mr. Oswald, but no one I knew had seen him.

When Mrs. Oswald came home, she was her old cheery self, though her arm was in a cast and her face looked like it still hurt a lot. Her lower lip was all split and some parts had been sewn together. The little black ends of the thread looked like bug feelers hanging out of her mouth.

Lena told James and me that, when she got home that day, her father was in the kitchen drinking coffee. There was blood all over, but he was just sitting there. Mrs. Oswald was on the floor in the living room, and by the time Lena had helped her mother to the chair, her father had left.

Mrs. Oswald finally got her arm out of the cast, and it looked okay, except it was bone-thin and white. Her face took a while longer to heal and her lip hung off to one side like part of it had died. She smiled and talked about her "accident". If you looked, you could see where there were teeth missing.

The RCMP called Jake's death a suicide. Elwood and Leroy said they figured that January had shot him because Jake was a hunter and knew his way around guns and wouldn't have made a mistake like that. And besides, they said, he had everything—good-looking wife, nice kids, good job.

"People like that," said Elwood, "don't shoot themselves. Shit. Only mistake Jake made was turning his back on January. That women's liberation's what's doing it. Fellow puts a woman in her place once in a while don't give her any call to shoot him. Hell, we'd all be dead."

Leroy's sister was married to one of January's brothers. "Sure, Jake pushed a little bit. That's what men do. But January should have said something. Jake would've stopped. No good letting things build up like that."

Everyone had an opinion, and most of them got back to January. Harlen and me figured that Jake

probably shot himself maybe because he hated himself for beating on January or because he was angry
at the time and didn't have anyone but himself to hit.

It was funny, in a way. Jake's suicide, I mean. For a
month or so after the funeral, everybody mostly worried about him, as if he were alive. We all had Jake
stories, and even January was anxious to tell about
the times Jake had taken the kids shopping or made a
special dinner or brought her home an unexpected
and thoughtful present. I wasn't sure how, but she
seemed to have forgotten the beatings and the pain,
and in the end, all of us began talking about the letter
as if Jake had written it.

"Jake really had a way with words."

"You can see he cared for his family."

"Hard for a man to say those things."

You could see that January wanted it that way, and
when you thought about it long enough, I guess it
wasn't such a bad thing. After a while, we all forgot
about the Jake January found lying on the bed, his
head hard against the wall, the shotgun pressed
under his chin, one hand on the trigger, the other
holding a pen, trying to think of something to say.

five

Big John Yellow Rabbit was Evelyn Firstrunner's blood nephew. Her father had married Rachael Weaselhead, which made Harley Weaselhead Big John's great-grandfather on his grandmother's side, which meant that Eddie Weaselhead, whose grandfather was Rachael's brother, was blood kin to Big John.

Evelyn's sister, Doreen, had married Fred Yellow Rabbit just long enough to produce Big John before Fred went off to a rodeo in Saskatoon and disappeared. Doreen married Moses Hardy from Hobbema, who wasn't related to anyone at Standoff, but that doesn't have anything to do with the trouble.

"You know John Yellow Rabbit, don't you, Will?"

"Director of the Friendship Centre?"

"Know Eddie Weaselhead?"

"Charlie's cousin?"

"You been down to the centre lately?"

Whenever Harlen had something important he wanted to tell me, he'd sort of float around the subject for a while like those buzzards you see above

Blindman's Coulee all the time. He'd start off cold and slow and have to warm to whatever he had to say.

"Martha Bruised Head came to see me yesterday. You know Martha?"

I nodded. "Sure."

"She's the secretary at the centre. Her mother's Rita Blackplume, Mike Bighead's granddaughter. You know, she married with Buster Blackplume who used to call all the rodeos on the reserve and over in Cardston."

Sometimes Harlen would circle for hours.

"Martha was there when it happened. She called the police."

Three years ago, the Friendship Centre was in bad financial straits. An Ojibway fellow from back east had been the director before Big John. The guy was nice enough, but he didn't watch the books—great ideas, no sense of money. Spent more than the centre had. Big John turned all that around. Most everyone was grateful because he had kept the centre from closing. There were a few complaints. Some of the traditional people didn't care for the three-piece suits that Big John liked to wear.

"Them suits make us think of Whitney Oldcrow over at DIA," Bertha Morley told Big John at one of the powwows. "And why'd you cut your hair?" And the staff at the centre grumbled about the no smoking signs Big John put up around the place.

"People going to mistake you for a Mormon." Bertha had a whole armload of opinions. She'd go around and collect them and give them to you all at once. "You maybe should get rid of that poodle, too."

"Will, do you know why two friends would be trying to kill each other?"

"Who?"

"Big John and Eddie."

"They're not friends."

"They're related. Like you and James."

"But they're not friends."

"Maybe not good friends, but that's no call for Eddie to go and throw a knife at Big John."

My mother's best friend was a white woman she worked with named Erleen Gulley. Once a week, on Thursday, Erleen would show up at our apartment in a good blue print dress and high heels. She would bring the newspaper, and the two of them would sit at the kitchen table and cut out the coupons for Safeway's and IGA and Woodward's. Then my mother would put on her green dress and her good shoes, and the two of them would go grocery shopping.

Most of the time, James and me had to go along. But it wasn't much fun. Mom and Erleen would get a cart, and both of them would push it up and down the aisles. They'd go up and down those aisles from the meat section at the one end to the fruits and vegetable section at the other. The first time through, they wouldn't put anything in that cart.

"You guys didn't get anything."

"We're just getting started," said Erleen. "You can't just grab the first thing you see."

Erleen would wink at Mom and toss her head like she owned the world. My mother would laugh and tell James and me to run along and play.

"In a grocery store?"

The two of them would go back to pushing the cart, and James and me would sit by the magazine rack and read comic books. Later, we'd help Erleen and my mother carry the groceries to Erleen's car.

The two of them would laugh, tell stories, and sing songs all the way home.

I didn't mind going with them. James was always willing to stay home.

Eddie Weaselhead was the social director of the Friendship Centre. He had been there a long time. When the Ojibway fellow left, Eddie applied for the director's position. He thought he should have got it, but Indian politics are complex. Eddie wasn't raised on the reserve like Big John, and he didn't speak Blackfoot either. At least, not very well. Eddie was raised in Red Deer, which wasn't his fault. And he was a half-blood, which also wasn't his fault. But you can see how things just pile up sometimes. And then there was the way he dressed. He always wore a ribbon shirt to work and a beaded buckle. He had four or five rings and an inlaid watch-band that he wore all the time and a four-strand choker made out of real bone with brass ball bearings, glass beads and a big disc cut from one of those shells.

"You look like a walking powwow poster," Bertha told him. "You got more jewellery and stuff than that queer guy used to play piano on television. You maybe give us a bad name."

"How about it, Will? What would make two good friends act that way?"

"A woman?" I was guessing. I figured that Harlen had the answer all along.

"A woman? Damn, Will. How come I didn't hear about her? Who is she? Wait, don't tell me. Let me guess."

Well, I guess it could have been a woman, but it wasn't.

"Did he hit him?"

"Who?"

"Eddie . . . with the knife?"

"Nope, bounced it off the wall. Not even close."

"What happened to Eddie?"

"That's the other thing I came to see you about, Will."

Eddie was looking pretty tired when I got to the jail. The police had taken his beaded buckle. They had taken all his rings, his watch with the inlaid band and the bone choker. They had even taken his ribbon shirt and given him a faded blue shirt. Eddie looked drab, like someone had plucked him.

"Will, what are you doing here?"

Which was a very good question.

"Just thought I'd see if I could help."

"I'm okay. They're just holding me till I cool off. Said I could go in the morning. No charges."

I didn't have Harlen's finesse or his patience.

"So . . . you threw a knife at Big John," was as close as I could come to gliding around a subject.

"Hell, it was just a jackknife."

"Good thing you missed, eh?"

"Blade wasn't even open." Eddie laughed and shook his head. "Just threw the whole thing. Scared the piss out of him." Eddie wiped his hand across his face. "Son-of-a-bitch called me a pretend Indian."

I really hate it when Harlen decides to help somebody with a problem. Generally, the first thing he does is to come see me. It was his idea for me to go see Eddie. And of course I had to see Big John too.

"Will, come on in. Hey, put on a little weight." Big John Yellow Rabbit had on his dark pin-striped suit with a white shirt and a burnt-orange tie with ducks stitched into it. I had seen one of those ties in Hunt's Men's Store. They called them club ties, and they

were expensive. Bertha had told him if he was going
to wear a tie like that that he should stay off the
reserve. Someone might mistake him for a flock of
geese and take a shot at him.

"Thought I'd drop by and see how things were
going."

"Heard about Eddie, huh?" Big John was more cat
than buzzard.

"Saw him at the jail last night."

"What'd he say?"

"Said you called him a pretend Indian. Said the
jackknife wasn't even open."

"Could have put out an eye or broken a tooth.
Eddie doesn't like the truth. You see how he dresses
all the time. You ever listen to him? Good thing the
cops got here when they did. You know me, Will.
Don't get angry much. Nobody throws a knife at
me." Big John leaned back in his chair and looked out
the window. "Nobody calls me an apple."

I guess Erleen was older than my mother, because she
had three kids who were grown. She had a husband,
too. His name was Herb, and she liked to tell stories
about the time they went to Waterton Lake on a fishing trip or the time they went to Florida on a fishing
trip or the time they went to Mexico on a fishing trip.

James and me liked Erleen's stories. She'd sit at the
kitchen table and cut out coupons and tell stories.
The one bad thing about her was she smoked.
Whenever she'd start a story, she'd light up a
cigarette, take a couple of puffs and set it on the edge
of the saucer. She'd leave it there until it burned
down to the filter. Then she'd stab that one out and
light another.

One evening, when Erleen was over, James said

that her husband must be one great fisherman, and
before I could stop him, he asked Erleen if Herb
would take us fishing some day. Mom didn't like us
doing that, and James knew it.

"Herb's dead, honey," Erleen said. "Cancer got
him."

Mom gave me a hard look, but I hadn't done anything. It was James who wanted to go fishing.

Later, when the two of them got back from the
store, James and me helped with the groceries. Erleen
sat down in the chair and took a package out of her
purse and handed it to my mother. Mom gave it back,
and Erleen gave it to her again.

"Come on, Rose," Erleen said. "We're friends.
Friends do things for each other." But my mother
laughed and shook her head, and Erleen said okay
and put the package back in her purse. After Erleen
left, I asked my mother what Erleen had given her.

"Some nylons," my mother said.

"How come you gave them back?"

"You shouldn't be wasting your time watching
everything people do."

"That was nice of her to get you nylons, wasn't it?
I'll bet they were expensive."

"Friends don't need to get each other presents."

"Erleen must be rich or something."

"Erleen's poor, just like us."

The next Thursday, Erleen brought some photographs of her and Herb. She brought a package of
cookies, too, the expensive kind that come in long,
thin cartons with bright green-and-silver foil. We all
sat at the kitchen table and looked at photographs of
Herb and Erleen and a bunch of dead fish and ate
cookies until they were all gone and it was too late to

go shopping.

I talked to Big John for almost two hours. Rather, he talked to me. I came away knowing all about the trouble he and Eddie had been having ever since Big John became director. I learned all about the centre budget, all about the new basketball uniforms, all about Big John's new car. I had to buy two tickets to the Friendship Centre annual party, and he walked me to my car so he could tell me about the new building the Friendship Centre was considering.

"Cops arrived just in time." Big John shut my door and squatted down on the curb so he could see my eyes. "Nobody calls me an apple."

Harlen came by my apartment that night.

"You sure it isn't a woman, Will?" Harlen shook his head. "A woman would be easier. You know, we got to get Big John and Eddie back as friends again."

"They've never been friends, Harlen."

"Big John does a good job of running the centre and talking with the government and those folks at the DIA. Got us a lot of money this last year. And Eddie, he takes good care of the socials. Old people got respect for him now. He got the bingo games going and organized that bus that takes them to the hockey games twice a month. Centre needs the both of them. Can't have them trying to kill each other. You got any ideas, Will?"

Harlen sat there and let his eyes wander around the room like he was waiting for me to find a good idea somewhere. He wasn't fooling me.

"Can't think of one," I said. "How about you? You must have an idea."

"Have to think some more." Harlen's eyes were

still gliding. "You doing anything Friday night? Having a social at my place. Hand game, too. Be lots of fun."

Almost anyone could come along to Harlen Bigbear's once-every-so-often, pot-luck-eating, cash-and-other-valuables hand game. For a long time, I thought the hand games that Harlen ran were why Frankie Manyfingers and Louie Frank called Harlen Bingo. But they weren't.

"We went down to Green Bay across the line for one of them Indian conferences," Frankie told me. "And the first thing we see when we get off the plane is this big sign that says, Indian Bingo! $25,000! Boy, you know, Harlen sees that sign, and he slaps Louie and says, 'That's for me.'

"So, you know, the first night after those meetings, we got some dinner and a few beers, and we grabbed a cab out to the reserve with the big bingo game. Real nice place, too, you know, not like down in the basement of the Labour Club. Real plush. Soft-bottom folding chairs and 100 percent glass ashtrays. We played a couple of cards each, and pretty soon that $25,000 game started. Harlen bought himself eight cards. Me and Louie only took two. Blackout game and damn if one of Harlen's cards didn't start to fill up. Seemed like every time they called a number, Harlen would X it out.

"Neither of us was even close, so we watched our cards with one eye and Harlen's with the other. All of a sudden, there was only one number left: B5. Harlen begins wiping his hands on his pants and shifting around as the lady who's calling the numbers sings out, 'G48 . . . O66 . . . I20 . . . I22 . . . N37 . . .' Louie and me were sweating and waiting for the next number. And then that woman, she calls out, 'B3.'

And Harlen leaps out of his chair, knocks it over and yells, 'Bingo!' He leaps up and waves his arms around and yells, 'Bingo . . . Bingo . . . BINGO . . . BINGO!!!'

"Well, you know he was real embarrassed. We left after that cause they never did call B5, and some fat guy from Tulsa, Oklahoma won. We went back to the hotel and stopped off at the café for some coffee and pie, and when the waitress came over, Louie says, 'Coffee and pie all around. Bingo Bigbear is buying.'

"We got back to Medicine River, and me and Louie went to that place in the mall and got one of them make-your-own T-shirts. Bought one says Bingo Bigbear printed across the chest."

I'd been to Harlen's hand games before, and he always wore that T-shirt. Said it brought him luck. He had it on when I got there Friday, which wasn't surprising. What was surprising was to see Big John standing in one corner of the room with his three-piece suit and duck tie and Eddie in another corner with his ribbon shirt and flashy choker.

"*This* your idea?" I said to Harlen.

"Sure, do it once a month if I have the time and money. Hope you brought some cash for the game," and Harlen slapped me on the shoulder and disappeared in the kitchen.

I never saw my mother and Erleen fight. They didn't get angry with each other, either. Sometimes I'd get angry with James, and he was my brother. Erleen and my mother weren't related. Whatever one of them wanted to do was always fine with the other. They were always playing games, you know, like kids. On the shopping trips, Erleen would dump a box of powder-sugar doughnuts into the shopping cart and my mother would fish them out.

"You eat these, Erleen Gulley, and they'll be hanging on your hips by morning."

Erleen would pat her stomach and run her hands
down her thighs. "I don't eat to please men."

"Men," my mother would say, "aren't worth the
time or the trouble."

"They have no appreciation of a bountiful figure."

"They have no appreciation of anything."

"Two raisins and a noodle, and a cupcake for
brains."

"There you go exaggerating again." And the two of
them would start to giggle until they had to park the
cart at the side of the aisle and blow their noses.

You could hear them all through the store, Erleen's
voice booming up and down the aisles.

"Christ, Rose, if meat gets any higher, we're going
to have to start eating cat again.

"What do you think, Rose, doesn't this remind you
of Misssssster God Almighty Anderson down at
work?

"Rose, you ever in your entire life see a cucumber
this ugly?" And all the time, there was the laughter.

It was a little embarrassing, listening to the two of
them going on like that. They talked as though no
one else was in the store, as though they had the
world all to themselves.

One evening, I had just finished a Batman comic
and was getting ready to read the new Superman,
when I noticed that it was quiet. I mean, there were
the usual noises, but I couldn't hear Erleen's voice. I
read Superman, but I was listening at the same time.
Then I got up and went looking.

I walked through the store three times. They were
gone. I remember thinking that they had left me, that

they had got to the check-out stand, talking and
laughing the way they did, and walked right out of
the store and got in the car.

I looked at the clock. The store was going to close
in another fifteen minutes, and I could see I was
going to have to walk home. They had forgotten all
about me.

"Your name Will?" The guy was dressed in a suit,
and he looked sweaty and uncomfortable. I didn't
answer right away.

"Your mother asked me to find you."

"Yeah," I said. "Her and her friend drove off and
left me. Now I got to walk home."

"Your mother and her friend are upstairs. You better come along with me."

We went through a couple of swinging doors and
up a flight of stairs. My mother was sitting at a small
table. A policeman was sitting on the edge of a desk.
"This the kid?" he asked.

My mother wasn't smiling. I stood there in the
middle of the room not knowing what to do.

"You might as well sit down, son," said the policeman. "This is going to take a while."

Big John and Eddie spent the first part of the evening
in opposite corners. If Eddie moved around to the
right to get some more salad, Big John would move to
the left to get a beer or a soda. They bobbed and
wove their way through the rest of the people, keeping the same distance between them—like fighters
looking for an opening.

I caught up with Harlen just as Louie and Frankie
were warming up the drums for the hand game.

"Big John and Eddie don't look any friendlier."

"Give 'em a chance, Will. Things are going to be

okay. Nothing like a hand game to get people together. You watch, pretty soon they'll be singing and having a good time, and they won't remember why they
were angry with one another."

"How'd you get Big John and Eddie to come?"

"That was the simple part. You know how those
two love to gamble."

I couldn't remember either one of them being a big
gambler.

"So I just told them that I had a new game to show
everyone tonight. Northwest-coast game. Bone game.
Told Big John that Eddie was going to head up one of
the teams. Told him that Eddie fancied himself something of an expert on Indian gambling games. Said he
could head up the other team, if he wanted."

"What'd you say to Eddie?"

"Same thing. Big John said no at first, but I kept
talking about how good Eddie figured he was, and
pretty soon Big John said, sure, he'd come. Maybe he
would head up the other team, make some easy
money."

There were dangerous curves and corners in
Harlen's mind, and none of them was marked.

"You check them for weapons?"

Harlen laughed. "Will, you are a joker. Come on,
whose team you want to be on?"

"I just want to watch."

Harlen got everyone's attention and announced
that they were going to play a different game tonight.
"Called a bone game. They play it on the coast. Got to
play in one when I was out there last month. Lots of
fun. You'll like it. Pretty much like a hand game, but
you use bones. Trick is to guess where the unmarked
bone is." And Harlen went on to explain the game.

Everybody got their money down, and the game

began. Big John and Eddie sat across from each other. Big John had taken off his jacket and loosened up the bottom button on his vest. Eddie got the bones first. He sat there straight up, moving his hands across his chest, looking right at Big John. Ray Little Buffalo had the other set of bones.

Big John put his arm out, looked over at Eddie, and pointed to the floor, meaning he wanted to see the inside hands. Eddie kept on singing some more of the song and then opened his right hand just a crack so we could see the bone, but we couldn't see if it was marked or not. Ray opened his left hand, and we saw that Big John had guessed one right. Then Eddie opened his hand up all the way, and there was that marked bone. Louie hit the drum and yelled, "Ho," and picked up the beat, and Eddie's team sang harder. Big John had to throw Eddie one of his counters and guess again. The next time, Big John guessed right, and the bones were passed to his team.

This game was tight. Nobody could get ahead. First, Eddie lost three of his sticks, and then Big John lost five of his. Back and forth. There was a good pot of money, too. Somebody had thrown in a ring. There was a watch and maybe two hundred dollars. Everyone was sweating.

"Hey, Will," said Harlen, "getting hot in here. Maybe open the windows."

Big John's team got the bones again, and he looked over at Eddie and loosened the top button of his shirt and pulled the tie down. Then he undid his sleeves and rolled them up, like he meant business. He picked up the bones and held them so Eddie could see them. Sort of a challenge. And he started singing and moving the bones from hand to hand.

You could actually see what hand had the

unmarked bone. But as Big John sang, he began to move the bones faster. By the time he stopped, I couldn't tell where the bone was, and I was looking hard. Eddie called the right hand, and it was there.

At two o'clock, the police stopped in to say the neighbours had complained about the drum and the singing, and could we finish up. No one was winning, and some of the folks had already left, so Harlen said we could do it again later and everyone should take their money and bring it back next time. Some of us grumbled, but most of us were tired. Everyone got up and stretched their legs. Big John and Eddie just sat there.

Then Eddie got a real friendly smile on his face, and he said so the rest of us could hear, "What say we play one quick hand, one guess, winner take all?"

Everybody had already taken up their bets, but Eddie didn't want to play teams.

"One on one," he said, and he took out five twenties and fanned them out on the floor in front of him.

Big John pulled out two fifties and laid them down. He took a twenty out too and held it up. "What say you throw in that plastic choker of yours," said Big John, pointing the twenty at Eddie's neck like it was a knife. "This should cover it. Couldn't be worth more than a dollar or two."

Eddie snapped his teeth together and waved his hand like he was getting rid of flies. "Keep your money, cousin," said Eddie. "You haven't got enough to cover this bone choker. But maybe if you put in that white-man polyester duck tie of yours and another hundred, I could think about it."

Slow as you please, Big John started to take off that tie. Just slid it out of the knot and folded it up nice and neat and put it down in front of him. Eddie, he

reached up behind his neck and undid the leather
thong.

"Give us a song, Louie. You take the bones," said
Big John, and he threw one of the sets to Eddie.

Eddie took those bones and held them up so everyone could see. He waved them around in Big John's
face. He held them close to Big John, so he could see
them. And he began to sing. And Big John started his
own song, which surprised us because it wasn't
exactly the way Harlen told us a bone game was
played.

Eddie moved his hands back and forth. He put one
on each knee; he held one up and the other down. He
moved them across his chest. Those hands were
always in motion. Louie had really got that drum
going, and Big John and Eddie were singing and
looking right at one another. I was a little afraid that
the police would come back.

Big John put his hand out like it was a divining rod
looking for water, and Eddie smiled and kept on
singing. Big John's hand just stayed there, looking for
that bone.

"Ten dollars says the bone is in his right hand,"
whispered Harlen, but I ignored him.

Then, slow as you please, Big John turned his hand
palm up and swept his arm to the left. Eddie stopped
singing and held both hands out, stretched his hands
out as far as he could reach and slowly uncurled his
fingers, so we could see both bones at once. Eddie's
right hand held the marked bone.

"I meant *our* right, *his* left," said Harlen, whispering again. "Christ, Big John lost."

And he had. Big John looked at the bones and
rocked back on his butt and shook his head. Then he
smiled and leaned forward and pushed the hundred

dollars and that silk duck tie to Eddie. Eddie was smiling pretty hard, and he let Big John push it all the way over.

"Good game," he said, and Big John nodded.

Eddie picked up the tie and his bone choker, and sort of weighed them in each hand.

"Here," says Eddie, and he tossed that bone choker in Big John's lap. "Just so people won't mistake you for a white man."

Oh hell, I knew we were going to get the cops back now. I heard Harlen suck in his breath, and everybody there in the room tensed up.

Big John sat there looking at that bone choker in his lap and then back at Eddie. And then he started to smile. And then he started to laugh. And Eddie started to laugh. Those two were sitting on the floor, laughing their heads off. Even Harlen started to laugh, but it was probably out of relief that Big John and Eddie weren't going to break his place up. Damnedest thing.

Big John got to his feet and slipped the choker in his pocket. "We'll play again some time, you know." And he thanked Harlen for the hospitality and left.

"See, Will," Harlen said, after both Big John and Eddie had gone. "Blood's thick around here. Good friends, those two now. Damn, I get some good ideas, don't I?"

I wasn't sure what had happened, but I was sure Harlen didn't have much to do with it.

They had caught Erleen shoplifting. That's what the policeman said. We stayed in that upstairs room for about two hours. The man in the suit and the policeman asked my mother a bunch of questions. They asked me some questions, too.

"You ever see Mrs. Gulley take anything?"

"No."

"You ever take anything?"

"No."

"You know that stealing things is a crime?"

"Sure."

"You know you could go to jail."

"I didn't take anything."

Erleen was in another room with the police. You could hear her voice every so often. My mother sat there and didn't say a word. The guy in the suit stood by the stairs, in case we tried to run, I guess. The policeman would get up every so often and look down the stairs as if he expected someone else to come along.

You couldn't hear the other people in the room with Erleen, but her voice came right through the walls. Later, the door opened, and Erleen came out. There was another man in a suit and another policeman in the room and one of the check-out clerks.

The man in the suit who had been in the room with Erleen motioned to the policeman sitting on the desk. "Would you escort Mrs. Gulley and her friend to their car?"

"I can find my own way," said Erleen.

"The store is closed now," said the man. "We'll have to let you out."

Erleen ran her hands over her hips. "I think you owe Rose here an apology."

"I'm sure we do," said the man.

"You sure as hell owe me one."

"I think we've settled that."

"In a pig's eye."

The policeman led us through the store and let us out a back door. Our car was the only one left in the lot. Erleen unlocked the door, and I got in the back. Erleen stood in front of the car for a moment and then turned and flipped up the back of her dress and stuck out her butt. On the way home, she couldn't stop talking.

"What a bunch of jerks. I always put nylons and cosmetics and stuff like that in my purse. Keeps them separate from the food. You know I do that."

"That's right," my mother said.

"Lots of people do that. And when I get to the check-out stand, I get them out and pay for them."

"That's right."

"That snot-nosed clerk was just trying to make a name for herself. She was just mad because the last time we were here, I told her she'd be a good-looking woman if she lost a few pounds."

"Was she the same one?"

"I was just trying to help. Take it from me, I told her. You put on weight when you're young, and you carry it around with you the rest of your life."

"You're not fat."

"Not as fat as that blonde pimple." And Erleen started to laugh. "Would you believe it? Didn't even give me a chance to take that stuff out of my purse like I was going to do when I got to the check-out stand."

"They'll probably fire that clerk," said my mother.

"It took that cute cop almost two hours to calm me down. I was really mad. Maybe I should sue them."

"You should get a thousand dollars or so."

"They do it because we're women, you know. You'll never see them treat a man that way."

We got all the way home before we remembered the groceries. "Those groceries are probably still sitting in that cart. By tomorrow, the meat will be starting to rot." And the two of them burst into waves of giggles. "And they'll make that fat clerk clean it up."

Erleen dropped us off at the apartment. Mom looked tired, and you could tell she didn't want to talk. But I did.

"Was Erleen taking stuff?"

"Just a mistake."

"Did they arrest her?"

"Nothing but a silly mistake."

"Is she going to jail?"

"Like she said, that manager was embarrassed."

Erleen came by the next Thursday as usual, but this time, they left me home.

I didn't see Harlen for about two weeks, and you know, I felt bad about not giving him some credit for bringing Big John and Eddie together. After all, it was his idea to invite them to that bone game, and it was his idea that being related was more important than some small difference of opinion or a little name-calling. So when he came to the studio on Tuesday, I felt obligated to say something complimentary.

"Harlen," I said, "you know, I've been thinking, you get some good ideas sometimes. Sometimes you really surprise me." Which wasn't exactly the way I had practised saying it, but the more I practised saying it, the more I remembered some of the ideas that he had had that weren't very good.

Harlen didn't look in the mood for compliments. "Will," he said, "you remember that idea you had about Big John and Eddie?"

"What idea?"

"The one about their being kin and all and good friends, too."

"That was your idea."

"Don't think it was a good idea, Will."

"Big John and Eddie . . . again?"

"You ever see Big John's poodle? Big black one. Damn, you know that dog can jump up as high as your arm. You ever see one of those dogs, Will? Can do all sorts of tricks, too. You ever see Big John's dog do her tricks?"

I could see Harlen spreading his wings.

"Got that poodle maybe four years ago. Called her Licorice. Not the kind of dog for a grown man."

"Harlen, I've got an appointment with the bank in two hours."

"Doesn't even look like a dog. Big John got her shaved like one of those hedges in front of the museum. Wouldn't have a dog like that. Bertha said it wouldn't even make a good stew. But can it do tricks. Sits up real good."

"Harlen . . ."

"You know what Eddie said when he saw that choker?"

"What choker?"

"The choker that Eddie gave Big John, you know, his good bone choker."

I was going to be late.

"Will, Big John went and tied that bone choker around that poodle's neck. Brought it down to the centre to show it off. It was pretty sad, Will. You know, I knew there would be trouble. I told Eddie not to wear that ribbon shirt."

There's no point in rushing Harlen. We sat there and drifted together. Harlen floated around lazily touching on this and then on that. Eddie had had a new ribbon shirt made up, and he had cut up Big John's duck tie for the ribbons. And he wore it to the centre—all those little silk ducks cut into thin strips like jerky and hanging off Eddie's chest and shoulders.

"Will, Big John gave that poodle a new name, too. Indian way of doing things, he told Eddie. Weasel—that's the dog's new name. Do you believe that, Will? Weasel, because she sits up and begs whenever she wants attention. What do you think?"

I didn't think anything. But I tried to imagine Eddie sitting at his desk stroking those silk strips and Big John getting Weasel to jump up and down so the choker around her neck would rattle.

"Blood kin and good friends too. What are we going to do?"

Erleen moved to Edmonton to be near her daughter. "Peggy divorced that one bum and married another," Erleen told us. "The good news is this bum's rich."

"Edmonton can get real cold," my mother said.

"I got my own room and a colour television."

"Sometimes those winters last until June or so."

"I figure they want me to help out with the kids, but that's okay."

Then the two of them started to cry, and James and me headed for the basement. We heard from Erleen regular, and every so often, she'd drive down to take my mother shopping. Erleen would wait at the kitchen table and smoke cigarettes and shout out stories, while my mother got dressed up. Then they would go clacking down the stairs in their high heels. James and me could watch them from the window, as they got in the car and roared off for the supermarkets.

The next year, Erleen's daughter called to say that Erleen had had a stroke and wouldn't be coming down for a while. She died before Mom had a chance to get up north to see her.

We didn't do anything. Eddie stopped wearing that shirt. Said the ribbons didn't hang right, that that was what happened when you used polyester. Big John took the choker off Weasel. Said it hurt her neck and it made her look cheap.

The following week, things were pretty much back to normal. Big John was wearing another of those club ties with the ducks on it, a blue one, and Eddie was wearing another bone choker. All of which made Harlen happy, because it was his idea that got Big John and Eddie back together and that was the way it should be, Harlen told me, with good friends and blood kin.

six

I was standing under the basket trying to catch my breath when Raymond Little Buffalo split Frankie's head open. The two of them were going after a rebound. Frankie dove for the ball, and Ray jumped on top of him, cocked his arm and threw an elbow into Frankie's face.

Ray was all apologies. He got a towel and told Frankie to hold it against his head. He even drove Frankie to the emergency room and waited while they put fifteen stitches in the gash above Frankie's eye. The whole time Ray stood around telling jokes, offering encouragements and rubbing his elbow as though it hurt.

"Ray used to be a regular," Harlen told me. "Then he got that job in Calgary. Big oil company. Should have seen the car they gave him. And all those credit cards. Ray took me to lunch once. You know, it cost sixty-five dollars. And the soup was cold. You believe that, Will? Ray said that's the way they do it."

I tried to stay out of Ray's way. On the court, he

was unpredictable. He'd slap you on the back and tell you what a great move you had made to get by him. The next time he'd put a knee in your thigh or try to catch you in the face with the back of his head.

"Should have seen him, Will, skinny and fast. He got a little fat sitting at that desk in Calgary."

Most of the time, I got to guard Ray. He wasn't fast any more, but you had to be careful when everyone got crowded in the paint.

"People who start off skinny," Harlen told me, "have a tough time being fat because they haven't had time to develop the muscle to carry the extra weight."

Ray still had some good moves, and I generally played off him out of range of his head and elbows and took the rebounds off his missed shots as they came my way.

"People may think you're a little heavy, Will. But you been like that all your life so you got the muscle to manage it."

Off the court, Ray was as friendly as a puppy. Watching him sitting around after practice at Tino's Pizza, laughing, drinking beer, telling the boys about the time he wasn't looking and caught a basketball with his face or the time he had to sleep on the floor in a motel in Medicine Hat because Floyd was in the only bed with two women and how one of the women rolled off the bed in the middle of the night and landed on top of him, you'd never know this was the same Raymond Little Buffalo who forty-five minutes earlier had tried to put you in the hospital.

Harlen, who could always find allowances lying around, said that Ray was still angry about losing that job. "Oil bust put a lot of people out of work. Ray's working for Canada Packers in town now.

Must have been hard to give up that Lincoln." Along with allowances, Harlen always had a pocketful of suggestions. "Maybe you could talk him into coming out and playing regular, Will. Ray likes you. Basketball is a great way to forget your problems."

I never said a word to Ray about that. He'd come out about once or twice a month and play, and that was plenty.

I suppose if you don't like someone, you're willing to go looking for faults that most people wouldn't ever see. For instance, Floyd smoked, but I liked Floyd, so I never said much. Ray smoked too, and whenever he'd light up, even if he was clear across the table from me, I'd snort and cough and wave my hand around.

Most of the boys bragged on themselves from time to time: the games they had won with last-minute shots, the women they had slept with, the times they had outrun the cops, the amount of beer they could drink before they passed out. We'd all laugh as though we believed every story. But with Ray it was different. Anything you had done, Ray had done it before and had done it better. If Floyd had a story about a woman with large breasts, Ray would have a story about another woman with huge breasts. If Elwood told about the time the cops threw him in jail in Browning and someone in the drunk tank stole his new sneakers, Ray would have a story about the time he was in jail in Penticton and someone stole all his clothes, and when he woke up the next morning, he was bare-assed naked.

Whenever Ray would start in on one of his stories, I'd snort and cough and wave my hand around.

The stories that Ray liked to tell best were the ones where he won basketball games with incredible last–second shots. Harlen didn't help.

"I remember that alright," Harlen would say. "You were a great player, Ray. Should come back out. Look at Will. Will wasn't too good when he started, but look at him now."

"Ain't no Clyde Whiteman."

"That's for sure. But he's got a pretty good hook."

"Ain't no Clyde Whiteman."

I can remember exactly when it started. I was flying back to Toronto. I hate flying, and whenever the plane hit a bump, I'd grab the seat in front of me. There was an older woman sitting across the aisle.

"I have a son who hates to fly, too," she told me. "And when he flies, he gets just like you. And then, sometimes, he throws up."

I laughed and told her I didn't think I'd throw up, and we started to talk. She told me about her husband, Morris, and her children. Her daughter was a doctor in Victoria, and her son was a dancer in Winnipeg. I told her I had a brother who was an artist. And then she asked me what my father did.

Maybe it was the way she asked the question, smiling, expecting that I had a father and that what he did was worth talking about. Like Morris.

"My father is a senior engineer with Petro-Canada."

"That's wonderful," said the woman. "Morris teaches at the university. English. You must be very proud of your father."

"He's gone a lot of the time. Engineers have to travel around."

"I'm sure he thinks about you and your brother all the time." And she took a plastic folder from her purse and stretched it out on her lap. There was Morris and Laura and William and Pooch the cat.

Ray got himself elected to the Native Friendship Centre board. He was popular, and it didn't hurt that he had had all that executive experience in Calgary. We didn't see him at practice for about two months after that, but when he did come out, he was driving a brand-new Lincoln.

"Didn't know the centre paid that well," said Floyd.

"Didn't know the centre paid at all," said Ray.

"No wonder you ain't been playing with us," said Elwood. "Been too busy collecting bottles and cans from behind the American."

Ray was all smiles. "Once you drive one of these babies," he said, "you can never go back to Fords or Chevys." Ray opened all four doors and turned on the stereo. "You can't buy a home system that sounds any better. Put your head in there. What you smell is leather."

It was a nice car if you liked that kind of thing.

"The salesman is still picking horse shit off his shoes. Poor bastard didn't know what hit him." Ray put his arm around my shoulder and gestured with his chin towards the car. "You still driving that truck?"

Ray said he'd drive the boys over for pizza. Harlen was going to ride with me, but Ray insisted that there was enough room. "You can ride shotgun," he told Harlen. "You can pick the first tape, too. We'll meet you over there, Will."

I had to stop for gas, and when I got to the pizza parlour, Ray's car wasn't in the parking lot. I sat in my truck and waited for half an hour, and then I went home.

I mean, I wasn't a kid. I was at least twenty-five when I told that woman on the plane that my father was a

senior engineer. And there was no reason to do that. I
didn't miss him. I didn't even think about him. I had
never known the man.

So, I began to invent him.

"My father's a pilot. He flies the big jets for Air
Canada.

"Dad's in stocks and bonds.

"He's a career diplomat.

"He's a photographer.

"He's a doctor.

"He's a lawyer."

He was never a rodeo cowboy, and out of consider-
ation for Morris, he was never a university professor
either.

Sometimes I'd sit in my apartment and try to think
up new professions for my father. And then I'd tell
myself to quit fooling around. I'd laugh at myself,
shake my head in disgust, promise that I'd stop the
whole stupid business. What if I got caught? What if
someone back home heard about my father being a
rich opal miner in Australia?

Ray stopped practising with the team altogether,
which was okay with me. Instead he started going to
the American Hotel. The American was the local
Indian bar, a tall, skinny, brick building wedged in by
a surplus clothing store on one side and by an old
wood-floored Kresge's on the other. The two floors
above the bar were rooms that no one ever rented
overnight.

The place had a lot of character. The original owner
had been something of a collector, and the walls were
hung with Indian artifacts from the 1920s. Before he
died, he told Harlen that he had been offered almost
a million for his Indian stuff by some big museum

back east, but he had told the museum people to piss
off, he was going to give it all back to the Indians.

The new owner, a businessman from Edmonton
whom no one had ever seen, left everything the same.
Tony Balonca ran the place, and most of us thought
he owned it, until the night he got a little drunk and
told Floyd that if the bar were his, he'd take down the
beads and feathers and the rest of the shit and put up
a big mural of the Italian coast. Harlen said he'd take
the stuff away for Tony, no charge, but Tony said no,
the owner liked the quaintness. When Tony said
quaint, he curled his lips so you could see his teeth.

I didn't go to the American much, and I wasn't
particularly interested in what was happening to Ray.
But Harlen's theory on information was that the more
you had, the more you knew, which made good sense
as far as it went.

"Will, did you hear about Ray?"

"They repossess his Lincoln?"

"His Lincoln? Why would they do that? Where did
you hear that, Will?"

Ray had come up with a plan to raise money. The
Friendship Centre was always needing money for
their community programs, and there wasn't much in
yard sales and car washes. Ray's plan was to produce
a calendar that featured prominent Indian people of
Canada and maybe a few from the States and sell it to
companies in Calgary and Edmonton.

"Ray says there are hundreds of businesses that
give away calendars every year. You know, Will, like
the banks or the auto-supply stores. A lot of those
businesses are always saying how much they appreciate Indian people. Ray figures you can sell the calendars in blocks of, say, five hundred for the small
businesses, one thousand for the medium-sized

companies and two thousand for the oil companies
and the government. What do you think, Will?"

"Beats another bake sale."

"That's the spirit, Will. Ray wants you to do the
photography work. I told Ray what a great photographer you are, and he said, sure, might as well give the
business to one of our own people. He's got a lot of
respect for you, Will."

I told Harlen it wouldn't be cheap, that that kind of
photography with colour separations and everything
was going to be expensive. And then there would be
printing costs.

"Not to worry, Will. Ray figures we can maybe get
a grant to pay for most of the costs. That way there
won't be any risk. Louise is going to do the account-
ing, and Elwood has a friend in Winnipeg who owns
a press."

"Am I doing this for costs?"

"No, Will. Ray said that was bad business. He said
to make sure you add in for your time."

"What's Ray going to do?"

"He's going to be in charge. Ray's got the brains for
this kind of thing. We're driving over to Calgary next
week to talk with the oil companies. Figure while
we're in the city, we can look at basketball uniforms,
too."

"Uniforms?"

"Sure. Big John said some of the money could go to
the team. There might even be enough for new shoes
and socks and stuff like that."

Ray stopped by the studio the following week. He
wanted cost estimates on the photography work. He
was dressed in a good-looking dark blue suit, and he
didn't waste any time on words.

"Could mean a lot of money for the centre. We

need a top-quality product. The big companies don't buy second-rate stuff. You know what I mean?"

I said that I did, and I said I'd get an estimate to him the first of the week. His Lincoln was parked on Third. I could see it through the window.

The cost was over five thousand dollars, and with my time, it came to almost six thousand. Ray came by with a folder with twelve photographs in it, dropped it on my desk, and said, "Do it."

Three months later, we had our calendar, and it looked good. The first print run was ten thousand. The second run was twenty thousand, and according to Harlen, they were all gone in two months.

"Ray's a great salesman, Will. Thirty thousand calendars. Do you know how much profit that means for the centre?"

"No idea."

"Oh," said Harlen. "Neither do I. I was hoping you knew how these things work."

I only told strangers, but there was always the chance that something would get back to my mother or to James.

"My father is a television producer.

"My father is an investment consultant.

"My father is a physicist.

"My father is a computer designer."

I ran out of interesting professions fast, and instead of trying to top each new career I created for him, I began to imagine long and elaborate stories that I could tell again and again, adding to them as I went along.

It was best on airplanes, where everyone was a stranger. The conversation helped to take my mind off the fact we were in the air. I even began to look

forward to the next opportunity to talk about my
father and slowly, over the months and years, he
began to take on a particular shape, a distinctive
sound.

He was a tall man with a low, pleasant voice. I
imagined him best as a free-lance journalist who
roamed the world taking his own pictures and writing his stories. He had a slight limp, the result of his
plane coming down in the Yucatan. (He was a pilot,
too.) Most of his stories were about oppressed peo-
ples, and he wrote about them with grace and wit.
His stories had been published all over, but he generally wrote under pseudonyms because he was a shy
man. You've probably read some of his pieces in
Saturday Night, *Time*, or *Newsweek*, I told the people I
met, and you didn't even know it.

Most of all, I liked to point out, he loved his family,
and I was always getting postcards and letters with
pictures of him standing against some famous place
or helping women and children take sacks of rice off
the back of trucks.

There was the time in New Zealand when he spent
four months around Rotorura living with a group of
Maoris. He had taken over five hundred pictures for
National Geographic and had written a superb piece on
traditional and contemporary Maori life, how the two
flowed into each other, how the culture continued to
maintain itself in spite of the inroads that technology
had made. Two days before he was to leave, a delega-
tion of the elders came by the house where he was
staying and told him that they had talked and would
prefer that he didn't put their pictures in a magazine.
That evening the village had a feast, and after everyone had eaten, my father took the story he had
worked on for four months and all the film and

placed them on the fire.

That was my dad.

Then, for my twenty-seventh birthday, my mother sent me a white shirt and a photograph.

By the end of the month, things were getting a little thin, and I kept hoping for the cheque to arrive. I could have called the Friendship Centre, but I didn't want to appear anxious. By the time the fifteenth rolled around, I was closer to desperate.

"Hi" I said. "It's Will. This Martha?"

"Yep."

"You know, I was just looking over my records, and I don't think I ever received a cheque for that calendar project. Have those cheques gone out yet?"

"Yep."

"Well, did my cheque go out?"

"You have to ask Ray."

"It was that bill I dropped off about a month ago."

"Ray took all that stuff. Said he was going to take care of it."

I couldn't bring myself to call Ray and ask him about my money, so I called Harlen.

"Sure, Will," said Harlen. "I can do that. Must have been a mix-up with the cheques. Could still be in the mail. Ray'll be real embarrassed."

Harlen didn't call back that day, and he didn't call back the next day either. When he did call, he told me that he had been right, that Ray was real embarrassed.

"Ray paid all the bills. But he said he didn't see your bill in the folder Martha gave him. Said he paid everyone. What was left over went to the centre."

"I can send him another bill."

"No need to do that, Will. Ray said we could just

take what you're owed out of what the centre got."

"That's fine with me."

"Boy, Ray was real embarrassed. How much was your bill?"

"Almost six thousand dollars."

"That much, huh?"

"How much did the centre get?"

"Three hundred and forty dollars. Looks like we're going to have to wait on the uniforms."

The photograph was of my father. He was leaning against a fence with four other men. He had on a pair of jeans, a work shirt and a hat that was pulled down over much of his face. There was a short letter from my mother with the photograph that said, "Happy birthday. Found this picture. Third from the right. That's him." And she signed it "love" like she always did. That was it. He had a cigarette hanging from his mouth. My mother had drawn a circle around him with an arrow pointing at the side of his head.

I had to take a loan out with the bank. Harlen spent the next two weeks apologizing for Ray.

"He feels awful, Will. Blames himself for what happened."

"What happened to all the money the centre was going to make?"

"Expenses, Will. The expenses took a lot of the profit."

"Yeah, but we sold, what, thirty thousand calendars?"

"Not quite that many in the end."

"How many?"

"Don't know. Ray said it wasn't as good as it might have been. Ray had to put in five thousand dollars of his own money."

"Ray lost five thousand dollars on the calendar?"

"Not exactly."

"So, how much did he lose?"

I ran into Ray about a month later in the American. I had just finished work, and it was hot, and a cold beer sounded good. Ray was sitting at a table near the back. Harlen was with him.

Ray had on his suit. He looked clean and neat sitting in the chair. "Sorry to hear you had to take out a loan," he said. "Harlen and me figure that as soon as the money starts to come in next year, you'll get paid first with interest. Damn, but I wish I knew what happened to that bill."

I guess I wasn't smiling when I sat down. "Expenses will sure eat into the profits quick."

Ray wasn't smiling either. "They sure will."

Ray ordered another pitcher, and I sat there staring at him until he disappeared in the smoke and the noise of the evening.

My mother normally sent me a shirt for my birthday. She sent shirts at Christmas, too. Generally, they were used, shirts she had found at yard sales. Sometimes they were new. New or used, she would wash them, iron them, and pin them up in a neat rectangle. She didn't make a distinction between new and used. There were clean shirts and dirty shirts, and that was it. She never missed my birthday.

She had pinned the photograph to the shirt pocket. "That's him," the letter said, as if knowing was an important thing for me to have.

seven

After a six-year courtship and a four-month pregnancy, Jonnie Prettywoman and Cecil Broadman got married. Cecil's parents were Catholic in a reasonable sort of way and were pleased that the ceremony was performed before they had to make plans for the baby's baptism. Bud Prettywoman hired me to take the pictures. It was a large wedding, just friends and relatives, and Jonnie wasn't showing at all, which is probably one of the reasons that both sets of parents were smiling at each other like toothpaste advertisements.

The wheat had been good that year, and the tables at the reception were stacked with food. Frankie Greysquirrel and Eddie Weaselhead were home in bed with the flu, but Floyd and Elwood and the rest of the boys on the team were there, and for the first five or six hours, they floated around the tables like a flock of crows.

"Hope you boys like the food," Bud told Floyd and Elwood, as they stood by the main table with a sandwich in each hand, a beer stuck in their jacket pocket and a mouthful of food. I got a candid shot of the three of them, Bud smiling with his thumbs tucked into his shiny cummerbund and Floyd and Elwood staring blankly into the camera with thin pieces of ham and cheese hanging out the sides of their mouths.

The reception was about half-way over when I noticed that Harlen wasn't there.

I caught Big John Yellow Rabbit at the punch bowl. "John, have you seen Harlen?"

John looked around the room once. "Harlen not here?"

"Haven't seen him."

"That's strange, Will. Can't imagine Harlen missing this."

Neither could I. Harlen went to everything. He went to all the powwows. He went to all the funerals. He went to all the weddings, the births, and most of the court cases. Any time there was a gathering of two or more Indians in a hundred-mile radius of Medicine River, chances were one of them was Harlen.

"Cecil's Harlen's cousin, isn't he?" said John.

Which was another reason that Harlen wouldn't miss the wedding.

The reception didn't break up until almost nine that night. Cecil and Jonnie left about six, but nobody missed them. Floyd and Elwood and the rest of the boys stopped floating about seven, and there was actually some food left. Bertha and Mary and Betty wrapped it up and gave it to some of the families.

"Real fine wedding, Will." Bud Prettywoman had taken off his bow-tie and loosened up his shirt. The cummerbund was riding up over his belly, and it looked as though he was wearing a flat inner tube around his chest. "Bet you got some real good shots."

"Sure did," I said. "Maybe next week I'll have the proofs for you folks to look at."

"Those two wait any longer," said Bud, fixing the deep-red tie on one of his braids, "you could have taken pictures of the baby, too."

Both of us laughed, and Bud handed me a beer. "Too bad about Harlen," he said.

"Yeah. Can't imagine him missing the wedding. Must have had to go somewhere or something."

Bud sighed and sat down on the table. "Floyd didn't tell you about Harlen?"

"Probably too busy eating."

"You're his friend, I know. Guess everybody thought you knew already."

"Harlen okay?"

"You know, Will, when Harlen was a young man, he was pretty wild. Used to call him Crazy Bear." Bud shook his head. "I can't tell you how many times his father threw him out of the house." Bud settled himself on top of the table.

"Course Harlen wasn't near as wild as Jesse Plume's boy. You ever know David? He joined that AIM movement, went all over the States. Got himself thrown in jail in South Dakota. Wears that jacket everywhere he goes."

Bud paused to drink his beer.

"And Harlen was never mean like Oxford Lefthand. You ever know his wife, Will?"

"Oxford Lefthand's?"

"No, Harlen's."

"No."

"Nice woman, Doris. Harlen settled right down when he married her. Stopped drinking just like that.

Not like Bennett Chase. You know Bennett, don't
you? Bennett married that white woman from down
in Santa Fe. Met her when he was a student at that
Indian art school. She had money, you know. Didn't
stop Bennett from drinking. He just drank better
stuff. . . . Bennett's father used to make his own
liquor. Did you ever know Peter Chase?"

"What happened to Harlen?"

"Well, you know Doris got herself killed in a car
accident. Happened near Banff. Real sad that. Harlen
took to drinking again. Drank pretty heavy. Almost
killed himself. Did something to his stomach. Doc
Calavano told him next time he drank like that, he
wouldn't have to worry about sobering up."

Bud leaned back and looked out across the empty
room and settled into the story about how Harlen
took up hard drinking and how he almost killed himself. Harlen always did this to me. I wondered if he
had learned it from Bud.

"You had to know Harlen when he was young. . . ."
Bud began.

I had first met Harlen years ago when my mother
died. I was living in Toronto at the time. My brother
James called, and I caught the first plane to Calgary. It
was evening when I arrived in Medicine River. James
met me at the airport. His eyes were red, and his hair
was greasy and matted. I wanted to do something,
but we both just stood there. Finally, he grabbed my
bag and threw it in the trunk.

There were quite a few people at the funeral. All
my mother's brothers came with their wives, and
Auntie Claire and her three girls were there. There
was a tall man I didn't recognize who kept smiling at
me. He was all chest, perched on long, thin legs. His

hands were stuck in his pockets, his elbows turned
out like wings. From a distance, he looked like a
stork. The priest stood across from James and me,
leaning into the wind, his garments trailing out
behind him as though he were preparing to fly. He
had to shout to be heard over the warm, rolling wind,
and there were tears in his eyes. Near the end of the
service, he raised one hand towards the sky and
extended a single finger as if to mark a spot, and in
that instant, his gown billowing around, his head
cocked to one side, he reminded me of Mary Poppins.

After the service, James asked me if I would mind
catching a ride back to Medicine River with a friend
of his. "I need to get away for a bit, Will. I'll stop by
later and take you to the airport." James waved to the
stork, and Harlen Bigbear glided into my life.

"Hi," said Harlen, "James said you need a ride
back to town. You smoke?"

I told him I didn't.

"James smokes," said Harlen, "so you never
know."

Harlen had an old green-and-white 1955 Ford
sedan, and we drove to Medicine River with the windows rolled down and the radio going.

"James tells me you been living in Toronto. Big
city?"

"Pretty good size."

"I never been to Toronto. Many Indians live there?"

"Some."

"Many Blackfoot?"

"No," I said. "Mostly Cree and Ojibway."

"You like it there in Toronto?"

"It's okay."

"James said you went there to get away."

"Wanted to be a photographer."

"That's a good thing to do," Harlen said. "I should have done that."

"Photography?"

"No. Get away."

"My job's in Toronto."

Harlen turned the radio down a bit. "Can't see Ninastiko from Toronto," he said. "So, when you think you'll be moving back home?"

"Here?"

"Sure. Most of us figured that, with your mother and all, you'd be coming home soon."

There was no logic to it, but my stomach tightened when Harlen said *home*.

"James says you take pictures. People pay you for doing that?"

"Well . . . yeah."

"You take the pictures of all those disasters that you see in the newspapers?"

"No, I take pictures of people mostly. Weddings, portraits, things like that."

"That's good. We got a lot of people out here but not many disasters. You could start your own business, you know."

I told Harlen I liked Toronto. There were good restaurants, places to go. Things to do. Medicine River was small.

"American Hotel is a great place for a beer. Baggy's just opened a sit-down restaurant. You got the Rockies, too. You see over there," Harlen said, gesturing with his chin. "Ninastiko . . . Chief Mountain. That's how we know where we are. When we can see the mountain, we know we're home. Didn't your mother ever tell you that?"

Harlen dropped me off at the Travel Lodge. Later that evening, James came by, and we had dinner together. He had washed his hair, but his eyes were still slick and dull.

"I may go to San Francisco," he said. "Always wanted to go there. What do you plan to do?"

"Stay in Toronto, I guess."

"Pretty exciting?"

"I guess."

James looked over my shoulder. "Been a long time, Will," he said, softly. "'Man of the house', wasn't that it?"

"Christ, James."

"Man of the house."

James drove me to the terminal and sat in the car with the motor running, while I got my bags out of the back seat. I remember saying that we should stay in touch, and then he was gone.

I sat in the airport that evening. It was only then that I began to feel my mother's death. I was slipping from melancholy to depression when Harlen walked through the double glass doors of the terminal. He had a folder in one hand, and he waved it at me.

"Will, good, you haven't left yet." Harlen sat on the seat across from me, the folder on the chair beside him.

"You know, Will, I've been thinking about you wanting to start up a photography business here in Medicine River. I was talking to Bertha Morley. You know Bertha? She's Sadie Bruised Head's grand-daughter."

"Harlen," I said, "I'm not starting a business in town. You have lots of photographers here already."

"No Indian photographers, Will. Real embarrass-ing for us to have to go to a white for something inti-mate like a picture. Bertha says you got a lot of rela-tives on the reserve. You think they'd go to a stranger for their photography needs when they can go to family?"

The loudspeaker came to life and announced the departure of my plane.

I got up and shook Harlen's hand. "I've got to go, Harlen. If you get to Toronto, look me up."

"When you decide to come home, Will," Harlen said, handing me the folder, "you just call. That's what friends are for."

I was half-way across the tarmac to the plane when I stopped and looked back. Harlen was standing by the window waving. I found my seat, and as the plane taxied out to the runway, I could see Harlen settled against the glass, smiling.

I didn't look at the folder until the plane levelled off. There was an information package about Medicine River from the Chamber of Commerce. It had a map of the city and a colour brochure that pointed out the amenities that the city had to offer. There were also several xeroxed sheets that Harlen must have copied from the local phone book.

It was the photography section, and Harlen had made notations next to each advertisement. Alongside Lynn's Photography, he had written "too expensive." Next to Fred Dillar's Photographic Studio, he had written "not too friendly on the phone." Across the large advertisement that Pierre du Gua's Photography and Salon had paid for, Harlen had scribbled, "Eddie says the guy doesn't like Indians." On the last page, after Terry's Studio, Harlen had printed in bold, block letters, "No competition for an Indian photographer."

Bud Prettywoman stood up and pulled his cummerbund down. "What do you think, Will, boy or girl?"

"Jonnie?"

"The wife thinks it's going to be a girl."

"What's happened to Harlen?"

Bud smoothed one of his braids and set his beer down. "Floyd says Harlen's drinking again. Saw him at the American the other afternoon. Looked pretty bad, Floyd said. Heard him in the bathroom throwing up."

"Harlen doesn't drink."

"Something must have happened. Figured you might know, you being good friends and all."

I got back to Toronto just in time to become unemployed. Walter Zneick ran a commercial photography studio. What kept us going were the large commercial contracts. But Mr. Z had started out as a portrait photographer, and he kept a small studio at the front of the building. I more or less ran the studio. When I got back from the funeral, Mrs. Callaghan, the secretary, told me that Mr. Z had sold the business and that the new owners weren't going to keep the portrait studio. "He feels awful, Will, but there's nothing he can do about it."

I looked around Toronto for a few months, took the occasional free-lance job, but nothing seemed to settle. I was sorry I had thrown out the folder.

So that's the way it happened, coming home, as Harlen said. I packed my things in wooden crates and cardboard boxes and arranged to have them sent west. I didn't call Harlen. _____

There was a four-hour layover in Calgary, and by the time we left, it was evening. We caught the sun as it started to drop behind the Rockies. There was a young girl sitting next to me by the window. You couldn't see a thing for the clouds, but as we began our descent, she pointed through the glass and said, "That's Medicine River, mister. That's where I live."

It was dark when the plane landed. In the glow of the lights, I could see people standing around in the terminal. There were children, excited, running back and forth and couples huddled up in one another.

I was walking across the tarmac when I saw him. Harlen Bigbear. He was leaning against the glass, smiling.

"You know," said Bud Prettywoman, "it's hard to get someone to stop drinking once they've started. Floyd figures that Harlen is depressed about Doris."

"Doris died fourteen years ago."

"Floyd figures that it's what they call post-partum depression. You know, where something happens, but it doesn't hit you until some time later."

"Bud, post-partum depression is what women get after they have babies."

"They get it, too? Maybe you better ask Floyd. He read a book or something. Floyd's pretty smart, you know." Bud looked around the room. "Pretty good wedding. Jonnie looked real good. Hope the baby don't look like Cecil."

Bud wandered across the empty floor to the door. "Catch the lights when you go, would you, Will? And maybe, if you see Harlen, tell him hello for me. Tell him it was a good wedding."

I packed up my gear, turned off the lights and went looking for Harlen. The American Hotel was busy, and it took me a good twenty minutes of looking before I was sure that Harlen wasn't there. Floyd and Elwood were sitting at a table with a couple of women.

"Hey, Will. Sit down. Never see you in here. Have

a beer. Maybe you want to buy the next round."

The smoke in the American was thick and blue. I could hardly breathe. "No, thanks. You guys see Harlen?"

Floyd looked at Elwood, and Elwood looked at the table.

"Haven't seen him tonight," said Floyd.

"Someone says they thought he was drinking again."

"Yeah, I heard that, too," said Floyd. "Heard he was at some bar the other day. Looked real bad, I heard. Throwing up in the toilet."

"Anybody know where he is?"

"Could be anywhere, Will. Man starts to drink, he loses track of where he is," and Floyd turned to the women. "Am I right?"

I left Floyd and Elwood drinking their beers and chatting up the women. The American was the Indian bar in town, but there were others that I had heard the boys talk about. I stopped at each of them. Harlen wasn't there. At about midnight, I figured I'd stop by his apartment on the off chance he had come home. His car was parked in front. I knocked on the door, but no one answered. Harlen kept a key on the back porch. Everyone knew where it was. Anyone who needed a place to stay the night could just come by, help themselves to the key and curl up on the couch. I had slept there for the first three weeks after I came back to Medicine River.

The place was dark, but I could smell the acrid odour of vomit. Harlen was lying on the bed in just his undershirt and shorts. There was a bucket next to the bed. He looked awful.

There was really no point in waking him, so I went to the kitchen and started some coffee. "Coffee'll make you feel better," Harlen liked to say. "Drives the blood right to your head." I took the bucket to the bathroom and emptied it and left it in the tub to soak. I found a blanket in the closet. It was going to be a long night.

When I arrived back in Medicine River, Harlen insisted that I stay at his place. The next morning, he took me around to the DIA people and began talking about a small-business loan. "Man's a world-famous photographer, you know. Worked in Toronto." And he took his time with each syllable in Toronto, as if the word was magic. Whitney Oldcrow shook his head and explained to Harlen that his office couldn't make loans to non-status Indians, that he was sorry but that was the way it was. We went to three banks that afternoon and out to the reserve the next day.

Harlen was indefatigable. "This is Will, Rose's boy. Will, this is . . ." By the time we headed for town, I'd met sixty or seventy people.

"You watch, Will. Few days and word gets around that there's a world-class Indian photographer in Medicine River, and people will be asking you to take their money. Couple of the banks we saw yesterday are probably trying to call us already. You got a name for the studio yet?"

The banks didn't call, but I was able to arrange a loan with a local credit union that was looking for new business. I had my own equipment, so I didn't need all that much.

"How about Redman Studios?

"Maybe you should call it Chief Mountain Photography.

"Ought to have something catchy like First People's Photography.

"Need a name that's personal like Will's Photographs."

I settled on Medicine River Photography. Harlen wasn't all that keen on the name. "Doesn't have much zip, Will. Maybe you should add *and Salon* and pick up some of the French business." I found a place across from the old post office, and in four months, I was open.

Harlen was my first customer. He wanted a photograph, a portrait of himself in his dance outfit. "You can put it in the window, if you like. Pierre du Gua does that, and so does Fred Dillar. Helps to bring the business in. People coming by the window and seeing me in my outfit, sure to bring in business."

I put the picture in the window, told Harlen there was no charge, but he insisted on paying the full price. "No good to give it away, Will. You won't stay in business long." When the business cards came, Harlen took them out to the reserve. He took some down to the Friendship Centre and passed them out to anyone he met. At the end of the first month, he stopped by and took me to lunch. When the waitress brought the check, he left two business cards along with the tip.

By the end of the first year, I was making money.

I was having my second cup of coffee when I heard Harlen moan. He had rolled over on the bed and was leaning over the edge.

"Harlen," I said, "you okay?"

Another moan.

"You want the bucket?"

"God, Will, I feel awful. What are you doing here?"

"Thought you might need some company. I've got some coffee on."

"Couldn't drink it."

"What can I get you?"

"Maybe some soup. There's some chicken soup in the cupboard. Soup would be real nice, Will." There was a pause, and Harlen's body tightened. "Maybe bring the bucket, too."

I was searching through the cupboard, when the front door opened and Bertha Morley walked in. "Will," she said. "What are you doing here?"

"Thought I'd come by and see if I could help."

"That's nice," said Bertha. "People should help like that. How's he doing?"

"Still pretty drunk. You want some coffee? I'm making him some soup."

"Drunk?"

"Don't know what started it. Bud Prettywoman said Harlen just started drinking. Didn't know why. You got any idea?"

"Bud see him drinking?"

"Floyd told him."

"How was the wedding?"

"Nice."

"I was supposed to be there, but my boy's got that flu. I really wanted to see the wedding. Did Jonnie show much?"

"Couldn't tell."

"Harlen's not drunk, Will. He's just got the flu. You had it yet?"

"Flu?"

"Everybody's getting it. Harlen got it Friday. It was my birthday. We went to the American for lunch. He was pretty sick then, but you know Harlen. Spent most of lunch in the bathroom."

Bertha found the soup and put the water on, and I went back into the bedroom. Harlen was sitting up. I wondered if he had heard me.

"Hey, you're looking better. How you feeling?"

"Pretty rough, Will. Wouldn't get too close. No sense you catching it, too. Was that Bertha?"

"Yeah, Bertha's making the soup."

"How was the wedding?"

"Good wedding."

"Lots of food?"

"More than enough."

"Real nice of you to stop by, Will," said Harlen, and he lurched forward and retched over the bucket.

"That's what friends are for," I said.

"You bet."

Bertha and I sat with Harlen while he tried to eat some of the soup, and I told him about the wedding and who was there and what the bride wore. I told Harlen that Bud Prettywoman said to say hello.

As we talked, I remembered the night I came in from Toronto, getting off the plane in Medicine River, and walking towards the lights in the terminal. I was almost to the doors when I saw Harlen leaning against the glass, looking as though he hadn't moved in all the months I had been gone. And as I stepped into the terminal, I remember wondering just how long he had been standing there waiting.

eight

Harlen had an ear for depression. He could hear it, he said. "You know, Will, women can hear their babies even before they start to cry. And Barney Oldperson's dog, Skunker, can hear Barney's half-ton coming across the river eight miles away. Bobby DuLac says he can hear voices, but that doesn't count. And people all the time are saying that they can hear a pin drop."

Harlen and I were driving back from a basketball tournament in Salt Lake City. Every year, the Native Students' Association at the University of Utah holds an invitational basketball tournament. Money tournament. Good money, too. And every year, the Medicine River Friendship Centre basketball team goes to the tournament. And every year, we lose.

"So, how come you're depressed, Will?"

"I'm not depressed."

Normally when we go to Salt Lake, we take the Friendship Centre van, but this time, Big John Yellow Rabbit needed the van for the elders who were going to Calgary to see the hockey play-offs against Edmonton.

"She just needs some time, Will."

It was just as well. Neither of us smoked; all the rest of the boys did. You can only drive for so long at sixty miles an hour with your head hanging out the window.

"You think the boys will be all right?"

"Sure," I said. "They got Leroy's wagon, the drum, a case of beer, a bunch of those cheap cigars, and a general idea of which way north is. What else could they need?"

"That's pretty serious depression, Will. Maybe you want to talk about it?"

"I'm not depressed."

Well, maybe I was a bit down. I didn't like losing, especially close games. And I didn't like talking about it.

"I just don't like losing close games, Harlen."

"Will, they beat us by twenty points. Hell, they're the team that took the championship. Maybe it's about Louise?"

"It was close at half-time. It has nothing to do with Louise."

I was probably a little upset about the shortcut we had taken, too. Harlen had looked at the map in Salt Lake and said we should go through Casper, Wyoming on the way home, since we had never seen that part of the country and it wasn't any longer. By the time we stopped for coffee in Rawlins and I looked at the map, it was too late to turn back.

"Getting old's not so bad, Will. You can't play basketball forever. More important things in life. Wife, kids, good television set, hot shower."

I met Susan at the McMichael Art Gallery. A friend of
mine, Bob Hobson who edited a journal on cultures
and the environment asked me to take some candids
of an exhibit of contemporary Native art that the
McMichael was showing for an article he was doing.

"It's in Kleinburg. You can use my car."

"Okay."

"Just some candids. You know, people standing
around looking."

"Sure."

"Maybe a shot of one of Joanne Cardinal Schubert's
war shirts. Something like that. Use your judgement."

She was looking at a painting by a Cree artist, Jane
Ash Poitras.

"Nice painting," I said, because I couldn't think of
anything else to say.

She nodded and smiled the way you do when you
hope the other person will disappear.

"I'm photographing the show." I waved my hand
around the room as if the gesture would magically
transform me into something other than a toad. "For
a friend. For an article."

"It is a nice painting," she said. And she left. I went
back to my camera, relieved she had let me escape
with only minor bruising.

Two weeks later, I stopped by Bob's office to drop
off the slides of the show. Bob wasn't in, and his secretary said I should leave the slides with his assistant
in the next office. She was sitting behind the desk.

"I'm Susan Adamson," she said and held out her
hand. "You're the photographer."

"For Bob. For the article."

"Are those the slides?"

"Yes."

"Are you hungry?" Her hair was black and cut short. Her skin was light, pale, like heavy cream. "We could look at the slides over lunch."

I don't remember where we had lunch. Everything came with a wad of green sprouts on it. She looked at the slides. I made one or two inane jokes about cameras. She said she liked the slides, and I left my business card. If you need any more photography work done, I told her, just give me a call. The number is there on the card. So is the address. You can reach me at home, too. And I wrote my home phone number on the back of the card. I could hear my voice croaking along, the warts popping up everywhere.

I took a long shower that night and watched the late movie with a pot of spaghetti on my lap and a carton of milk and a bag of chocolate-creme cookies.

"A hot shower," said Harlen, turning on the dome light and looking at the map, "is great for depressions. In the old days, we used to have regular sweats just for that reason. The old people were pretty smart, you know. Did you know that Carter Heavyman still has a couple of sweats each year? Should ask Louise about them."

Having to listen to Harlen reminded me that there were a few advantages to travelling in the Friendship Centre van with the drum going and the great clouds of smoke billowing out the windows and everyone singing at the tops of their voices.

"Hey, Will," said Harlen, folding the map over the steering wheel so I could see. "Look at this."

"We lost already?"

"That's better, Will. Little humour always helps. No, look. We're going to go right by the Custer National Monument. Look, it's just outside Billings.

What do you say? Let's stop by and see it."

"You think they let Indians in?"

"Why would they keep us out?"

"Harlen, it's probably just a bunch of plaques and some farmer's field with a fancy fence around it."

"History, Will. It's part of our history."

"The Blackfoot didn't fight Custer."

Harlen shook his head and patted me on the shoulder. "Pretty hard to see the bigger picture, when you're depressed. Come on, Will. When we stop for supper in Casper, I'll get one of those tourist books that tells all about the Little Bighorn. I can read it to you as we head north. Get you in the mood. Maybe you can call Louise, too. Nothing like a phone call to smooth over a quarrel."

"Who said we had a quarrel?"

"Bertha."

"Bertha?"

"You know Bertha."

We stopped in Casper for supper. Harlen picked out a place called the Casper Café.

"Fancy that," I said. But Harlen ignored me.

"You got to eat at the local spots, Will. They got the best food. Looks like they're full up. Sure sign of good food. Good food'll cheer you up."

There were at least four tables empty. The waitress came over with the menus and told us that the special was meatloaf and that there was still some of the Casper Café's famous apple pie left in case we wanted to reserve a piece.

I looked at the menu, but I wasn't hungry. Harlen ordered the meatloaf and reserved two pieces of pie. "Good pie is hard to find," said Harlen, "and if I don't like the first piece, I can always pass on the second."

It wouldn't do me any harm to miss a meal. I might even lose some weight. I ordered a small dinner salad with no dressing.

"Long trip home," said Harlen, getting up. "Going to see about that book on the Little Bighorn. You know, you can smell that meatloaf from here. Maybe you should call Louise."

Susan called me a week later to say she would like my advice on a project that involved old glass photographic plates. "It's Susan Adamson," she said. "I don't know if you remember me. . . ."

We had lunch again, and it could have been the same place. There were sprouts on the sandwich and on the salad, too. This time, I wore my blue blazer and my grey slacks. You couldn't tell I was a photographer. We talked about glass plates and the upcoming show. We talked about the plays in town. I hadn't seen any of them, but I said I was going to. She had seen two, but they weren't very good. Had I read Basil Johnston's new book? He's Ojibway, she said, and the book's quite funny. I had heard about it, I said, and planned to read it soon. She was from Prince Edward Island. I told her I was from Alberta. You're Indian, aren't you? she asked.

Half-way through the meal, my nose began to run. Not fast. Just a slow drip. I tried dabbing at it, while I pretended to wipe my mouth. I had a handkerchief in my pocket, but I couldn't bring myself to blow my nose there at the table.

After lunch, we walked back to the museum. What are you doing Friday night? I asked her. Croak, croak. She was busy then, but would I like to go to an art opening with her on Thursday? Maybe dinner afterwards.

"I love art," I said.

We went to the art show that Thursday, and we went to dinner. I don't remember how we decided to go to my apartment. We weren't drunk or anything like that. We caught a cab, and Susan said something that sounded like "let's go," and I gave the driver my address. She went up the steps as though she knew exactly where she was going, and we went to bed as though we had been lovers for years.

"I'd like to see you again." During the week was best, she said. Did I like Japanese food? Had I ever been to Harbourfront? Did I have a favourite wine? Would I tell her if she snored? Did I think she was fast? She talked with that soft voice of hers and those blue eyes and that mouth that only bent at the corners when she smiled. I chased after the answers.

She left the next morning. I went into the kitchen and scrambled four eggs, fried two potatoes, grilled half-a-dozen sausages and ate warm toast and apricot jam until all the bread was gone.

The meatloaf arrived before Harlen got back. It was thick and greasy and covered with a white sauce. You got some puckered green peas with it and a wedge of mashed potatoes covered with more of that white sauce.

Harlen came back shaking his head. "Would you believe it, Will? They don't have any of those booklets on the Little Bighorn. The lady at the desk said that we should try after we cross the line into Montana. All they had was a postcard."

"So, where's the postcard?"

"I didn't want a postcard, Will. Hell, we're going to see the real thing." Harlen whacked off a large forkful of meatloaf and shovelled it into his mouth.

"Mmmmmmmm," he said, squeezing his eyes shut and dragging a bit of sauce off his lip with his tongue. "Nothing like these local places for good cooking. What'd Louise have to say?"

"Too late to call."

He ate both pieces of pie.

By the time we left, I was beginning to get a little hungry. Harlen hadn't even offered me a bite of the second piece of pie.

The road from Casper took us up through Sheridan and then across the line into Montana. By the time we got to Lodge Grass, the sun was dropping down behind the mountains, and Harlen was looking at the map again.

"The Little Bighorn is just up the road. And look at this, Will. We're on the Crow Indian reserve. Maybe we should drop in and say hello."

"Maybe they have a basketball tournament we could donate some money to." I was still thinking about that pie.

There was a storm waiting for us to the north. As we left Lodge Grass, I could see the occasional lightning flash in the mountains.

"You still got some film in your camera, Will? I want to get a picture of us standing over Custer's grave. Maybe send it to the *Kainai News*. Put a big caption under it says, 'Custer Died for Your Sins.' What do you think?"

I wasn't that depressed.

"Dumb idea," I said.

"Should have had that meatloaf, Will."

Harlen turned on the radio, and we listened to some cowboy sing about his pick-up truck and how bad life was since his girlfriend ran off with a long-haul trucker.

"Saw Louise and South Wing at Woodward's last week. How old is she now, Will?"

"Nine months."

"Pretty girl. Looks like her mother."

"So they say."

"You see them regular, don't you?"

"Sure."

"Floyd says he thought he saw her and that Cree guy at Casey's, but you know Floyd."

"Sure."

We caught the weather report, snow flurries in the mountains. There was more lightning now, and each bolt sent the radio crackling.

"There it is, Will."

The big green highway sign said, Custer National Monument, One Mile.

"Slow down, Will. Don't want to miss the turnoff."

Harlen was rocking back and forth in his seat and looking out the window.

"I'll bet Custer wasn't even close at half-time." I don't know why in the hell I said that.

Harlen laughed and slapped his legs. "Hell, Will, Crazy Horse slam-dunked that bastard. Whoooeeee, slam-dunk."

"Time out," I shouted. "That's what Custer was yelling when all those Indians came riding out of the hills."

"Time out," shouted Harlen.

We missed the turnoff. We had to drive another five miles before we could turn around and come back. The Custer Monument was up a hill, and we got there just in time to see some fellow in a Bronco closing the gate.

"Stay here, Will. I'll go see what's happening."

In the headlights of the car, I could see Harlen

talking to the man. Harlen pointed off to the hill, and the guy shook his head. Harlen held his hands out, and the guy shook his head. Harlen turned around once, took a step or two back to the car, and then went back to where the guy was throwing a chain around the gate. Harlen pointed back to the car, and the fellow looked into the headlights. And he shook his head.

Harlen came back to the car. "It's closed for the night, Will."

"What?"

"Young fellow, friendly enough. Told us to come back tomorrow."

"We won't be here tomorrow."

"I told him that."

"Did you tell him we drove all this way just to see the monument?"

"I told him that."

"Shit!"

"He said he was sorry."

"Did you tell him," I said, rolling down the window and shouting into the night, "did you tell him we're Indians!"

"I told him that, too, Will. He said he was sorry."

I got out and stood by the car and imagined I could see that kid hiding in the dark, hunkered down behind the fender of the Bronco, his hands shaking around his rifle, waiting for us to come screaming and whooping and crashing through the gate.

Susan and I went out once, sometimes twice a week. A poetry reading, a meal, and bed. An art opening, a meal, and bed. A play, a meal, and bed. And we talked about everything. We talked in bed, especially, and always before we made love, sometimes for

hours, until it became part of foreplay. We joked
about that and laughed.

She brought some of her clothes by and hung them
in my closet. I'm not moving in, she said, so don't
worry. I told her I wasn't worried. It's just more convenient, she said, and she was right. She was telling
me to be patient, I knew that. It would be a slow pro-
cess of trying each other out, and in the end, she
would move in, and we would talk about other
things.

"Will," she said, "If you don't want me around, just
say so."

I could smell her everywhere in the apartment, and
I began to miss her when she wasn't there.

I called her at her office one afternoon. Leon Rooke
was reading at Hart House that night. She had
bought one of his books, she said, but hadn't read it
yet. She's not here, the secretary told me. She wasn't
feeling well and went home. Did I have her number?

I called when I got home. I let the phone ring.

"Yes, may I help you?"

"Susan?"

"Nope. Mummy's sick. Who's this?"

"I'm a friend of your mummy."

"You want to talk to Daddy?"

I saw it too late, and I was caught like a thief in the
middle of a room with all the lights suddenly thrown
on.

"Can I help you?"

"Hello, yes, I'm a business associate of your wife's.
I'm calling about a photography project that we're
working on."

"Oh. She's lying down right now. But if you call
back in about an hour, I think she'll be up."

"Great. Why don't I do that."

"Can I tell her who called?"

"Tell her it was Zneick's Photography."

I wasn't going to call back. I was going to leave it alone, but I rang the number at seven and at eight and at eight-thirty. The line was busy. I tried it again at nine, nine-fifteen, nine-thirty, quarter to ten. I gave up at eleven, the busy signal sounding for all the world like an alarm.

"Do you believe this?" I shouted.

"It's okay, Will."

"Hell, we should just drive right through that gate."

"Pretty big chain."

"That chicken-shit bastard is probably pissing his pants. I'll bet he can see us."

"Don't think so, Will. He said you can't see a thing in the dark. Said he'd let us in but the hockey play-offs are on tonight. Series is tied at three games all."

I got back in the car.

Harlen had the map out. "You think we could get to Billings before the third period starts?"

We drove back down the hill. Harlen could talk to himself for all I cared.

"Better get some gas, Will. There's that station we passed. Looks like a restaurant, too. Maybe you're hungry now."

We got out of the car and stretched.

"I'll bet they got good food here. You know, Louise is probably still up."

There was a phone next to the washroom. Harlen had a big piece of apple pie in front of him when I returned.

"Even better than that other pie. They got some chicken-fried steak left, too. You get hold of Louise?"

"Too late to call."

I had some soup. I had some pie, too.

"What if we stay here overnight, Will? Pretty late anyway, like you say. Get a room, watch the game, see the monument in the morning."

We finished our coffee. I went and washed up, again. The line was still busy.

We got a room at the Big Chief Motel. It had a neon sign that flashed Vacancy and You Like-um. Harlen chose it because he figured that, since we were near the Crow reservation, the tribe probably owned it.

"Got to help each other out when we can."

The room was clean. The bathroom had a shower. The television worked, and if you looked hard out the window, you could almost see the top of the iron gate at the Custer monument.

"Fellow said we got the best room, Will. Has a view, he said, but you can't see it at night. What do you think, Will? He could have been Indian."

Calgary won the game. Harlen fell asleep on the bed and began to snore. I left the television on and turned off the sound. I lay there in the dark on my side and dreamed about driving up the hill to the monument, busting through those gates, the tires squealing, bullets flying all around me, the kid yelling for reinforcements, the phone ringing busy in my ear.

chapter

nine

Basketball practice for the Medicine River Friendship Centre Warriors was on Monday and Wednesday evenings at the Adams High School gym. We got the gym after the girl's volleyball team finished around nine, and we practised until we were exhausted or the janitor threw us out.

Wednesday night, Floyd and I were shooting free throws, when Harlen walked in with a tall kid I didn't recognize. I nudged Floyd. "Another one of Harlen's recruits." Floyd looked and then looked again. "Holy cow," he said. "That's Clyde Whiteman."

Harlen was forever recruiting someone who was going to help propel the Warriors into a league championship. Two years ago, he had talked Peter Black Elk into playing with us. Peter was a track star. He could run circles around everyone on the team. But he couldn't shoot. Paul Moon could shoot. Every scrimmage we had, he'd score thirty, forty points. But he froze during the games. Al Frank was a great shot and could move quick as a trout, but he had a girl-friend in High River who didn't like him spending three nights a week with a "bunch of bums".

So most of us didn't get too excited any more when Harlen showed up with another recruit. "Damn," said Floyd. "It *is* Clyde Whiteman." Harlen walked out to the middle of the court like he always does when he has an announcement to make.

"Some of you boys know Clyde Whiteman. He's Harper Whiteman's nephew. He's going to play for us. Pretty good player, too." And Harlen smiled, as if someone had called him up to say that he could borrow Magic Johnson for the rest of the season.

Clyde Whiteman was tall, as tall as me, maybe even taller. But he knew how to play. He was smooth and quick. The ball left his hands effortlessly, sliding into the net from all angles and distances. I tried to guard him. He shot over me. He moved around me. He muscled me off the boards. By the end of practice, I was bent over grabbing my knees, feeling as though I had been dragged along behind a large horse. Clyde had barely cracked a sweat.

I leaned against the cool ceramic wall and let the water run over me. Floyd was standing at the next shower. "Who did you say that was?"

"Clyde Whiteman. He's Freda's boy."

"Good player."

"The best. When he graduated, he had all kinds of offers from the big schools."

I stuck my head back under the water. "Where's he been?"

"In jail," said Floyd.

Harlen came into the studio the next day. "What do you think, Will?" he said, sliding into his favourite chair.

"About?"

"Clyde."

"Good player."

"Good, hell, Will. You're good."

Harlen had a way around words that would rattle a weasel. "Okay," I said. "Clyde's better than good."

"Will," Harlen said, leaning over so his chin was about an inch off my desk. "He's going to help us win a championship."

"I hear he was in jail."

It was my own fault. I could have let the matter die, admitted that Clyde was a better player than me, agreed that, with Clyde at centre, the championship was a cinch. I could have done all that without mentioning jail. But I didn't, and Harlen didn't leave for another two hours. By then, I knew Clyde's life story, and I had missed lunch.

Clyde had been a great high-school player. Everyone figured he'd go off and become famous. But on graduation night, he took off with a couple of friends, "borrowed" a car, and drove it to Edmonton, where they wrecked it after a high-speed chase with the cops. The cops caught Clyde; his friends got away. Clyde wouldn't tell who the other kids were, so the judge gave him a year in jail.

"It wasn't his fault, Will. Just out with the wrong people."

Seven months after he got out, he was involved in a robbery. Clyde drove out to Cardston with Marvin Weaselback, Jerry Rabbit and River Johnson. Everyone was drunk, and when they stopped to get gas, River took the 30-30 out of his trunk and helped himself to the cash register as well. Clyde was sound asleep in the back seat. They got about twenty miles before the cops caught them. When Clyde woke up, the police were putting cuffs on him.

"Clyde's unlucky, you know. Wrong place, wrong time. I knew his mother, Will. Real good woman. You know, I do some counselling down at the jail for the Indian kids. I've known Clyde since he was little. He's a good kid. Bad luck, that's what it is, Will. Bad luck."

Just before Christmas, Clyde tried to stick a portable television under his coat and walk out of Sound Warehouse with it.

"You should see him play basketball. The inmates play pick-up games on Tuesday nights. Those baskets over there are a little too high, you know, and crooked. And the nets are those chain things. Noisy. The ball is always getting stuck, so you have to stop the game and knock it loose. And the floor is made up of those tile squares. Hard as hell. He was still getting forty points a game. Can you imagine what he'll do on a good court?"

It didn't take long to find out. Our next game was against one of the real powers in the league: Bolton. They always beat us. But by the time we left the Bolton gym that night, whatever doubt anyone on the team had had about Clyde Whiteman's value was gone. He put in forty-two points, blocked half-a-dozen shots, and we beat the Wheat Kings by ten.

Harlen couldn't stop talking and slapping Clyde on the back. "Faked them right out of their shorts. Nothing between us and the league championship."

Clyde was more modest. "You guys play good without me, Will. Probably could have beat those guys. I'm just happy you don't mind me playing with you. You know, me being an ex-con and all."

I drove the van home. Harlen and the boys sat in the back and beat on the drum and sang songs. Clyde sat up front with me. "I just want to stay out of trouble, Will. Turn my life around. Already lost too much. Playing with you guys is going to change my luck. I can feel it."

Clyde sure changed our luck. We began to win our games. Harlen was insufferable. He sat on the bench with a towel draped around his neck and just grinned. He had never been a great coach, but with Clyde on the floor, whatever pretensions he had just slipped away. He would sit there, grinning, occasionally clapping his hands. Every so often, he'd yell out an encouragement.

"Atta boy, Clyde.

"Way to drive.

"Great rebound."

But mostly he sat there quietly and watched, and we were left to substitute for ourselves.

Clyde would grin back at Harlen, but he didn't look particularly happy.

"Maybe you could talk to Harlen, Will. Don't want you and the boys to think I'm stuck up."

"Don't worry," Floyd told him. "Harlen'll calm down. Soon as you make a few mistakes, he'll start yelling at you like the rest of us."

But if anything, Harlen got worse. He began comparing us to Clyde.

"Watch Clyde, Floyd. He knows how to make that move.

"You got to box out better, Elwood, like Clyde.

"Maybe you should work out with some weights, Will. Lose a few pounds. Get those legs in shape so you can get more rebounds, like Clyde does."

We all had pretty tough skins, and we had all been through Harlen's coach's talks before. But they were affecting Clyde. His game began to fall off. We were

still winning, but Clyde wasn't running as hard, and
he wasn't getting as many points. Then we played the
Nanton Antelopes, a team in sixth place, and lost.
You'd think that someone had shot Harlen's mother.
Clyde took most of the blast.

"Christ sakes, Clyde. You looked like you were
asleep out there.

"You ran like Will. You been drinking again? You
on drugs again?

"You play like that in the play-offs, and we'll be
out in the first round."

I finished showering and got dressed. Harlen was
out in the van with the rest of the boys. Clyde was sitting on the bench by himself.

"Come on, don't worry," I said. "Harlen gets like
that whenever we lose. It's just noise."

Clyde looked at me and smiled. "Just don't want to
disappoint anyone, Will. Want to do it right this
time."

We played Cardston on Thursday. I got to the gym
late. Floyd caught me as I came into the locker room.
"Come on, Will. Get dressed. Game starts in another
two minutes."

"No rush," I said, looking at Floyd. "Harlen never
starts me."

Floyd sighed. "Clyde's in jail."

"You're kidding."

"Got drunk and took a swing at a cop."

"Hell."

"Got thirty days."

"For hitting a cop. Damn, he was lucky."

"He missed the cop. Hit a parking meter. Hurt his
hand pretty bad."

"Harlen know?"

Harlen knew. He was sitting on the bench, bent

over looking at the floor. I sat down next to him.
Neither of us said a thing.

"Don't worry, Harlen," I said, putting a hand on
his shoulder and trying to throw some humour on
the situation. "I've been watching Clyde play and
there's nothing to it. You watch. I'll score forty points
tonight." Which should have been enough to get
Harlen laughing, because we had already played half
the season, and I didn't have thirty points yet.

I didn't really expect Harlen to laugh, and he
didn't. But he did look up. And he sighed. "Why do
you think he does it, Will?"

"Does what?"

"Gets himself in trouble like that?"

"Just bad luck, like you said."

"Nothing to do with luck, Will."

The game started, and I left Harlen sitting on the
bench with his thoughts. I played hard that night. So
hard, I fouled out, which I never do. And I scored
fourteen points, which I never do, and we won. But
Harlen was inconsolable.

"Hey, Harlen," said Floyd, as we were dressing.
"You see Will hit that hook? Fourteen points, too. Not
bad for an old man."

Harlen didn't even join us for coffee after the game.

"Harlen'll get over it," said Floyd, pouring three
creams into his coffee. "He takes things personally
sometimes."

"Clyde a relative?"

"Nope."

"Doesn't make sense. Remember when you and
Elwood got thrown in jail in Browning just before
that big tournament?"

"That was Elwood's fault."

"You were both drunk."

"That was Elwood's fault."

"Okay, but Harlen didn't get upset about that. Not like this."

Floyd put another cream and two sugars in his coffee. "He was angry, alright. Told us we let him down and that sort of stuff. You know Harlen."

"But not like now. Why's he so upset with Clyde?"

Clyde was out in thirty days, and we were still in first place. Clyde wasn't even rusty. The first night he was back, he put in forty-three points, and Harlen was happy again.

Harlen caught me after the game. "Play-offs are coming up, Will. Maybe you could have a talk with Clyde. He respects you, Will. Maybe help keep him out of trouble. You know, like a father."

"Don't know him very well," I said.

"Bet your father had some great stories about staying out of trouble, the kind that made you laugh, but then when you looked underneath them, you could see they were serious, and you knew he was trying to help."

"Never knew my father."

"I've done all I can do, Will. Maybe tell him how much the team needs him. You know, like a father."

My mother never talked much about my father, and James and me knew it wasn't a good idea to ask. But every so often, she would get in a story-telling mood. Most of the stories were about when we were little.

"When you were a baby," she would say to James, "you always wanted to be tossed in the air. You'd lie in that basket and kick your feet and wave your arms until someone came along and picked you up."

James always liked hearing the stories.

"I was scared that you'd get dropped, but you just

laughed and laughed. Used to really scare me to see you flying through the air like that. It scared Will, too. Will would stand there ready in case someone dropped you."

I didn't remember any of that, but I liked the idea of trying to save James.

"And Will, you liked to drive. Any time someone would come by with a car, you'd beg to sit behind the wheel. You could hardly see over the dash, but that didn't bother you none. Off we'd go down the road with you sitting on someone's lap, holding onto that wheel like you were in the races."

I knew the someone in the stories was my father.

Normally, Clyde rode home with Harlen, but as Harlen was stuffing all the uniforms into the bag, he said, "Clyde, I got to stop at a friend's house. How about catching a ride with Will?"

Clyde lived way over on the north side. It was late, and we were both tired.

"Good game," I said. "You got a great jump shot."

Clyde sat there and looked out the window.

"You okay?"

In the flash of the street lights, I could see Clyde's face. "You think Harlen's still mad at me?"

"No. That's just Harlen. He always yells at us. He likes to yell."

"I screwed up again."

"No, you did great. Forty-three points. Wish I could shoot like that."

"You know what I mean."

"Hell, Clyde, there isn't a man on the team hasn't been in jail."

Clyde looked at me. "You ever been arrested, Will?"

"Floyd's been arrested," I said. "So has Elwood and Frankie. Just like you. Too much to drink, you know."

"You ever been in jail?"

I was stuck. "No, but I screw up all the time. You've seen me play. Hell, the team could get as much offence out of a beaver."

Clyde turned back to the window. "Just can't seem to change things, no matter how hard I try. Keep disappointing everybody."

"You're doing fine. Hey, we're going to win that championship."

I dropped Clyde off at his apartment. He took his bag out of the back of the car and leaned on the door. He was smiling.

"Will, you tell Harlen I'm going to try, just like he said. I'm going to try hard." And he turned and walked away.

As I pulled into my driveway, I saw the front of Harlen's car parked just around the corner of the block. I put on some water for tea and threw some clothes in the washer. The doorbell rang, just as the kettle began to whistle.

"Saw your light on as I was driving by, Will. You weren't in bed?"

"I was just making tea."

"You got any coffee?"

Harlen wandered around a bit. He asked how Louise and South Wing were doing.

"They're doing fine, Harlen."

He asked after my brother James, who had left San Francisco and taken off for Australia for no other reason than that he had read an article on Aborigines in a copy of *National Geographic*.

"James was headed for Australia, last I heard."

And he asked about the business, how it was doing.

"Business is fine, too."

Harlen stirred his tea for a while, nodded his head a couple of times and looked around the kitchen, as though he had lost something that he expected to find any minute.

"You gave Clyde a ride home, didn't you?"

"Just like you asked me."

"You get a chance to talk with him?"

"Just like you asked me."

"How's he doing?"

"He's doing fine, Harlen."

Okay, I was being mean-spirited. I knew what Harlen wanted to know. Sometimes when he went around in circles, I'd wait and see how long it took him to ask the questions he wanted to ask. But it was late, and I didn't have the patience for a two- or three-hour circle.

"I think he'll be okay, Harlen. He thinks a lot of you and your opinions, you know. Afraid he's going to disappoint you. Maybe you should take it easy with him. The rest of the boys understand when you yell at them, but I don't think Clyde does."

"I don't yell at the boys, Will."

"You yell some."

"When was the last time you can remember me yelling at someone on the team?"

I was sorry I started this. "Last game, Harlen. You yelled at Clyde."

"That wasn't yelling."

"Okay."

"Sometimes I just talk loud, you know, encouragement."

"Okay."

"Some people have a hard time staying out of trouble, you know. Clyde's like that. He needs a lot of encouragement. You tell him how much we need him for the championship?"

"I told him."

"What'd he say?"

"He said he was going to try hard. Didn't want to disappoint us."

"You know, Will, Clyde could have been my son. Freda and me almost got married."

"What happened?"

"She married Gary Whiteman."

Sometimes you needed a map of Harlen's mind to keep up with him.

"That's it?"

"You know me, Will. I don't mess around with married women."

I threw Harlen out around two. Maybe he felt responsible for Clyde because of all the talking they had done when Clyde was in jail, or maybe he just wanted to win the championship. Clyde's father had died of cancer, and Freda never got remarried. Maybe Harlen decided to fill in for Gary.

Sometimes the stories were about when she was younger, before she had us. "One time," she told us, "we all went over to Waterton Lake. It was a weekend, and we had nothing else to do. George Harley had his father's truck, and he and Wilma Whiteman rode up front, and I had to sit in the back with one of Harley's friends, a white guy named Howard Webster.

"He was a goofy guy. George had met him at the rodeo in Edmonton. He wanted to see some Indians, that's how goofy he was, so George brought him along."

Every time my mother would say "Howard Webster", she'd look at the floor or look away and then, after a second, she'd keep going. "So we got to the lake and that Howard wanted to go swimming. George told him that the water was cold, but that Howard was real goofy, and he took off his boots and his shirt, and before we could say anything, he ran and dove into the water."

Henry Goodrider told James and me that he had been to Waterton with his uncle and that the water there was so cold that it would freeze things like apples and bananas and that if you dipped a peach in the water and then dropped it on the rocks, it would shatter like a piece of glass.

"So Goofy Howard jumps in the lake and goes all the way under, and we don't see him for a couple of minutes, and just when we think he's killed himself, he comes out of the water like he's seen a half-dozen grizzlies. And he runs up and down the shore shouting that it's cold and where's the blanket, and then he starts chasing Wilma and me, trying to catch one of us so we can warm him up.

"Wilma and me are laughing too hard to get away and that goofy guy gets us wet, too. So George has to grab the tarp from the truck and the four of us lie down in the sun until we're warm again."

Each time my mother told her stories, they got larger and better. Sometimes, it was Howard. Sometimes, it was Martin. Sometimes, it was Eldon. But she never used my father's name.

When the championship came around, we were in first place, so we didn't play the first game. We won the second game. Clyde had thirty-five points. "Good game," Harlen told us. "Only three more to go."

The next one was a breeze. Clyde scored fifty-five points. I scored eight. Harlen was elated.

"Great game, Clyde. Going to be easy. I can see you guys all dressed up in those championship jackets."

We played Bolton in the semifinals. It was tough. They led most of the way, but Floyd came on strong and scored fifteen points. Clyde only scored twenty-four points.

"Not to worry," said Harlen. "Tough team, those guys. Tough to work around a double team all the time, Clyde. You did real well."

"Floyd did real well, too," I said.

"You bet," said Harlen. "Floyd did real well, too."

Clyde sat on the bench with his head down.

"You tired?" I said.

"Yeah, a little tired."

"You want a ride home?"

"No, I'm going to walk. Need to get out."

"Long way."

"Walk it all the time."

"Maybe you want some coffee. Maybe talk some."

Clyde pulled his sweatshirt on over his jersey. "No, just need to walk."

I caught Harlen as he was leaving the gym. "You say anything to Clyde?"

"Just encouragement."

"Anything in particular?"

"Just encouragement."

When the phone rang at two in the morning, I knew it had to be Harlen. It was Floyd. Floyd always comes to the point.

"Guess who's in jail?"

"Not Clyde again."

"Give that man a basketball."

"Drunk?"

"Nope."

"Do I keep guessing?"

"Borrowed a car."

"Shit."

"I haven't called Harlen yet. You want to do the honours?"

"No."

"Should I call him?"

"Yes."

I turned off the light and took the phone off the hook.

There was one story, in particular, that my mother liked to tell again and again.

"When you kids were real small, George Harley and that Howard Webster took all of us to a rodeo. He had some money, you know—Howard, that is—and he was always trying to impress us Indian girls. Wilma's sisters thought he was cute, but Wilma and me thought he was just goofy. But he was nice, too. He bought you one of those little cowboy hats, Will. Do you remember that?"

"Sure, I remember that."

"James, you slept through the entire rodeo. All that noise, and you slept right through it."

"I remember that, too."

"Well, we were all sitting there and pretty soon they call the bucking-horse contest. That was my favourite part. Those horses would come out flopping around like fish on a rock and those smart-alec cowboys would go flying in all directions.

"So we're sitting there watching the show, and the announcer calls the name of the next cowboy, and it's Howard Webster. George tells Wilma that Howard is doing it because he loves her, and Wilma gets embar-

rassed and tells George to shut up and starts whacking him on his shoulder. But just then, Howard comes
out of one of the chutes on this big chestnut.

"I got to say he looked pretty good. He had his legs
up high on that horse's neck, and his arm was in the
air. And he was smiling. Then that horse turned hard,
and Howard took off and landed right on a big pile of
horse poop.

"He got up out of the dirt, and you could see it all
over his nice shirt. He tried to brush it off, but it was
pretty wet. The worst thing was that that goofy guy
had only one shirt, and we had to drive home with
him smelling like a horse. George wanted to make
him sit on the hood, but it was Howard's car, and he
just laughed and said he'd smelled worse.

"And you know what you did, Will? You begged
him to let you drive. You sat on his lap all the way
home and turned the wheel. There you were with
your head against Howard's shirt, horse poop and
all, pretending you were bringing us home."

Harlen was already sitting on the bench when I
arrived for the championship game the next evening.
He didn't say a thing. I dressed and warmed up with
the rest of the boys. It didn't take me long to get up a
sweat. I went back to the bench and sat down.

"Don't worry," I said. "We're going to win this
game."

"You bet, Will."

"Clyde's just unlucky. Like you said. Runs around
with the wrong crowd."

"He was by himself."

"Some people are just unlucky."

We won the game. None of us could believe it. It
wasn't even close. There we were, league champions.

It didn't sink in until we were back in the locker room, and Floyd began prancing around in his bright red-and-blue championship jacket and his jock strap.

"The Warriors . . . champiooooons. How do I look, boys, in my new jacket?"

"You look like a fruit," said Elwood.

"Hey, Harlen. You buying?"

Harlen took out two twenties and gave them to Floyd. "Here, buy a couple of pizzas and some soft drinks. You boys did real well."

"You not coming?"

"Don't feel too good. Maybe the flu."

The season was over, and everyone sort of forgot about Clyde. I guess I figured that someone should go out and see him. When I finished work on Thursday, I drove out to the jail.

"Whiteman's in the gym," the guard told me.

A bunch of the inmates were playing a game of four on four. Clyde was moving through the defence smooth and sure. I walked over and sat on the bench. The game ended, and Clyde came over and sat down.

"Hey, Will. You didn't have to come out. Hear you guys won the championship. Didn't need me at all."

"Could have used you, Clyde. How you doing?"

"Okay. Keep screwing up. But I'm okay."

"You going to be okay?"

"Sure. Harlen stopped by, you know. Brought me a championship jacket. Real good looking. That was pretty nice of him."

"What'd he say?"

"You know . . . talked to me. Hey, it's going to be okay. Learned my lesson this time. Not going to disappoint anyone any more. You watch, just like that jump shot of mine. Swooosh! No rim."

"Sure."

"You watch. Going to be different. I can feel it."

Clyde went back to the game, and I watched him for a while. He moved from side to side with the fluidity of a dancer. Everyone else seemed half a step behind, as he wove his way through their arms and legs.

I always meant to talk to my mother about Howard Webster, and the time I rode home from the rodeo on his lap. I started to once, just before I left for Toronto, but she laughed and turned away and said I was probably too young to have remembered, and anyway, it was a long time back.

I walked over to the door. It was nice that Harlen had brought Clyde a jacket. After all, Clyde was one of the reasons we had got to the championships. I knocked on the door to get let out and looked back to see Clyde float to the top of the key and take that jump shot of his. I watched as the ball left his hands and arched smoothly towards the hoop, spinning backwards as it dipped over the lip of the rim and fell tangling in the chains.

ten

Every so often, Harlen could be as blunt as a brick. "Morning, Will. I bet Bertha a cup of coffee that you forgot."

Harlen had a favourite chair in my studio. Sometimes it would get moved out of position—a large sitting, the cleaning people, furtive decorating. Wherever it was, Harlen would drag it out to the centre of the room in front of my desk and sit down.

"Tomorrow's South Wing's first birthday," said Harlen, dragging and sitting all in one motion. "Have you got your daughter a present yet?"

Harlen's being direct always set me back a few seconds.

"She's not my daughter, Harlen, and no, I haven't bought her a present yet. But I'm going to."

"Bertha says that South Wing can almost say *Daddy*."

"Bertha can talk, but South Wing can't. I'm her uncle, just like you."

"She's always happy to see you."

"She's happy to see anyone."

"That's close enough. You're just crabby because you almost forgot her birthday."

"I didn't almost forget her birthday."

"Bertha was afraid you'd forget."

"I didn't forget."

"Well, we better get moving then."

I had lost Harlen. Somehow he had gotten away from me. "I came to take you shopping."

"Harlen, I have to work."

"Stores won't be open tonight. Tomorrow'll be too late." And he sat forward in the chair with his hands on his knees, looking at me with his mouth closed. Harlen chewed on a lot of people this way. It was best to cut your losses and give up.

We started at Eaton's.

"If you had planned ahead, you could have got her a beaded dress or a ribbon shirt."

"Harlen, she's one year old."

"You could have got it large, for later on."

"I could get her a pair of moccasins. Friendship Centre might have some."

Harlen shook his head. "Already looked."

The salesclerks were no help either. The current rage, so one woman told us, was Fiona Faithful, a doll with a built-in cassette tape-recorder and a Velcro strap that went around your waist so you would never be without her. Harlen didn't stick around to hear the price, which almost made me laugh in spite of the good manners my mother raised me with.

We looked at teddy bears at Woodward's and a Fisher-Price tub toy that squirted water and made six different noises. Woolco had a toy lawn mower that also made noise. Harlen found a little red drum with white maple leaves around the sides that he thought

South Wing would like.

It only took us an hour to exhaust Medicine River.

"Maybe the drum wasn't such a bad idea, Will."

"It was a bad idea."

But it wasn't as bad an idea as it had been an hour before.

"Maybe you should call Louise."

Louise and I hadn't gone out much since South Wing was born, but I would generally go over for dinner about once a week. We still joked about the mistake the nurses had made.

Louise wasn't in. Harlen and I were left to our own devices.

"You know, Will, I'm not one to butt into other people's business, but you and Louise should probably get married."

"Harlen . . ."

"I know you like being single, but everybody can see how much you love South Wing. Bertha figures you're pretty fond of Louise, too."

"I like being single. Louise likes being single."

Harlen shook his head. "Maybe you two could try living together."

"I like living alone. Louise likes living alone."

Harlen nodded, jammed his hands in his pockets and looked back down the streets towards the river.

"I guess we better go out to the reserve then," said Harlen.

"What for?"

"The present. I just thought of where we can get one."

"You thinking about Grey Horse Crafts?"

"No. Got another place in mind."

I didn't have any afternoon appointments, and Wednesdays were always slow.

"We better take your truck, Will," said Harlen. "We got to go out past Rolling Fish Coulee."

We were half-way to the reserve, before I figured out exactly where we were going.

"Harlen," I said, in as friendly a voice as I could manage, "who lives out past Rolling Fish Coulee?"

"Not to worry, Will. You'll see."

"Wouldn't be we're going out to see Martha Old-crow, would it?"

"Lots of people live out there."

Which was a lie of sorts. Lots of people lived on the reserve, but only Martha Oldcrow lived out past Rolling Fish Coulee, and Martha Oldcrow and South Wing's birthday present didn't seem to have much in common.

Martha was a doctor. People with problems went to see her. She was known as the "marriage doctor" because that was what she fixed best.

"Harlen, is this about Louise and me?"

Harlen had the window rolled down. He was sitting there singing to himself, which is what he does on long trips or when he's trying to ignore me.

The road past Old Agency out to Rolling Fish Coulee was always a surprise. I'd only been on it once before. It was a standard joke on the reserve. The council didn't bother grading it like they did the other dirt and gravel roads, because no one lived out there except Martha, and she didn't drive. Every year, the snow and run-off would cut new gullies through the road, and the road itself would change as the pick-ups and four-wheel drives found new ways around the cuts. Last winter, there was a slide that took the road out about ten miles from Old Agency. From there, you went cross-country and found your own way.

"Slide's up ahead about two miles, Will. Better head west."

We left the road, climbed a low embankment, and headed out on to the prairies.

"This is just like the explorers, Will," said Harlen. "Head south. Those trees over there look familiar."

We headed south. We got lost. We headed north. We got lost. We headed west. We got lost.

"Those trees over there look familiar, Will. Head east."

I looked at the gas gauge. With any luck, we could just make it back to Standoff. And Harlen's luck held. We came to the edge of a coulee and couldn't go any farther.

"There it is, Will."

Martha's cabin sat on a small flat across the river.

"Just have to walk down. Best to leave the truck here."

It was almost a mile down the ridge to the river.

"Water's not too deep this time of the year." Harlen was ever the optimist. The river was only about twenty feet wide, but you could see it was going to be over our heads. We looked at it for a while, Harlen measuring it up for a jump. "What do you think, Will?" In the end, we took our clothes off, tied them up in a ball and threw them across. The water was green and murky and freezing.

"Something to tell your kids about, Will."

Martha Oldcrow was sitting in a white Naugahyde Lazy Boy recliner under a cottonwood tree.

"You boys come all this way to go swimming?"

"Afternoon, Granny," said Harlen. "No, we didn't come to swim. Came to see you about a present for a little girl."

"You get lost or something?"

"Big slide across the road. We had to come around."

"Council fixed that two months back."

I looked at the river and my truck up on the ridge.

"We need a present, Granny," said Harlen. "You know Louise Heavyman's little girl, South Wing. Her first birthday's tomorrow. Wanted to get her a real Indian rattle. Like the ones you make, you know."

"This her father?"

I jumped in, before Harlen got started. "I'm a friend."

"Don't need a friend," said Martha. "Needs a father, that one."

"This is Rose Horse Capture's boy, Will. Granny Pete's grandson."

"Sure, I know him. No father that one, too."

Martha got up and headed for the house. "Maybe you boys want to swim some more?" As she got to the door, she stopped, turned around, and looked me up and down like she was measuring me for a suit. "That little girl needs a father. You see her born?"

"I was there."

"Okay. That'll do. You love her?"

On the way back, when we crossed the river again, I was going to drown Harlen.

"Sure."

"Don't sound too sure."

"I love her."

"Okay. How about the mother? You love her?"

I was going to drown him slow. Let him up a couple of times, before I shoved his head all the way into the mud.

"You deaf or you thinking?"

"No. Yes, I like Louise."

"Okay. Like is close enough. Come on. The present's inside."

Martha's house was one big room, and it was dark and cool. There was an old stove in the middle of the floor and a bed near the south wall. There was one window and a table underneath it. All around the room were boxes, and in the boxes were books. There were novels, stacks of Harlequin romances, chemistry textbooks. There were travel books, books on physics, a box of English textbooks, a couple of French dictionaries, a Greek grammar book, along with dozens of *Reader's Digest*s, newspapers and a 1964 *Farmer's Almanac*.

"You read all these?"

"Nope."

"Where'd you get them?"

"Found some of them," said Martha. "Others, people just bring them by."

"What do you do with them all?"

"Look after them," and she said it as though it was the stupidest question she had heard for a while.

"Real nice place," said Harlen.

Martha went over to a dresser and rummaged around in the drawer.

"Here's what you boys want. Good present, this one."

It was a small leather rattle made out of willow and deer hide. It was painted blue and yellow and had several strands of horsehair tied to the side. There were stones or seeds inside. Martha shook it and sang a song. "You know that song?" she asked.

I shook my head.

"Good thing you know how to swim then," and she handed me the rattle. "Young boys don't know anything today. Anyway, you give this to your daughter. Everything will be fine. You'll see. No cost. Next time you come maybe bring a book or maybe some oranges. Better learn that song."

"How about that," said Harlen, as we took off our clothes again. "I told you Granny Oldcrow would have something."

I carried the rattle in one hand as we crossed the river. The water cut into me, and my legs began to cramp, but when we got to the middle, I reached out, and with my free hand, shoved Harlen's head under water.

He came up spitting cold, green river water and cursing. "Damn, Will. Why'd you do that?"

Everybody came to the party the next day. South Wing was in her high chair with ice cream all over her face and her dress and the chair.

Louise had some in her hair.

"You've got ice cream in your hair," I said.

"And you don't," said Louise, and she handed me the spoon. "Everybody gets a turn."

I put the present with the others and sat down next to South Wing, who gave me a big smile and opened her mouth. The first spoonful of ice cream wound up on her nose. The second wound up on the floor. I reached out and rubbed her head, but she was having none of that. She leaned forward in the chair and squealed and opened her mouth.

We lit the cake and sang "Happy Birthday", and Louise began to open the presents.

"This one's from Grandpa and Grandma.

"And this one's from Auntie Sue.

"And this one's from Uncle Leroy."

When Louise opened the rattle, she began to blush and stammer.

"And . . . this one is . . . from . . . Uncle. . . . This one's from Will."

"Hey," said Carter Heavyman, as he set his Instamatic, "that looks like one of Granny Oldcrow's rattles. Real hard to come by, those. Looks just like the one you got for her, Louise."

Louise looked at me, shook her head, and reached into her apron pocket and pulled out a rattle.

"Bertha took me shopping yesterday. Harlen take you shopping?"

I looked around for Harlen. He was gone.

I stayed until after everyone else had left. I figured someone should apologize. South Wing hadn't made it through the cake, before Louise had to put her down.

"You want some tea, Will?"

"Sure."

"Granny talk to you?"

"She did."

"I suppose they mean well."

"I'm going to kill Harlen."

Louise laughed and leaned over the table and kissed me. "That old woman is dangerous," she said. "You know what she does for a living?" Louise didn't pull away. She stayed there, leaning on the table, close to me. And she kissed me again. "Why don't you see if South Wing is okay, first."

I stood up, and Louise put her arms around me. "You ever have a girlfriend before me?"

"Sure."

"In Toronto?"

"I guess."

"What was her name?"

"Susan."

Louise pressed her fingers against my lips. "Maybe I'll make us something to eat. You want something to eat?"

South Wing woke up in the middle of the night and started to cry. She was standing in her crib. One of the rattles was on the floor. I picked it up and shook it, and South Wing smiled and reached out. I took her out of her crib. Her diaper was wet, so I changed it. She didn't make a sound. She lay there playing with the rattle, watching, and it reminded me of the morning she was born. Later, I put her back in the crib, but I stayed in the room until it got light and tried to remember the song.

eleven

Spring was the worst season in Medicine River. The snow would melt. The days would warm. And just as you started thinking about all the things you could do outside, the wind would arrive. It blew every day. It blew every night.

"Old people used to be happy to see those chinooks, Will," Harlen liked to tell me. "Boy, here comes that chinook, they'd say. Real happy to see them."

Every winter, the city threw dirt and gravel on the ice to keep the cars from sliding into one another. When the snows melted in the spring, the wind would blow the finer dirt all the way to Regina, leaving the larger pieces free to be kicked up by the cars and trucks. Glass shops in Medicine River did their best business in the spring.

James's letter arrived the same day as the wind. "Dear Will," it said. "Thought I'd write to let you know I'm still alive. Didn't get to Australia yet. Stopped off here in New Zealand. It's a real nice

country. Hey, it even has Indians, but they call them
Maoris down here. I'm taking off for the South Island
tomorrow. Going to climb a glacier. How are you
doing? Next time, I'll send some pictures. Say hello to
everyone for me. Probably be back in San Francisco in
December."

After Mom died, I didn't hear from James for a
long time. Then I began to get postcards and letters.
They were from all over the world: Mexico, South
America, Hawaii, France, Japan. Most of them were
funny, and he seemed happy enough. The return
address always said, "Bentham Reserve," and each
letter was signed, "Your brother, James."

I was standing by the window of my studio, reading the letter and watching shoppers being blown up
and down Second Street, when Floyd called.

"Joe Bigbear's back in town," he said.

"Who's Joe Bigbear?"

"You kidding?"

"No, who's Joe Bigbear?"

"Harlen's brother."

"Harlen's brother?"

"Yeah. You never met him?"

"I didn't know Harlen had a brother."

"American Hotel, eight tonight. Joe's buying."

The bar in the American is a great dark hole filled
with blue smoke and dead people. At least, they
should be dead. When you enter the American, the
trick is to hold your breath and close your eyes.
Harlen, who has the lungs of a whale, can walk into
the American, sit down, and talk and laugh for hours
without having to surface. Each time I go there, I
swear it will be the last.

"You got to meet Joe, Will. He's a great guy.
Nothing like Harlen."

"Don't know if I can hold my breath that long, Floyd."

"You don't have to drink if you don't want."

"Figured I'd go for a walk this evening," I said.

"In this wind?"

Curiosity and the wind are powerful movers, and it was a Thursday night, too. With luck, the American would be empty.

Everyone was there. Floyd caught me at the door.

"Hey, Will. Glad you made it. Hey, everyone's here. Good party, huh? Here, have a cigar. Joe brought them all the way back from Cuba."

All the boys from the basketball team were in one corner drinking and smoking their cigars. Big John Yellow Rabbit and his wife, Estelle, were at a table with Bertha Morley and Bertha's boyfriend, whose name I couldn't remember. Eddie Weaselhead and Crystal and their oldest boy Peter were at another table. Ray and Elwood and Frankie were sitting near the jukebox with three women I had seen at some of our games.

"Where's Harlen?"

"Harlen's not here," Floyd said.

"Is he coming?"

"Don't know," said Floyd. "Come on, I'll introduce you around."

I followed Floyd through the crowd. We worked our way to a heavyset man in a leather vest.

"Will," said Floyd, throwing his arm around me, "this is Joe."

There was no family resemblance that I could see. Joe Bigbear was shorter than Harlen by a head and stouter. He had one of those cigars stuck in the corner of his mouth.

"Good to meet you, Will." Joe stood, shook the

ashes off his vest and stuck out his hand. There are people, whites mostly, who understand handshaking as a blood sport. The trick is to give them the fingers and no more. Joe caught my hand by surprise.

"Damn good to meet you, Will." And Joe squeezed my hand like he was trying to find all the bones at once. "You know what," he said, still squeezing my hand and leaning over and whispering in my ear so most of the people at the table could hear. "You shake hands like a damn Indian." And he roared, and everyone else laughed, too. "Sit down, Will. Heard a lot of good things about you. Sit down."

Joe pulled out a couple of the cigars from his vest and tossed them into my lap. "Try one of these, Will. Cuban."

"Don't smoke," I said.

"Course you don't. Neither do I. But there are the exceptions. You ever had a Cuban? You only live once. You got to let go, try everything at least once." And he turned to the rest of the people at the table. "Am I right?"

"Maybe I'll try it later."

"There is no later, Will. Here . . ." And he leaned across the table and stuck out his lighter. "Just bite off the end there and spit it on the floor. That's the way the Cubans do it."

I choked on the first puff and started coughing. Earl Manyfingers and Jerry Fox began whacking me on the back, and Joe boomed, "Man's dying over here. Better bring us another pitcher."

The beer helped, and as Joe's attention slipped away from me, I was able to let the cigar die a well-deserved death in the ashtray.

"So I was in Australia," said Joe. "And I was riding along the coast with these two Aussies, and it was early morning. Well, all of a sudden, this pig comes trotting across the road and scampering behind her were about eight little piglets."

"UUUUUUEEEEEEE," someone shouted, "bacon!"

Joe twirled that cigar around in his mouth. "You bet. One of those Aussies says, 'Boy, I sure would like some fresh pig.' And I says, 'Well, stop the car, boys, and I'll show you how an Indian brings home the bacon.'"

Floyd leaned over to me and said, "Pay attention, Will. This is a good story."

Joe blew a giant smoke ring and watched it for a second, as it rose towards the ceiling.

"So there I was with just my knife, and I began stalking that pig. I wasn't after the momma. Hell, I'm not that stupid. But I figured that one of them babies would be just right."

Floyd started laughing and nodding his head up and down. "It gets better," he whispered.

"There was no wind," Joe continued, "but every time I got close, that momma pig would snap her head up and look around. She didn't see me, but she knew there was trouble somewhere. Pretty soon, though, she finds something really tasty at the base of this tree, and she begins to work her snout down under a root, and I see my chance. I stay low, like this. . . ." and Joe got up and crouched down by the table. "Those little pigs don't see me, and I begin to run. No sound either. Just floated across the ground.

"I get maybe thirty feet from the little pigs, when old momma jerks around and spots me. Damn . . . she's off like a shot. And all those little piggies go squealing after her. Should have heard them. Squeal . . . squeal . . . squeal.

"You see those movies about lions and cheetahs.

You guys get those movies up here, don't you? Well, those cats can only run so far, maybe a couple hundred yards. But boy, for that hundred yards, they can fly. So that's what I figure. Those pigs can outrun me, but maybe I can catch one before they got going.

"So off we went. Momma pig leading the way, the eight little piggies trying to keep up, old Joe Bigbear beginning to close the gap, and those two Aussies standing on the roof of their car so they can see, yelling and waving their arms."

Floyd stuck an elbow in my ribs. "Here comes the part I like."

"Well, I got to admit, I was beginning to tire. But right then, one of the little piggies gets itself tangled up in a bush. Tried to run through it and got hung up. It was trying to free its back legs, when I slid in for the tackle."

"Uuuueee, uuuueeee, uuuueee." Floyd sat in his chair, tears running down his face. "Uuuueee, uuueee, uuuueeeee."

"That's right, Floyd," said Joe. "That little pig begins to squeal, loud enough to break your ear drums, but I had him. Joe Bigbear, Indian hunter. I held that piggy up and sort of waved him at the Aussies, who were waving their hands and shouting.

"Well, the next thing I know, I'm flat on my back, and when I look up from the dirt, momma pig is just making her turn and is coming back to have at me again. I don't know where in the hell the little piggy went, and right then, I don't care.

"Australia's sort of like around here, you know. They don't have much in the way of trees. Just a whole bunch of skinny things that you could almost pick your teeth with. Well, the only thing between me and momma pig was this sorry-ass excuse for a tree, but I wasn't particularly picky and up I go. The thing only stood ten feet off the ground and had a trunk no bigger around than Floyd's pecker.

"So there I was, about four feet off the ground in this skinny damn tree, thanking Napi that pigs can't climb, when this pig starts chewing at the trunk. You believe it! She starts chewing on the trunk! I'd have been pig food, if those two Aussies hadn't stopped laughing and chased her off."

Floyd roared and fell out of his chair. Beer and cigars went flying, and everyone started laughing, even Joe, who ordered another round.

"But that's old stuff. I just tell that story because Floyd there likes it." Joe rolled his cigar in his mouth and pulled at his moustache. "You boys want to guess where I've been for the last nine months?"

"Most likely in jail," said a voice, and there was Harlen, standing beside me, smiling.

"Harlen, hey, you made it," and Joe jumped up and moved his chair to one side. "Come on, sit down, grab that chair there."

Even through the smoke and noise, I could hear the snap in Harlen's voice. He sat down stiffly and waved off a large Cuban that appeared from Joe's vest.

"You got here just in time, Harlen," Joe said, lighting his own cigar, which had gone out during the saga of the wild pig. "Now, where do you suppose I've been for the last nine months?"

"Hey, don't be too fast with the story, Joe," said Floyd, standing up. "I got to see a man about a horse, you know. Be right back."

Floyd got up and headed for the bathroom.

"Me, too," I said, and followed Floyd.

When I got to the bathroom, Floyd was at one of

the urinals trying to find his zipper.

"Hey, Will, what'd I tell you? Great guy, Joe. Been everywhere. Done everything."

"What's with him and Harlen?"

"Oh, nothing. They just don't get along very well, I guess. You know, brothers."

"Harlen doesn't seem too happy to see him."

Floyd finally found his zipper and got it down. "Hell, Will. You know Harlen. Pretty straight. Joe's done it all. He's famous. You know, he got one of his jokes published in *Reader's Digest*. I guess it's hard to have a famous brother. Harlen always gets like that when Joe comes to town."

Floyd chewed on his cigar and chuckled to himself and sort of swayed back and forth at the urinal, as though there were a song playing in his head.

I was at the sink washing up, when I heard him shout.

"Jesus!" Floyd was wearing a pair of white pants, and there was a long telltale wet spot that ran from mid-thigh to past his knee. He looked over at me with that cigar. "Jeez, Will. God! Look at this." I must have been smiling, because Floyd got all serious. "Hey, Will . . . you won't say anything . . . you know . . . to the rest of the guys. They won't notice anything, if you don't let on."

The smoke and noise were making me mean. "Okay, Floyd," I said. "So what's the problem with Harlen and Joe?"

Floyd smiled again, almost laughed, and waved the cigar around in a circle. "Like I said, Will, broth-ers. You know."

Harlen Bigbear was one of the most charitable peo-ple I had ever known. No matter who it was, Harlen would always go looking for the good in a person.

And even if he couldn't find it, he assumed that it was there, buried somewhere. If anyone knew why Harlen was sitting across the table from his brother, stiff and tense, it was Floyd.

"I hear little kids stop doing that when they're about two."

"Come on, Will. Shit, you wouldn't do that?" Floyd's vanity was legend. He loved good clothes, and whenever he came into town from the reserve for a big night, he'd wash his car out there first, and then he'd stop off at Elwood's house on the north side of town and wash it again.

"Sure I would, Floyd."

"Honest, Will," said Floyd, his arms extended, the dead cigar hanging in his mouth. "There's nothing to tell."

"Tell me anyway."

When we got back to the table, Joe had already started the story. I ran interference for Floyd. I walked in front, and Floyd kept as close to me as good manners would allow. Moving through the bar like that, back to our chairs, we must have looked like Siamese twins.

". . . so there we were, ten gorgeous women just waiting for us down by the stream. And there we were up on the bridge trying to explain to these French soldiers with machine-guns just what we were doing there. . . . Hey, you guys almost missed the best part. What'd you do, get married in there?"

"Floyd proposed," I said. "But I said no."

Joe went on with the story about Tahiti and then told one about being in New Orleans during Mardi Gras and another about the time he worked on a fishing trawler off the coast of South America. Harlen sat there through all of Joe's stories looking at the floor or staring at the Molson sign on the wall above Joe's head. Every so often, he'd sigh and turn to look at me and then turn back to the floor or the wall.

". . . but you know, the time I almost bought it was on the Navajo reservation. I met this fellow, Mike Begay, in a bar in Gallup and . . ."

I leaned over to Harlen. "Never knew you had a brother."

Harlen nodded yes and went back to staring at the floor.

"Seems like a nice guy."

"Hey, Harlen," said Joe, "you remember that time when we were kids and we went down to the old bridge. They tore that bridge down, boys, before most of you were born. That thing must have been fifty feet in the air, all wood. They got that new metal one now. Well, old Harlen says, 'Let's climb that sucker. We can jump from the top.' Hell, I didn't want to go, but I was older, and you know how that is.

"So up we went. The first part was easy. You could just walk along the planks, but once we got out over the river and I looked up, I was scared. Old Harlen, he wanted to go up to the top, but I chickened out. The water was only about twenty feet below us, and I figured it was better to jump from where I was than to slip on one of those planks near the top. So I jumped. Christ, that water felt like concrete. I must have gone all the way to the bottom, because I was spitting water when I finally came up for air.

"The worst part was that the river was still pretty high, like now, and the current was fast, and it started taking me down river. Well, you know, I looked up, and there was Harlen leaning out, holding on with one hand, just like a damn monkey, waving me good-bye.

"It took me maybe three miles before I could get to shore and, boy, was I cold and tired. Took me another three hours to catch a ride home.

"When I got home, there was Harlen sitting on the couch, reading a book. I'm standing there, my clothes are still wet, and he looks up like nothing ever happened and says, 'You enjoy your swim?' Ha! You believe that? Just as calm as you can be. 'You enjoy your swim?'"

Everyone laughed, and even Harlen laughed a little.

About two, Joe began to run out of gas. He'd had more than enough to drink, and he looked tired. Most of the people had left. Joe closed his eyes and leaned back in the chair.

"Should probably take him home," I said.

"He's got a room at the Marquis."

"He's not staying with you?"

"No."

"Hey, Harlen." And there was Joe, wide awake, leaning over the table with the butt of one of those cigars sticking out of his mouth like a brown carrot. "Time to go. Will, you come too. You got your car here, Harlen?"

"Most every place is closed now, Joe," I said.

"Not in town . . . going out to the reserve."

"Right now?" I said.

"No time to argue, Will. It's time to drive." And Joe got out of the chair, stuffed the cigar into the ashtray and headed for the door.

"It's not a good idea, Joe," said Harlen.

"It's a great idea. Come on, you guys, live a little."

It was the wind that did it. That damn wind was blowing hard when we came out of the American, and it blew us into Harlen's car. I wouldn't have gone, but there was the wind, and the reserve was as good a hiding place as any.

"Where exactly are we going?" I said.

Joe crawled into the back seat and laid his head on the armrest. "Vernon Heavyman's place," he said, and he went to sleep.

I looked over at Harlen. His hands were on the wheel, and the key was in the ignition.

"You okay?"

"Yeah," he said, and he started the car.

As we pulled away from the American, Joe began to snore. The wind howled, and Joe snored, and Harlen set his lips against his teeth and drove into the night.

Floyd hadn't been much help. He had stood there in the bathroom with the one wet pant leg, pleading ignorance. I was left with my curiosity, Harlen, and the wind.

I tried Harlen's trick of strolling around a topic.

"So," I said, "Joe's your brother."

Harlen looked in the rear-view mirror.

"So," I said, "how come you never mention him?"

Harlen looked at the speedometer.

I was already tired of strolling. "You don't seem to get on too well with him."

"Joe's okay, Will," said Harlen. "We're just different."

"You want to talk about it?"

"Nothing to talk about."

"Floyd said . . ." And I couldn't think of what Floyd might have said that would help to crack Harlen's shell.

Harlen began to laugh a little. "Will," he said, "I've never seen anyone so curious about other people's business."

"Well, Floyd said . . ." I said, sticking with the original lie, hoping Harlen might finish the sentence for me.

"Floyd probably told you that Joe and me don't get on so well, and that's true. And he probably told you that I more than likely wouldn't be at the American tonight. And that's true, too. He may have even said that I don't like Joe, but that's not true. Joe's twelve years older than me, you know. He was out of the house and gone before I really got to know him. He always had different friends and did different things than me. How good of friends are you with James? He's only four years younger than you."

James's letter was in my pocket. I tried to imagine him in New Zealand, standing on top of a glacier, waving.

"Joe's got great stories, though. That one about the pig. . . . Did he tell the one about the pig?"

Harlen talked about Joe for a while, and then we listened to the radio. By the time he turned off the gravel road onto the dirt road that led to Vernon Heavyman's house, the sky was beginning to lighten behind us.

"Pull in there," said Joe, "next to the corral."

"Damn, Joe," said Harlen, swinging the car around. "You almost scared the hell out of poor Will. Thought you were asleep."

"Feel great. Come on."

Harlen barely got the car stopped, before Joe was out and stretching.

"Come on, Harlen," said Joe.

Harlen turned around in the seat. "Listen," he said, "why don't you stay here?"

"Something wrong?"

"Nothing's wrong. We're just going for a walk."

"Come on, you guys," Joe shouted. "We got some climbing to do." And he headed down the slope to the river.

Harlen got out of the car. I got out the other side.

"Where's he going?" I said.

Harlen leaned on the car and shaded his eyes. "To the bridge."

"The trestle bridge?"

"That's the one."

"Why?"

"We're going to climb it," said Harlen. "Maybe you better stay here. Pretty high, that one."

"You guys are crazy. That bridge must be a hundred feet high."

Harlen nodded and headed down the slope after Joe. I looked around. There was Vernon Heavyman's house and his corral and the land stretched out to the mountains and Harlen's green-and-white Ford.

"Hey," I said, "wait up."

It was a long walk to the bridge. Joe was out in front, singing. Harlen was about twenty feet behind him, and I was right behind Harlen. The trestle had looked high from the bluff, but down in the river bottom, it seemed to stretch up forever.

"Why are we doing this?"

"Don't have to do it, Will. Maybe you want to go down to the river. Have a nap."

"I'm not sleepy. This have anything to do with when you two were kids?"

Harlen waved me off with a hand. "Nope. Joe just likes to climb around on things. Me, too."

It was going to be a hot day. Joe kicked up clouds of dust as he walked, and the grasshoppers and dragonflies in the willows along the bank began warming to the day.

Joe was waiting for us at the foot of a huge concrete abutment.

"Okay," he said. "You coming, Will?"

"Sure," I said. "Wouldn't miss it for anything."

Joe took off like a monkey. Up the side of the abutment and onto the first steel beam. Harlen followed him. I had some trouble.

"You got to find the toeholds, Will," Joe said. "That's the secret."

That first girder was as high off the ground as I ever want to be.

"Hey," said Joe, "that was the hard part. The rest is easy."

I was going to say something, but Joe began moving out on the girder. Harlen was right behind him.

"You guys are crazy," I shouted, but I kept moving along the girder.

When Joe and Harlen got to the centre of the bridge, Joe began walking up a transverse beam that went from the girder we were standing on to the one above us. The beam was set at about a thirty-degree angle and you had to hold on to it and climb at the same time. Joe was half-way up when I caught Harlen.

"You okay, Will?"

"Sure. Always wanted to climb a trestle."

"The next part's tricky," Harlen said. "You got to hold on to the beam and use your feet to push yourself up." Harlen spit into both his hands. "The hard part is near the top. When you get close, you have to grab on to the girder and then pull yourself up. . . . Look . . . watch Joe."

Joe was almost to the next girder. His head was right up against it. Suddenly, he let go of the beam and grabbed the girder. His feet slipped, and for a second, he was dangling in mid-air above the river.

"Uuuuuuwweeeee," he shouted. "Come on up!"

Joe threw one leg over the girder and pulled himself up.

Harlen's mouth was set on a line. "That's how you
do it," he said, and he turned away so I couldn't see
his face. Then he spit into his hands, again. "You
want to go first?"

"What happens if you fall?"

"I won't fall," said Harlen.

"Not you. Me. What happens if I fall?"

"Push off if you can. You don't want to hit the
beams. Water's a little cold this time of the year."

I looked down at the river. "You go first," I said.

Harlen didn't manage as well as Joe. He dangled
over the river and waved his legs for a while, but he
got up.

"You guys are crazy," I shouted. And then I started
up.

The first few feet went okay. It was an awkward
position, bent over at the waist, trying to hold onto
the beam and walk up it at the same time. I was half-
way up, when my arms began to cramp. The beam
seemed to narrow as I got near the top.

"Come on, Will," Harlen shouted. "You can make
it."

"Come on, Will," shouted Joe. "Fun's just starting."

My head hit the girder.

"Almost there, Will. Let go with your hands and
grab the girder. Got to do it quick, though," said Joe.

"Don't look down, Will," said Harlen. "It'll make
you dizzy."

Which is, of course, exactly what I did. The river
seemed a mile below me. I wasn't even sure I would
hit it if I fell.

"Told you not to look, Will," shouted Harlen. "Come on, you can do it."

And I did. I grabbed the girder. My feet slid out from underneath me. I waved my legs in the air for a minute, and after several attempts, I managed to throw one leg over.

"Damn, Will," said Harlen, "you tore your pants."

So, there we were, Harlen, Joe, and me, standing on a steel girder, twenty feet above the Medicine River. Actually, I was kneeling. The girder below had a cable that ran all the way across that you could hang on to. This girder didn't. It was about a foot wide, and, if you wanted to move along its length, you either crawled or trusted to your sense of balance. I was happy kneeling. The top of the bridge was another thirty feet above us.

"You guys go ahead," I said. "I think I'll just sit here for a while."

"We're here," said Joe, and he looked out over the edge of the girder. "This is where we jump."

It didn't register immediately.

"You got to do a safety jump. You put your arms like this and keep your legs bent, like this." Joe covered his face with one hand, locked the other one around his body, and stood on one leg. He looked like a flamingo.

"Jump?"

"Yeah," said Joe. "But you got to do it like this."

"I'm not going to jump."

"You don't have to, Will," said Joe. "But the climb down is pretty tricky. A lot easier coming up."

"It's a hundred-foot drop."

"Naw," said Joe. "Maybe twenty feet. I've done it five or six times. Pretty exciting when you first start to fall. But when you hit that water. . . . Smash! You can't imagine the feeling."

"Sort of like death," I said.

"Damn, Will," Joe laughed. "You are a joker. You guys ready? Come on, we can jump together. Like the Three Musketeers."

Harlen was looking off down the river. He wasn't smiling. "Maybe you should go first, Joe. Show Will how it's done."

Joe put his hands in his pockets. "How about the two of us jumping together. Like old times."

Harlen looked at me and shook his head. "Better stay here. Make sure that Will jumps. You know, encourage him. Somebody should stay behind to show him the way down in case he can't do it."

"I can get down by myself," I said. "I'm not going to jump."

"Come on, Harlen," said Joe. "You and me. Just like old times."

"I'll be right behind you, Joe. Just want to be sure that Will's okay."

Joe looked at Harlen and then at me. "Okay," he said. "Hey, it's like flying." Joe leaned over the edge, looked back at the two of us, winked and said, "See you in China."

And he jumped or rather he fell, screaming all the way down.

"YAHHAhahahoooooooo."

We were too high up to hear the splash. All you could see was a great boil of green water.

"You see him?"

And then, there he was, waving and floating down the river and shouting something up to us.

"There he goes," said Harlen, and he turned back to me. "You okay?"

"I'm okay," I said. "You go ahead and jump. I'll watch."

"Better I stay with you."

"Don't worry about me. Go ahead, jump."

Harlen sat down on the girder beside me and pulled his head down into his shoulders. You could barely see Joe now. He was floating towards the big horseshoe bend. Every so often, he'd wave his arm.

"Joe going to be okay?"

"Sure. He'll float down to where the highway crosses the river. We'll catch him back in town." Harlen didn't look like he was much interested in moving from where he was.

"You ever jump?" I asked.

"What do you mean?"

"Just what I said. Have you ever jumped off this trestle?"

"Ripped your pants pretty bad, Will. Hope those weren't your good pants."

"Harlen . . ."

"Too bad you didn't bring a camera. Could have got a great picture of Joe. Maybe win an award."

I wasn't in any mood for Harlen and his wanderings. "You never jumped, did you? That's what happened. Joe jumped, and you didn't, and you never have jumped."

Harlen shook his head. "Real tricky getting down, Will. Harder than coming up."

I looked down at the river. It didn't look *that* far away. Hold your hand over your nose, keep your feet spread a little. . . .

"Well, I'm going to jump," I said suddenly. "You can stay here, but I'm going to jump."

Harlen smiled. I stood up and wished I hadn't. The river looked farther away now; the girder seemed narrower.

"I'm going to jump, just like Joe. You coming with me?"

"Sure, Will," said Harlen. "You go first."

"That's right," I shouted, trying to keep my balance. "I'll go first."

I stood at the edge. Joe had made it. I could make it.

The wind came up. It must have been blowing all the time, but I hadn't noticed it.

"Wind's starting to blow pretty good, Will. We better start climbing down."

"No," I said. "I'm going to jump."

The wind blew a little harder. Harlen was holding on to the girder with both hands. The backs of his knuckles were pale.

"You going to jump?" I said.

"Don't think so."

"Why not?"

"Same reason you won't jump."

"I'm going to jump."

"Don't think so, Will."

A gust of wind almost blew me off the girder. I sat down next to Harlen. "I'd jump," I said, "if the wind wasn't blowing."

"Blowing pretty hard, that wind," said Harlen. "You got your good shirt on, too. No sense ruining it. Maybe we should climb down now."

Joe had disappeared around the bend. "Wind ruins everything," I said. "Got a letter from James. He's in New Zealand."

"New Zealand?"

"Going to climb a glacier."

"No kidding."

"He writes me all the time. We talk a lot."

The climb down was hell. I tore my shirt on a loose

rivet. My hands were scraped, and my shoes were badly scuffed from trying to hold on to the beam we had come up. Harlen didn't fare much better. When we got to the concrete abutment, I looked at Harlen and Harlen looked at me.

"You know, Will," he laughed, "we should have jumped."

"Next time," I said, turning away from the wind, "next time we'll jump."

I didn't see Joe Bigbear again. Floyd told me that Joe was off to Italy, this time, but then, that was Floyd. If Harlen knew, he didn't say. We never told anyone about the bridge. It was our secret, Harlen and me. By the time we got home, we had agreed that Joe had taken the easy way, that climbing down was harder than jumping. Joe had his way of doing things, Harlen said, and we had ours.

"You know," said Harlen. "We should go out there next week and jump from the first girder. You know, get the feel of it. By the time Joe shows up again, we'll be jumping off that third girder, sweet as you please."

We never went back to the bridge. At least, I never did. I was satisfied with the first adventure—the river miles below me, the wind whipping around the girder, Joe letting go of everything and plunging into the green water, and Harlen and me, perched on that narrow piece of steel like a pair of barn owls, hanging on for dear life.

twelve

I was in the back of the studio when the front-door buzzer rang. I stepped into the front shop, just in time to see Lionel James close the door.

"Oki, Will," said Lionel, and he helped himself to the padded chair by the window. "Boy, feels good to sit down." Lionel looked around the room. He smiled. "Pretty good chair, you know. Nice sign, too. Medicine River Photography."

Lionel was one of the elders on the reserve. He belonged to the Horn Society, and he owned a medicine bundle. I had only seen him in town three or four times before.

Lionel laughed and shook his head. "That's Jonnie and Cecil," he said, gesturing to one of the pictures on the wall. "That's a real good one of them." Lionel rubbed his knees. "Maybe you've got one of them credit cards, too."

"You want some coffee, Lionel? I've got some fresh," I said, just as Harlen Bigbear came in the door.

"Damn," said Harlen, pulling his hair out of his

eyes. "It's windy out there. Couldn't find a parking space. That coffee machine of yours working, Will? You got any coffee?"

"Coffee sounds real good, Will," said Lionel.

I went to the back room. The coffee machine was making its strange noises again.

"Hey, Lionel," said Harlen, "what do you think? Old Will's a wealthy man. A real success. Always willing to help out a friend, too."

I could hear Harlen clearly from the back room where the coffee pot was. Lionel wasn't deaf, and neither was I.

"Will is always helping someone. Takes pictures of all the weddings. Will could take your picture, too."

"It's a real nice place," said Lionel.

"You want your coffee black, Lionel?" I asked.

"Black's okay, Will," said Lionel. "Maybe some sugar if you have any."

"Black for me," said Harlen.

"Maybe some cream, too, if you have any," said Lionel.

"I've got both," I said. "Whatever you like."

"See?" said Harlen. "Rich and generous."

I brought the coffee out on a tray I had bought at a yard sale. It wasn't exactly a tray. It was the top of one of those stands that you eat off while you watch television.

"Say look at this," said Harlen.

"Looks real good," said Lionel.

Lionel put three sugars in his coffee. Harlen put four in his. Harlen held up the cream carton and looked at it the way you look at a glass of wine. The cream had been in the refrigerator for over a week. Bertha Morley had brought it by when she came to ask me if I knew anything about instamatic cameras.

Hers wasn't working. I didn't use cream, but I fixed
the camera. I hoped it was still fresh.

"Real cream, Lionel," said Harlen. "Not that white
powder you get at the truck stop in Reynolds and not
that cream substitute you get at the Lodge. Boy, I'll
bet you don't get real cream for your coffee every
day."

"That's right," said Lionel, "only at home."

I didn't know Lionel James very well, but I had
heard stories. Harlen said he was almost one hundred
years old. Bertha said he was about sixty-nine. Harlen
said Lionel had been a great athlete when he was
young, could run for miles. Bertha said he had had a
bad drinking problem, spent some time in jail. Harlen
said Lionel had been to some of the old-time Sun
Dances and had the scars on his chest to prove it.
Bertha said he got those in a car crash. But whatever
he had been in his youth, he was one of the most
respected men on the reserve.

"You got any cookies, Will?" said Harlen. "I'll bet
Lionel would like some cookies. Those black ones
with the cream centres."

"You mean Oreos?"

"Maybe some bread and jam, if you have any," said
Lionel.

"Lionel would like some bread and jam, too," said
Harlen. "What kind of jam you like?"

"Don't matter," said Lionel. "They're all good."

Mostly I kept film in the refrigerator, but there
were some cookies, oatmeal with raisins, and I had
some bread and butter and swiss cheese just in case I
got hungry at work. There wasn't any jam.

"Looks like I'm out of jam," I shouted.

"No jam?" said Harlen.

"That's okay," said Lionel.

"I've got some cheese."

"Cheese is real good, too."

George's grocery was just across the alley, and Harlen was right, it was windy. Harlen and Lionel were still talking when I got back. They never even knew I'd gone.

"Hey, I found some jam. Had some after all . . . strawberry."

"Great," said Harlen. "It's Lionel's favourite."

So we sat there in the shop, the three of us, and ate bread and butter and jam, and drank hot coffee. The wind picked up, and the gusts rattled the front window.

"You know, Will," said Harlen, "Lionel travels all over. He knows everyone." Harlen finished his bread and licked his fingers. "Did I tell you Lionel and your father were friends?"

"Your father used to rodeo," said Lionel. "One night in Calgary, after that big rodeo, he took me and Sam Belly out to dinner."

"So, you knew my father?"

"You bet," said Lionel. "You don't look much like him."

"How well did you know him?"

"You look more like your mother."

"Lionel goes everywhere," said Harlen. "Tell Will where you've been."

Lionel laughed. "Boy, you know, I never thought I'd go some of the places I've been. My mother never left the reserve. I was in Calgary a few times and up in Edmonton once, but that was before my wife died. Last few years, I've been all over."

"Lionel's been to Germany, Will."

"Yes," said Lionel, "that's right."

"And he's been to England and France."

"I was in Ottawa just last week," said Lionel.

"Lionel's been all over the world, Will. That's what we came to talk to you about."

"Need some publicity pictures, huh?"

Harlen looked at Lionel, and Lionel looked at me.

"What are those?"

"Will means pictures of you to advertise what a famous person you are."

"That's real nice of you, Will," said Lionel, "but I'm not famous. I just travel a lot."

"No," said Harlen quickly, "we don't need pictures."

"Pictures would be nice," said Lionel. "Your father got his picture in the *Calgary Herald* when he won the all-round title. He used to carry it in his wallet. Do I need a picture for a credit card?"

I was used to conversations with Harlen that didn't make much sense and didn't seem to go anywhere.

"That's what we came to see you about," said Harlen.

"My father?"

"No, credit cards," said Harlen. "You got one, don't you?"

"Sure, I have one."

"See, Lionel? Will knows all about them."

"I just have one."

"Good enough," said Harlen. "Tell Will what happened, Lionel."

Lionel smiled and leaned back in the chair. "Boy," he said, "it's good to talk about things like this. You know, first time I went to fly somewhere, I had to walk through this fence, and the police made me do it again, and then I had to take off my belt buckle. You know what? There was this woman who waved this stick all around me. She waved it around my arms and down around my boots. She even waved it up between my legs. Said she was looking for metal. I was real embarrassed, you know. I had to hold my pants up. It's real bad over in those European places."

"Lionel has been to Japan, too," said Harlen.

"That's right. I've been to Japan. People want me to talk about what it's like to be an Indian. Crazy world. Lots of white people seem real interested in knowing about Indians. Crazy world.

"So, I go all over the world now, and talk about Indian ways and how my grandparents lived, and sometimes I sing a little. I used to dance, too, but my leg hurts too bad now. Most of the time, I tell stories."

Lionel paused and looked out the window. The sky had darkened, and the buildings on Second Street hunkered down before the storm.

"This is real good jam," he said.

Harlen helped himself to a piece of cheese. "What kind of credit card you got, Will?"

"It's a Visa."

"Those are good."

"There's MasterCard, too."

"Those are good, too," said Harlen.

"You also have American Express," I said.

"See, Lionel," said Harlen. "Will knows about these things."

"I'm sure glad someone does," said Lionel. "I don't want to cause any problems."

"Tell Will what happened in Ottawa, Lionel."

"There was this big conference, you know, on Indians. Maybe two weeks ago. My friends asked me to come back and tell some stories. So I went to Ottawa. Real nice place. Hard to say no to friends. They had to work all day, so they said to take a taxi to this hotel, big one. Real nice one.

"I went up to the place that said Reception and said I had a reservation. So this young boy looks up in that computer, and he says, yes, I have a reservation. He gives me a form, and I fill it out. And then he asks me for my credit card.

"I don't have one of those, and I told him that I didn't have any credit card, and the boy said they couldn't give me a room unless I had one. You know, I told him I had cash, and he said cash wasn't any good.

"I hadn't heard that before, but we don't hear everything on the reserve. So I said, what do you use instead of cash, and he said, credit cards.

"So I figure I better get a credit card. You know, be a modern Indian."

I looked at Harlen.

"Lionel needs someone to help him get a credit card." Harlen put a piece of Swiss cheese on some bread and folded it over. "You know how these things work. Would you believe it, Will? The bank messed up my account last week. This is the third time."

"It's not hard to get a credit card," I said. "Generally, you just apply for a card at the bank where you have your chequing account."

"Lionel doesn't have a chequing account, Will."

"How about a savings account?"

"Don't have one of those, either," said Lionel.

"I think you'll have to have a chequing account before the bank will give you a card."

"You got a chequing account, don't you, Will?"

"Sure, over at the TD."

"I used to have an account," said Lionel. "But I don't know what happened to it."

"If you like," I said, "I can take you over to the TD

and see if we can get you an account."

"And then I can get a credit card?"

"I think so."

Lionel leaned back in the chair. "Boy, hard to keep track of this world. You know in Germany I told the story about how Coyote went over to the west coast to get some fire because he was cold. Good thing he went travelling in the olden days before he needed a credit card."

We all laughed.

Lionel straightened his jacket and smiled. "Well, you know Coyote ran along until his feet hurt real bad, and pretty soon he was in the trees and the prairies were behind. 'Boy,' he said, 'I'm real sleepy. Maybe I'll just lie down here and sleep for a while.' But you know, Raven saw Coyote, and she flew down, and sat on a limb near where Coyote was trying to go to sleep, and she said, 'You can't sleep here unless you got a credit card.'"

Harlen slapped his knee. "You're a good storyteller, Lionel."

"You know, sometimes I tell stories about today, about some of the people on the reserve right now. I like to tell about Billy Frank and the Dead River Pig. All the people back home like to hear that story. When I was in Norway, I told the story about the time your father and mother went to one of those chicken restaurants after a rodeo. Your mother was pregnant, and I guess the smell of all that fat and grease made her sick because she threw up."

"Threw up. At the restaurant?"

"That's right. She was sitting near the window, and she couldn't get out. It was real messy."

"My mother did that?"

"So your father, quick as he can, said in a real loud

voice, 'Hey! what's in this chicken, anyway?'"

"Sounds just like your father, don't it, Will?" said Harlen.

"The manager came over with a bucket and a mop, and he was all apologetic. Nice fellow. Young boy. He even bought our meal for us, and your father gave him two free tickets to the rodeo."

"What else did my father do?"

"But those people in Germany and Japan and France and Ottawa don't want to hear those stories. They want to hear stories about how Indians used to be. I got some real good stories, funny ones, about how things are now, but those people say, no, tell us about the olden days. So I do."

"It must be exciting to go to all those places," Harlen said. "See all those people. I'll bet they really like your stories."

"The travel is okay, but I've been thinking maybe I should just stay home. This credit card thing is real confusing."

"We can get you a credit card, Lionel," I said.

"People are real curious, you know. When I was in Japan, I told them the story about Old Man and Old Woman, and when I was done, everybody stood up and clapped."

"You're a good storyteller, Lionel," said Harlen.

"You know, it was my wife who knew all the stories. She used to tell them to the kids. Crazy world. Everybody on the reserve knows that story. Those people in Japan just got up and started clapping. Same thing happened in Germany."

"Tell Will what happened next."

Lionel smoothed his braids. "Well," he said, "everyone left."

"No," said Harlen, "before they left."

"Oh. Well, they gave me one of those boards with a piece of metal on it that said I was in Japan."

"A plaque?"

"Something like that, I guess. They gave me other presents, too."

"Cause you're such a good storyteller," said Harlen.

"I don't know," said Lionel. "Maybe cause I'm Indian. You know, I didn't see any white storytellers over there. I saw a Mohawk fellow in France. He was telling stories, too."

Lionel put his coffee cup down and looked out the window. "That travel is pretty tiring. Those jet planes don't have much room to sleep. Some of those hotels are real noisy, and everyone wants to take you out to dinner. Maybe it's okay I don't have a credit card. Maybe I should stay home."

"I'd like to hear some of your stories when you have time," I said. "We could talk about other things, too."

"Sure, Will. That would be good. Maybe you want to come to my house, have a meal. I tell those stories to my grandkids, when I'm home. Maybe you can come out."

"I'd like that."

Lionel leaned forward in his chair and got up. "Boy, that was good bread and jam. Good coffee, too. I guess I don't need that credit card, after all."

"Hey, Will," said Harlen. "Maybe you should take Lionel's picture while he's here. You could put it up on the wall. People who come in could see a real world-famous Indian."

So I took some pictures of Lionel, and they turned out good. I put one up next to the picture of Harlen and the basketball team. The next week, I took four of the best pictures out to Lionel's house. I had never been out to that part of the reserve. Harlen gave me directions, and I got lost. By the time I found the house, everyone had eaten, but Lionel took me in the kitchen and warmed up some of the moose-meat stew that his daughter had made.

Later, we sat around in the back yard, and Lionel told stories. There were some about Old Man and Old Woman, and some about Coyote and Raven and the rest of the animals. Lionel told a story about a white fellow from Cardston who tried to sell Alfred Yellow Rabbit a horse that was blind in one eye. He told me about the time my father hid me in a clothes basket at the laundromat and tried to convince my mother that he had put me in with the wash by mistake. And he told the story about the fence at the airport and the kid at the hotel.

"It's a crazy world," Lionel said, as he walked me out to my truck, "them people living in the past like that." He looked back at the kids, who were playing on the porch. "They all got up and clapped, Will. Just stood there and clapped. Like they never heard that story before."

thirteen

Bertha Morley was a thick, handsome woman with a talent for rescuing the truth from falsehoods and flights of fancy. There was no finesse in Bertha. The minute she heard an exaggeration buzzing around, her head would snap up, and her tongue would flick out and slap it against the wall.

"Person would have to be all blind and mostly dead to believe that," she told Eddie Weaselhead, after Eddie finished his story about outrunning six police cars and a helicopter in Winnipeg. "Good thing they don't put you in jail for trying to sell them mouthfuls of garbage to honest people."

Harlen, who had a great respect for the truth, though on occasion he had difficulty finding all the parts, tended to be more temperate in his insistence on the whole truth all at once. "Bertha's an honest woman, Will. No one can take that from her. But you know, the truth's like a green-broke horse. You can come running out of the barn and throw on a saddle, leap on its back and plant your heels in its side, but you never know which way it's going to run or who it's going to kick. Sometimes it's better to walk up slow, you know, with a carrot or an apple. Let it smell the saddle for a while, before you pull the cinch and slide up."

Bertha worked at the Friendship Centre, and every time the centre needed some publicity photographs, Big John would send Bertha over to see me. "You got responsibilities, you know," she'd say. "The centre needs some of them photographs, and we can't afford to pay anyone to take them." So when Bertha came to the studio on Thursday, I figured it was time for the office photograph. She was wearing a print dress filled up with tiny flowers, and she had on high heels.

"Looking good, Bertha," I said. "What's the occasion?"

"I need some photographs, Will. You got time to take some?"

"This for the centre?"

"No. These are for me. For the advertisement." Bertha took a clipping from her purse and put it on my desk. "They want a picture of me to pass around."

The advertisement was for the Calgary Centre for the Development of Human Potential. It was a glossy advertisement that showed a couple walking near a lake holding hands. The caption beneath the photograph said, "Develop your potential with that special person."

"This is a dating service."

"That's right," said Bertha. "You pay them some money. They find you a man. Here, you got an education. You think this is okay?"

Bertha handed me a form that said "Confidential"

across the top in large red letters. It asked for the usual information: name, address, phone number, all of which Bertha had filled in. But under weight, height and date of birth, she had printed "NOYB."

"NOYB?"

"That's right. It's none of their business, that stuff. They got a picture. They can see what I look like. The rest of that stuff is just nosy."

Under "General Description" Bertha had written: "I'm a Blood Indian woman in good health with lots of friends who say I'm good-looking. I'm not a skinny woman, and I graduated from high school. I got a good job and I've raised four kids and have no objection to a couple more. I got my own car. I like to go fishing and hunting, and I play bingo every Thursday."

"You don't need a dating service. You're a good-looking woman."

"Got nothing to do with my looks. Just tired of what's available around here."

Under the section, "Your Description of an Ideal Partner", Bertha had put down: "No drinkers or cigar smokers. Whites are okay. Should have his own job and not be married. I'd like someone tall so I can wear heels when we got out, but short is okay, too."

"Lots of single men in town and on the reserve," I said.

"Pickings around Medicine River," said Bertha, "would starve a vulture."

Toronto had snow flurries that night. I sat up and thought about Susan and watched the flakes fall and melt. I called her the next day. "This flu is horrible, Will, but I'm feeling better now." She sounded happy. "Well," she said, "I guess you know I'm married."

"I talked to your husband."

"I was going to tell you. It's all so silly."

Susan saw the surprises in life as either silly or cute. Silly surprises were events that caught you flat-footed and out of breath. Cute surprises were the ones that left you angry.

"We should probably talk, Will," she said.

We went to Queen's Park and walked. The leaves had begun to turn and fall. Susan put her hands in her pockets and looked out across the park as if she hoped to see someone she knew just beyond the trees. I had expected she'd apologize or cry.

"You know," she said, "we should take the ferry to the island. Go out to Hanlan's Point. Maybe rent a couple of bicycles."

"I was just surprised."

"I like winter. Ralph and I used to go skating at city hall. You know what he bought me for Christmas last year?"

"I was just surprised."

"A new washing machine. That's cute, isn't it?"

Susan began to walk faster, kicking at the drifts of fall leaves on the grass. "I'm glad you called, Will. I'm really glad you called."

We waded through the leaves, around the fountain, past the man on the horse, until my toes and fingers began to burn from the cold.

"I talked to your daughter."

"Was it Beth?"

"I suppose."

"It could have been Meg. Meg is my oldest. Meg is Ralph's favourite. I don't believe in that sort of thing. They're both wonderful girls. That's the big question, you know."

"The children."

"No, Ralph. I worry that Ralph can't raise two daughters on his own. Not when he likes one better than the other. Do you still want to see me, Will?"

"What about Ralph?"

"You'd like Ralph. He's quite witty."

"Does he know about us?"

"I love you, Will. I really think I love you."

I suppose that's what I was waiting to hear, what I was hoping to hear. And I came to the rescue, galloping across the grass, all sparkling and aglow in the autumn light. "I'll be here." I pulled Susan close to me and tried to find her body through the layers of clothing and coats. "When it's over, I'll be here."

"When it's over? Will, I want you here now."

"Don't want no Prince Charming," Bertha said. "I've had one of them. Want a regular man with a sense of humour. You know, someone who can make me laugh. You think those people in Calgary can find someone like that?"

"What about someone like Jack Powless?"

"That one's too young. Never been married. Eats too much, too. Don't want to be tied to no stove cooking all the time."

"There's George Cowley. He's divorced."

"Good reason for that, too. Betty says he was pretty mean to Lucy when they was married. You got any better ideas than that?"

Looking back, it would have probably been better if I had kept my ideas to myself. "How about Harlen?"

"Harlen Bigbear?" Bertha pulled her face up into a huge grin, and she started to laugh. She laughed until she cried, and then she laughed some more until her nose began to run. "Damn, Will, if Louise didn't have you already, I'd give you a try myself."

"Ralph had a heart attack, Will. We were in bed, and he had a heart attack."
    "God, is he alright?"
    "It was bad at first. The pain. I had to take him to the hospital, and they ran all sorts of tests. Actually, it wasn't exactly a heart attack. Ralph has something wrong with his stomach, and when he gets excited or drinks too much coffee or eats spicy pizza late at night, his stomach cramps up. He says it feels like a heart attack, that you can't tell it from the real thing."
    "Did you tell him about us?"
    "No. I didn't think the time was right."
    "Maybe we shouldn't see each other for a while."
    "Why would we do that?"
    "What about Ralph?"
    "He's okay. He always feels foolish when it isn't a real heart attack."
    "As long as he's okay."
    "That's sweet, Will. I wanted to tell him about the divorce, but he did have that heart attack. If you talk to him, it's probably best not to mention it."

Discretion was not one of Harlen's many admirable characteristics. He kept secrets poorly and was more concerned with the free flow of information than with something as greedy as personal privacy. "People who keep secrets," Harlen liked to say, "generally got something to hide." And I didn't know anyone who disagreed with that.
    He came by the studio on Friday, his face flooded with excitement and news. He looked like a dam eager to collapse.
    "You seen Bertha lately?"

"Saw her yesterday."

"You take her picture?"

"That's what I do."

Harlen shook his head. "It's embarrassing, you know. Bertha selling herself to that escort service."

"Dating service."

"We could turn up half-a-dozen names just here in town. Without even thinking hard."

I had been through this with Harlen before and so, rather than waste time coming up with names that would just make Bertha cross, I told Harlen how good she had looked and exactly what she had been wearing. I even added a nice pair of earrings, a pearl necklace and the same expensive perfume I had bought Louise for her birthday.

"Course she looked good, Will. She's after a husband. Women can do that when they want."

"She mentioned your name."

"Me? Why would she do that?"

"Well, you're not married."

"Hope you didn't say that to Bertha, Will. That sort of talk will just get her thinking wrong and give her false hope. We got to protect her."

"Don't think she needs protection."

Harlen pulled a chair up against my desk. "Will, she's already made two mistakes. She married Jason Black, and then she married River Johnson."

"Third time's a charm," I said.

"Jason was okay. Nice guy. Treated her like a queen. But he couldn't beat the drugs or the alcohol. River Johnson used to beat on her. He's still in jail, you know. Robbed a gas station, and the day he got out of prison, they caught him trying to lift a gun from Padfield's Sporting Goods."

"Bertha's a lot smarter now."

"Will, you're not watching. Things aren't getting better. Things are getting worse. The way Bertha's going, the next guy she picks could be a mass murderer."

I didn't see Harlen for a couple of days, and I probably wouldn't have known what was happening if Louise hadn't called me to find out why I had told Harlen that Bertha was crazy for him.

"What?"

"Has Bertha been by to see you?"

"No."

Louise started to laugh. "Then now's the time to take that vacation you're always talking about."

"I didn't do anything."

"I'd go to Toronto, if I were you, or better yet, Halifax. Get a cheap room and watch television and hope that Bertha doesn't have the air fare."

Louise was still laughing when Bertha walked in the door. She was wearing jeans and a flannel shirt. She didn't look particularly angry, but then she wasn't smiling either.

I hung up in the middle of Louise laughing and waved at Bertha. "Hey," I said, "I've got those pictures. They turned out pretty well."

"You tell that crazy Bigbear that I was hot for him?"

"No, I didn't do that."

"You tell him I was looking for a husband?"

"I don't think so."

"So why is that one hanging around wanting to take me out, all the time smiling like he knows something I don't?"

"That's Harlen. He wants to help."

"Don't need any help."

"That's what I told him."

"What'd he say?"

"He said he thought you were a strong woman."

"He said that?"

"Something like that."

"You tell him to keep them opinions to himself. How much I owe you for the photographs?"

I put the photographs in a bag. "You know," I said, "you could do worse than Harlen."

Bertha glared at me. "Figure I can do a whole lot better." She strode across the room, her thick arms swinging. She stopped at the door, pulled the photographs out of the bag and looked at them. "What else did he say about me?"

Susan's husband was a phantom, a one-time voice on the phone. I tried to imagine him, wondered if I had passed him on the street or taken his picture.

"What's Ralph look like?"

"My husband? Oh, he's average."

"I mean, is he tall?"

"Average."

"He's probably good-looking."

"My secretary thinks he's distinguished. It's because he has grey hair."

"Do you have a picture?"

"Do you remember St. John Rivers in *Jane Eyre*? He looks like St. John Rivers."

The next thing I heard, Harlen and Bertha were going out together. Louise told me all about it over dinner. "You'd never believe it, Will: Harlen all dressed up in a suit and tie, Bertha in a dress and heels. At bingo. Betty saw them."

"Wouldn't get too excited about that," I said. "Probably won't last."

Louise stopped eating and looked at me. "Harlen say something to you?"

"Like what?"

"You know."

"No."

"You sure?"

"It's just that they don't have much in common."

"Neither do we."

Louise and I didn't exactly have a fight. It was more a discussion about Harlen and Bertha, though in the end, the discussion didn't have much to do with them at all.

I saw Harlen the next week, and by then, I had decided to stop trying to help.

"Hey, Will," Harlen said, "that was good advice."

"What advice?"

"About Bertha. About taking her out. She signed up with that escort service only because she was getting tired of staying home. Wanted some excitement in her life."

"You don't want to give her false hopes."

"No. Nothing like that. She understands. We're just good friends, having some good times."

"You tell Bertha that?"

"What's to tell? She understands. Real practical woman."

Bertha caught me in front of the bakery counter in Woodward's. "You were right about Harlen, Will. Got no idea what to do with his life. Needs a woman around. That was a good idea."

"It wasn't my idea."

Bertha winked and leaned in close. "We'll probably get you to take the pictures of the wedding." And she smiled and wandered off into the dress section, leaving me standing next to the doughnuts and the puff pastries.

I called Harlen that night and told him what Bertha had said.

"Marriage? I never said anything about marriage. You sure she said that?"

Susan came by on Thursday. "I think it's time we told Ralph."

"You haven't told him yet?"

"And I want you to come with me. Be there when I tell him. I want you to meet Ralph."

"Maybe I could meet him later."

"There's nothing to be afraid of."

"I'm not afraid."

"Maybe I should wait until after Christmas. It would probably be better just after Christmas."

Susan bought me a new camera strap with maple leaves on it for Valentine's Day. I asked her how things were progressing and she said there had been a few complications, and I told her it was probably time to be making some decisions.

I didn't talk to Bertha. There was no sense in looking for trouble. I talked to Louise. "Bertha said something about her and Harlen getting married. Bertha say anything to you?"

"Did you ask Bertha?"

"I don't want to ask Bertha."

"Did you ask Harlen?"

"Harlen doesn't know."

"How come you're so upset?"

I wasn't upset, and Harlen and Bertha didn't get married. Harlen came by with the news. "She was only fooling, Will. Said she did it just to see your face. You remember that escort service?"

"Dating service."

The Centre for the Development of Human
Potential had sent Bertha a list of about a dozen
names with photographs along with a glossy pam-
phlet advertising their "Executive Class", the deluxe
part of their service which provided you—for a small
additional fee—with the names of professionals who
made over fifty thousand dollars a year. According to
Harlen, Bertha had said a few uncomplimentary
things and had thrown it in the trash. In the end,
though, she did find a couple of interesting men on
the list who Harlen said didn't look like criminals at
all.

"She's got a date next weekend with a tractor salesman from Nanton, Will. What about you and
Louise?"

"What about us?"

"Bertha says it's time you and Louise got married."

"We're happy the way we are."

"Bertha says it's because you're afraid of commit-
ment."

"No, I'm not."

"I know that. Bertha says you should give Louise
an ultimatum."

"That's a dumb idea."

"Not my idea, Will."

"What does Bertha know?"

"Well, she has been married twice, and you got to
figure she knows something about women."

Susan finally left Ralph in May. "You can't imagine
how it feels, Will," she said. "It's like I just got out of
prison."

We spent that evening in bed with a bottle of wine.
Susan couldn't sleep, so she got up and sat by the
window. "I feel so free, Will. It's wonderful."

"We're going to need a larger apartment," I told her. "Maybe one of those nice brick duplexes."

On the way home the next day, I bought a paper and another bottle of wine. I was going to make a big pot of spaghetti and some garlic bread. But Susan wasn't there. She had come by sometime in the afternoon, collected her things, and left.

Louise caught me off-guard over dinner. South Wing was smashing peas with her spoon, and Louise was buttering an ear of fresh corn. "So," she said, the cob held in front of her mouth so I couldn't see what her lips were doing, "when's the ultimatum? You know, the one Bertha tells me you're working on. The one about marriage or else."

"That's just Bertha."

"So, what do you think I should do with the advertisement for that dating service? Bertha gave me the address, in case I said no to your ultimatum."

Bertha did all right with that dating service, I guess. One guy took her for a ride in a hot-air balloon around Calgary. Another fellow took her horseback riding in Waterton Park. But she didn't get married. Harlen said she had had several offers, but decided that life was complicated enough.

Louise said she knew what Bertha meant. The truth of the matter, she told me, was that marriage was always more of a burden on women than on men, that women always had to take on extra weight, while men just fell into marriage as if they were falling into bed.

I tried to stay away from talk like that.

fourteen

Monday mornings, I usually tried to get to the studio early. It gave me a chance to straighten up the darkroom, vacuum the floors, look at the accounts. I didn't have a routine, and some Mondays, I'd just sit in the easy chair by the front window and think.

So it was a Monday, and I was sitting in that chair thinking, when I heard someone knocking on the window. Without turning around, I would have guessed it was Harlen, but I never knew him to be up before eight and I was right. The guy at the window was wearing a red jacket. He was smiling and bobbing up and down like a fighter. He had an envelope in one hand. His hair was tied back in a ponytail. I didn't recognize him, and I didn't think he was from the reserve. It was his clothes, I guess, and his gestures. If I had been in the back room, I would have ignored the knocking, but I was caught sitting in that chair in the window like a department-store display.

So I opened the door, wanting to say something clever and friendly about the business hours which were clearly posted.

"You must be Will," he said, and he glided past me into the studio, waving the envelope as though it were a wing. He stood in the middle of the studio and looked around, and I could see the back of his jacket, and I knew who he was. David Plume.

I had never met David, but I knew the jacket. It was an ordinary club jacket, red nylon with knit cuffs and waistband. Across the back in large white letters was the word *AIM*.

"Glad I caught you, Will," he said as though we were old friends. "I need some photography work done."

That jacket was famous. People who didn't know David, like me, knew the jacket.

"Harlen says you do good work on photographs that are beat up a bit." And he handed me the envelope.

The photograph was beat up a lot. It had been folded, and the emulsion had cracked and peeled. There was a tear that ran half-way down the left side.

"That's me," David said. "What do you think?"

James and me liked to play tricks on my mother. Nothing mean. One time, I put on one of James's shirts and walked into the kitchen with the shirt up around my chest. "Look at this," I whined. "You must have shrunk it. It was my favourite shirt."

Mom would look at me, and before she could say anything, I'd shout, "Ha, it's James's shirt. Had you fooled, right?"

"Boy, I guess you did."

"You thought it was my shirt, right?"

"I guess I did."

"You got to watch out for me."

"I guess I do."

Another time, I got James to crawl under the sink. He crawled way at the back where the pipes were, and then, I piled the soap boxes and rags and the bucket and stuff like that all around him. Even with the doors open, you couldn't see him, unless you got down on your knees and really looked hard.

James was supposed to stay there until he could hear Mom at the sink, and then, he was supposed to start meowing. I guess it was because he was young. After a while, he got scared of being in the dark and started to cry. Mom found him and hauled him out and held him.

"It was Will's fault," he cried.

"No, it wasn't. You were supposed to be a cat. Not my fault you're still a baby."

"Am not!"

"Are too!"

Sometimes our tricks didn't work out so well.

"The guy standing next to me is Dennis Banks." David held the picture and ran his finger across the image. There were four men and one woman in the photograph. David and two of the other men were holding rifles. "That's Carter Camp. I can't remember the other one. The woman is Gladys Bissonette."

The photograph was underexposed. Probably whoever took it shot it without a flash. But you could see David, alright. He was wearing a headband and a T-shirt.

"You see the jacket Dennis is wearing? This is the same jacket. He gave it to me. You think you can fix this?"

David had a big smile on his face, as though one of the other men had just told a joke. Dennis Banks wasn't smiling. He was turning towards David, caught in mid-gesture, his eyes half-closed, his mouth open, his head turning to the side. "I'd like to get a really big one. You know, poster size. Maybe a couple of wallet-size ones, too."

In the background, you could see a table. There were people sitting around the table. They might have been eating, but you couldn't see much detail. It was too dark, and the people were beyond the range of the camera.

"This is a famous picture," said David. "The FBI or the RCMP would love to get their hands on it."

There was nothing remarkable about the photograph. It could have been five friends on a hunting trip. I knew it wasn't, but it could have been.

"Wounded Knee," David said almost in a whisper, as if someone might be listening. "This photograph was taken at Wounded Knee."

Maydean Joe was retarded. She lived in the apartment building next door to ours, and every so often, Maydean would wander into our basement. We played in that basement in the winter, when it was too cold to go out, and in the summer, when it was too hot to stay out. I guess we figured we owned that basement.

When Maydean first showed up, we didn't know what to do. Henry Goodrider told her it was our basement, and that if she wanted to play in it, she would have to pay. Maydean just stood and looked at Henry with her mouth hanging open. Her arms hung in the air at funny angles, and every so often, they would jump as though someone had pulled on a set of strings. She sort of frightened me, her arms jumping about and her head jerking as if she couldn't control it. I think she frightened Henry, too.

We tried to play a couple of tricks on her. One day, James and Henry and me pretended we couldn't hear Maydean or see her. We walked around the basement, as though she wasn't there. We talked to each other as though she didn't exist. It was a joke, but all of a sudden, Maydean let out a scream and rushed Henry and pushed him into some boxes that were stacked in the corner near the washers and the large commercial dryer. He wasn't hurt, but he was angry as hell, and he got up and pushed Maydean. She fell down, and then she got up and pushed Henry, and Henry pushed her back, and then she pushed me. We all started pushing each other, and then we started laughing, and after that, Maydean was okay.

I don't mean she got better or anything like that. She was still retarded. She liked to hug us, and that was embarrassing. She'd run over in that staggering, falling, loose-limbed way she had of moving and grab Henry or James or me. She was strong, and she liked to squeeze us as hard as she could.

The other kids didn't like her much. Lena Oswald called her Little Miss Moron, and Bat Brain, and Slobberdean, because Maydean drooled a little when she got excited. Vicki Wright and her sister Robin started drawing pictures and writing things like "Will loves Maydean" or "James loves Maydean" or "Henry loves Maydean" on the basement walls with chalk they stole from school. Vicki said if you hung around retards like Maydean and let them slobber all over you, you would become a retard, too.

The kids said all those things out loud in front of Maydean, as if she couldn't hear or didn't care. One day, she sort of went wild in the basement and started scrubbing at a picture Vicki had drawn. Maydean tried to erase it with her bare hands, and she got most of it off, but not before she cut her hands on the concrete. They didn't bleed much, but you could see the faint fan of blood on the wall.

Harlen had told me the story of David Plume. As soon as the Indians took over Wounded Knee, David and Kevin Longbird and Amos Morley piled into Kevin's van and headed for South Dakota. They got stopped in Fargo and were thrown in jail there. After they got out, Kevin and Amos Morley turned back and came home.

Ray Little Buffalo figured that David was bullshitting everyone. "Once the feds closed down the highways and the secondary roads around Wounded Knee, no one got in. Plume probably just hung out in town and tried to convince the whores he was some big hero. Probably got that jacket at a surplus store."

According to Harlen, after Wounded Knee ended, David got himself arrested for aggravated assault in Lincoln and spent fourteen months in jail. When he came home, he had the jacket.

The photograph could have been taken inside Wounded Knee. But it could have been taken at someone's house, too, or in a bus depot.

"I can fix it," I said. "It won't be as good as new, and I can't print a poster-size copy. How about an eight-by-ten and some wallet size?"

"Kinda like something bigger. It's a historic picture."

"Don't have the equipment to do real big stuff. There might be some places in Calgary that can do that."

"It was taken the morning the cops really started shooting at us," David said. "This jacket has power.

You had to have been there."

It was Henry's idea that we put Maydean in the dryer. James wanted to be the one, but Henry said that he might bang his head as the dryer went around, and that if Maydean banged her head, it probably wouldn't hurt.

We'd put Maydean in the dryer and wait until my mother came down to put the wash in the dryer and just before she turned it on, we'd say, "Hey, isn't that Maydean?" or something like that. That was the idea.

But Maydean wouldn't get in the dryer. She got as far as the door, but she wouldn't get in.

"Come on, Maydean. It'll be fun."

"No," said Maydean.

"Look, tell you what. We won't let her turn it on."

"No."

"Maydean," said Henry. "If you want to play with us and be our pal, you got to get in the dryer."

Maydean didn't get in the dryer. She was stubborn sometimes, and this was one of those times. So we were stuck with James. Henry borrowed his brother's hockey helmet and a pair of gloves because, he said, you can't be too safe. James looked like one of those astronauts climbing into a space ship. He pressed his nose against the glass and stuck out his tongue. Maydean stood in front of the dryer jerking her head around and laughing, while James made fish faces behind the glass.

When we heard Mom coming down the stairs, we told James to be quiet, and we shut the door. Maydean stood in front of the dryer, and she wouldn't move. We thought she'd give the whole thing away. "You mess this up, Maydean, and you can just find some other basement."

Henry and me went and stood by the washers and tried to look casual. "We'll help you, Mom," I said as soon as she came through the door. Henry opened the washer, and we began carrying the wet clothes to the dryer.

My mother didn't say anything. She just watched us. Maydean started to laugh and sway.

"You kids break something?"

We got all the clothes from the washer into the dryer, and my mother took her coin purse out of her apron pocket.

"Maybe you should take a look to see that we put them in right."

"Don't know of a wrong way to do it."

"We may have made a mistake, you know."

My mother opened the purse and took out two quarters, but as she closed the purse, it slipped out of her hand and fell, the coins scattering across the floor.

Henry and me leaped on the quarters and the dimes and the nickels. Some of the coins ran under the washer. Others rolled to the far side of the room. We chased them all down, pouncing on them like hawks on field mice.

I was just starting to count my coins, when I heard a klunking sound and Maydean's crazy laugh.

"What's wrong with this dryer?" my mother was saying. "What'd you kids put in here?"

I made some coffee. David sat in the easy chair. He sat with his legs sprawled out in front of him as though he had walked a long distance and was tired.

"You ever been shot at?"

It was a casual question. David might have asked me if I'd flown in a plane or if I liked sushi or if I had ever been to Yellowknife.

"It's weird, you know. At night, you can see the flash and the tracers coming in. Every so often, you'd hear the bullets hitting something."

"There's a poster company in Calgary. I could make a negative and send it to them. They'll blow it up to any size you want."

"I was never scared at Wounded Knee. Most of the time we just sat around and talked. Most of the time we sat and waited. Most days, it was boring as hell. You know the cops killed Frank Clearwater while he was sleeping?"

I was trying to think of something sympathetic to say when David got out of the chair and tucked the tail of his shirt back in his pants. "You get close to guys when someone's trying to kill you. You know what I mean? Me and Dennis Banks were like that."

I nodded and started moving towards the door, hoping David would follow. "Give me a couple of days," I said. "I'll shoot a negative, touch it up and print a couple of wallet-size photos. I'll look up that address in Calgary."

"He gave me this jacket," David said, and he turned so I could see the letters on the back. "Harlen says you were in Toronto when we took Wounded Knee."

"That's right," I said. "I thought about going."

"Lots of people thought about going."

David walked back to the chair and sat down. I watched the window hoping Harlen would drop in. We talked about Wounded Knee. We talked about Medicine River and the reserve. David's parents lived in Cardston. They were both Mormons, and he didn't see much of them. It was a friendly conversation full of anecdotes and humour, but as he talked, his gestures became laboured and jerky as though springs were slipping inside, and his voice plunged and thrashed like someone dying in water. I wasn't sorry when he finally left.

I caught Harlen at the Friendship Centre. "David shows everyone that picture," Harlen told me. "He doesn't mean to make people feel bad, you know. He's the only one who went to Wounded Knee from around here. Kevin and Amos went with him, but they didn't stay."

"He didn't make me feel bad."

"That's good. Some of the boys don't like him. Ray figures David likes to show off. Those two almost got into a fight at the American a few weeks back. Things would be easier if he didn't wear that jacket all the time."

"You think that's the problem?"

"Sure. Jimmy Bruised Head went to law school, and Louise's cousin Alice got two or three degrees and went to teach at that university in Saskatoon. You and Louise own your own businesses."

"So?"

"So, none of you went to Wounded Knee."

"So?"

"David did. You can see how it all makes sense."

Henry and me got James out of the dryer. His nose was bleeding, and the helmet was jammed down over his eyes. We took him over to the sink and got most of the blood off his face. He was trying not to cry. I knew Mom was looking at me.

"He wanted to do it. I told him no, but he did it anyway."

"That's right," said Henry. "It's Maydean's fault. She was supposed to do it, but she didn't want to because she's crazy."

My mother stood and looked at the three of us, Henry and me and James, who was trying to stop the blood with a corner of his shirt.

"Where's Maydean?" my mother said.

She wasn't in the basement, and at first, I thought she had left. But then I heard her popping laugh. She was in the dryer. She was lying in the dryer on her back, her knees drawn up against her stomach.

"Hey, get out of there. You're going to get those clothes dirty."

"Yeah," said Henry. "You didn't want to get in the dryer before and look what happened. Now it's too late." Henry reached in and grabbed Maydean's arm. She jerked the arm out of Henry's grasp, rolled over, kicked at Henry and began screaming. Henry snapped his arm back and banged it on the side of the dryer. "Damn," he shouted. "You gone and done it this time, Maydean Joe. Everyone's going to know you're crazy. Wanting to stay in a dryer is real nuts."

The following Wednesday, just before closing, David pulled up in front of the studio in Kevin Longbird's van. Kevin was in the driver's seat, and I could see Amos Morley in the back.

"We're on our way to Ottawa," David told me. "Government wants to cut the money for Indian education."

"They're always trying to do that."

"You should come along, Will. You could take pictures."

"I don't know why the government does that."

"I meet a lot of Indians, you know, who are sorry they didn't go to Wounded Knee. That's what they tell me. They feel like they got left out. It feels good to be part of something important."

"Yeah," I said. "I know what you mean."

We stood around the dryer. James's nose had stopped bleeding. Maydean was rolled up on her side with her face against the back of the dryer.

"Go on," my mother said. "Go play outside. She just wants to be like the rest of you."

Mom pulled up a chair next to the dryer and sat down and waited. "Go on," she said again. "Going to take a while to fix this foolishness."

I walked David to the van. He got in the back. He left the sliding door open as if he expected I might change my mind at the last minute and jump into the van with everyone else.

"A person should do something important with their life. You should think about that."

"I will."

The van turned the corner past the American and headed for the highway. I stood at the curb and watched it go. Later, I went back into the studio and turned on all the lights and opened the doors.

chapter

fifteen

Harlen had a great many interests. He liked basket-ball. He liked cars. He liked golf. He liked fishing. He was a fair carpenter and a decent hockey player. He collected these interests the way some people collect stamps, and though they never seemed to last very long, the knowledge accumulated in Harlen's brain like brown grocery bags in a closet.

Harlen's latest interest was photography. For the last month, every time Harlen stopped by, I'd have to explain another aspect of taking pictures, or I would have to explain how a certain part of the camera worked.

"That's the shutter release, Harlen."

"Right."

"This ring sets your f-stops. It controls things like light and depth of field."

"Right."

"This is how you set your shutter speed."

"What is this?"

"That's the time-delay button."

"Those guys think of everything."

"I don't use it much."

"What does it do?"

Harlen was a good listener. I was a lousy teacher.

"Well, let's say you wanted a picture of yourself and the basketball team. You'd put the camera on a tripod and set the delay like this. Then you would push the button right here, and you'd have about ten seconds before the camera actually took the picture."

"So I could be in the picture, too."

"If you moved fast enough. I don't use it much."

"Damn," said Harlen, "those guys think of everything."

Near the end of June, Harlen decided that I should run a photography special. He hauled me over to see Leon Butler, who ran the local Woolworth store. According to Harlen, Leon knew everything there was to know about specials. Leon liked to tell anyone who would listen that specials helped to bring people in, and once they were in, there was no telling what else they would buy.

"You got to get them in first, Will," Leon said. "Run a special. Lose money on it. You'll get it back. Hell, give 'em a free photo. When they come by to pick up the picture, tell them how nice the picture would look in a custom-oak frame. Maybe someone in the family is getting married and they need a photographer. A special is always a good idea."

"Run a family-portrait special," Harlen said. "Something like that will bring in a lot of people from the reserve. Family is an important thing."

So I ran a special. Not for Harlen's reasons and not for Leon's. Business had been slow, and a small profit was better than no profit. So for the last two weeks in June, you could get a family portrait for twenty dollars. You got one eight-by-ten, two five-by-sevens, four three-by-fives and eight wallet-size photographs. It was a great deal. Joyce Blue Horn was the first one to call.

"Does that special mean all the family?" she said.

"Yes, it does."

"I got a big family."

"Doesn't matter. Just bring everybody in, and I'll take the pictures."

"Maybe we could come in on Saturday."

Generally, I only worked Saturday mornings. "Early Saturday morning?"

"We got to drive in from the reserve."

"Late Saturday morning?"

"That's fine. Going to be real good to get a picture of the family."

One summer, my mother decided that we should get a family portrait. I don't know where she got the money, but I do remember the guy who took the picture. He was a short, plump man in a thick, black sweater.

He said hello to my mother, looked at James and me, and held out a wet, pink hand. "Is the mister going to be coming along soon?" he asked. "I got more appointments, you know."

My mother shook her head and told him that there wasn't any mister coming along, that there were just the three of us, and he could take the picture now.

The guy took us into a back room that smelled of disinfectant and had my mother sit on an old piano stool. James and me stood on either side of her with our hands on her shoulders.

"Come on, you boys," he said, "get in tight to your mother. You love your mother, don't you?"

He took five, maybe six shots. Kept telling us to

wet our lips or to smile or to look at the camera.

About a month later, the portrait arrived in the mail, and Mom got four thumbtacks and stuck it up on the kitchen wall. It stayed there until the paper began to curl up and the colours started to fade.

When Harlen stopped by the studio, I told him about Joyce Blue Horn, and Harlen, who knew about these things, gave me the family history.

"Joyce is Mary Rabbit's daughter. She married Elvis Blue Horn. They got eleven kids."

Joyce, according to Harlen, was a minor celebrity on the reserve, but not because of the size of her family.

"There were the three girls first, triplets: Frances, Deborah and Jennifer. Then you had two sets of twins: Fred and Fay, and George and Andy. Robert was the only single, and he was followed by another set of twins: Christian and Benjamin. How many's that?"

"Ten, I think."

"Okay. Then there was John and Samuel, but Samuel died. You keeping track of everyone?"

"I'm trying."

"She say she was bringing everybody?"

"I can handle eleven people."

"Don't forget Joyce and Elvis."

"Thirteen is no problem either."

Harlen smiled and walked around the studio looking at the walls. He began to laugh, soft, low clucks like he was sitting on a half-a-dozen eggs.

"Something wrong?"

Harlen's eyes were squeezed down into two smiling slits. "Will, when Joyce Blue Horn said *family*, she wasn't just talking about her and Elvis and the kids, you know."

"Her parents alive?"

"Elvis's mom and dad, too."

"No problem."

"Elvis has nine brothers and four sisters."

"Come on, Harlen."

"And Joyce," said Harlen, trying to keep from laughing out loud, "Joyce has seven sisters and five brothers."

"The photo special is for immediate family."

Harlen wiped his eyes with his shirt sleeve. "Oh," he said, "then we're only talking about fifty people or so."

Harlen liked to exaggerate. I knew that. And there was no way I could get fifty people in the studio for a photograph, so I guess I didn't really think that fifty people would show up.

Friday night I took Louise Heavyman out to dinner. We went to the new Chinese place that had just opened up. Louise liked hot food, and the Pearl had some of those Szechuan dishes. I waited until we had finished the soup.

"You know Joyce Blue Horn, don't you?"

"Went to school with her."

"Joyce is coming by the studio tomorrow. You know, that special I'm running."

"The family portrait?"

"That's the one."

"You got room in the studio for everybody?"

"Studio will handle twenty easy."

Louise shook her head, reached across and patted my hand, and then she began to laugh.

"I know she has a large family," I said.

People at the other tables were beginning to look around. Louise blew her nose and said, "Eat your dinner, Will."

Saturday morning, I got to the shop early and began to move everything out of the studio, so I'd have enough room. At ten o'clock, Harlen arrived.

"Joyce here yet?"

"Not yet."

"Thought I'd come by and watch."

Louise and South Wing arrived at eleven. "I haven't seen Joyce and the kids for a couple of months," she said. "South Wing and Joyce's youngest boy John were born a month apart. You mind if we watch?"

Joyce Blue Horn and her kids arrived at eleven-thirty. Elvis was right behind them with a large cardboard box that said Huggies on the side.

"Where do you want this?" he said.

"What is it?"

"Lunch," said Elvis.

By noon, not counting Harlen and Louise and South Wing, there were thirty-eight people in the studio. Harlen knew everyone, and as people came in, he'd say hello and introduce them to me.

"Will, this is Charlotte, Joyce's sister, and her husband Mel.

"This is Elvis's brother Rodney, and that's Ann and Sonny and Jimmy.

"Clare Blue Horn, Will. Her husband Bender used to play for the team. You remember Bender?

"This is Cindy and Betty and Katie and John and . . ."

Well, I did make an attempt at remembering some of the names. And I tried to keep count. By twelve-thirty, there were in the vicinity of fifty-four people—adults and kids—in my studio. The kids were everywhere, in the bathroom, in the studio itself, in the kitchen. The adults stood around in groups, talking. Someone had opened the cardboard box, and Joyce Blue Horn was passing around sandwiches and potato chips.

Louise waved at me from behind a wall of people. "Will," she shouted, "why don't we take everybody down to the river? Should be nice down there. Wind's not bad. We can get some more food and soda, and you can take the pictures of Joyce and Elvis and the kids near the beach with the big cottonwoods."

"Horsehead Coulee?"

"Sure. Have a picnic, do some swimming, too. You could get a good picture of everyone."

There were probably lots of reasons why it wasn't a good idea to try to take a family portrait down by the river, but before I could think of any, Louise was over talking to Joyce, and Joyce was talking to Elvis, and Elvis was talking to his sisters. . . .

Harlen came by with a root beer. "Hey, Will, what if we took the picture down by the river?"

"Louise was already here."

Elvis waved at me above the crowd. "That's a great idea, Will," he shouted. "I'll call the rest of the folks."

"Can I borrow the phone?" said Harlen. "Might as well call Floyd and the boys. See if they want to come, too."

Louise was putting South Wing's jacket on. "On the way, let's stop by the centre and see if Bertha and Big John and Eddie want to come."

Spring and early summer were the prettiest seasons on the prairies, especially down in the coulees around the river. By May, if there had been a little rain, the hills would begin to come green. By early June, if we hadn't had any spring blizzards, the flowers would be out. It had been a good year, and the coulee bottom was green and bright.

By the time we bounced our way down the dirt road to Horsehead Coulee, Elvis and his brothers were already setting up some makeshift tables, and Joyce and her sisters were spreading out the food. The river was lower than I had expected, green and murky, slow-moving and shallow, occasionally dropping into deep, warm holes.

"Maybe we'll feed the grandparents first. Let them get settled in," said Elvis. "Kids'll just as soon swim, anyway. Maybe you could take the pictures a little later, Will. That okay?"

I said sure, and I found Louise and South Wing and me a flat place down by the river. The sun was warm. Louise snuggled down against my shoulder. "This is nice, Will."

I was just getting settled, feeling warm, thinking about a nap, when I felt the sun disappear, and there was Harlen.

"Will, get up. You're supposed to be working. Don't want to lose your good reputation by going to sleep where everyone can see you. Come on. People been asking about you."

Harlen took me over to a group of elders who were sitting in lawn chairs, watching the kids in the river. I knew Lionel James and Martha Oldcrow.

Harlen stood up straight and put his hand on my shoulder. "This is Rose Horse Capture's boy, Will." And Harlen pushed me forward a little.

Harlen waited for everyone to get a good look at me. Finally Lionel stood up and dusted his jeans.

"Real nice day, Will," he said. "You and your brother were raised up in Calgary, so maybe you don't know everyone. Maybe you should greet everyone, so you know the people."

We never knew many people when we lived in
Calgary. Mostly my mother stayed to herself. But
during the summer months, the Calgary Friendship
Centre would hold potlucks and social dances in the
basement of the Catholic church across from the Shell
gas station on Sixteenth Street. It was a cool, deep
hole, banked against the summer sun and the prairie
wind. Sometimes dancers on their way to the money
powwows across the line would stop in and give us
an exhibition for some food and maybe a little gas
money. But mostly those evenings were socials full of
food and round dances and talk.

James and me didn't dance. We had other games
we played with the rest of the kids up on the wooden
stage. We'd wrap ourselves in the heavy velvet curtains and twist around and around. Or we'd hide at
the back of the stage in the dark and watch the people
as they moved in the slow, shuffling circle. We were
safe and powerful there in the darkness. During the
evening, the mothers would come to the edge of the
stage one by one and call out a name in soft, low
voices. It wasn't like the white women in our apartment building who stuck their heads out the windows at supper time and squawked their children's
names as if the kids were playing on the moon.

"Johnnnnnnnnnnnieeeeeee!"
"Geooooooooooooorggeeeee!"
"Frrrrrrrrrrrrrred!"
These were coaxing calls, an invitation to come and
join the dance. The girls would always go right away,
and they'd drag the older boys with them. But the
rest of us would pull back farther into the darkness
and smile to ourselves and whisper and watch. We'd
only come out when the drum stopped.

"Bet you didn't know where we were." We liked to
tease Mom.

"Seems to me," she'd say, "you were up in those curtains again."

"Naw, we were at the back, and we could see you."

"Tyrone came and danced tonight. Maybe you should watch Tyrone."

"Tyrone goes cause of Rita."

"Maybe you should come next time."

"James and me got better things to do."

"Yeah! We got better things to do!"

"Maybe when you're older."

"We can see everything you do. It's like watching a movie."

"Then you can see what a good time we're having."

We stopped going to the socials when my mother lost her job at the Bay and had to take a night job cleaning offices in the Petro-Can building, but the memory of those evenings was like a series of photographs—the women leaning against the stage, calling into the dark, the dancers moving in the light, the children hidden and invisible, waiting back from the edge, listening and watching.

Lionel shook hands with an old woman and whispered something to her in Blackfoot. She looked at me and smiled and began to laugh to herself.

"This is Floyd's grandmother," Lionel said. "She knew your mother. She's happy to see you're alive and getting enough to eat." Lionel leaned over. "Her oldest boy died last year in a car wreck. She wants you to get her a sandwich."

"Sure," I said. "What kind does she like?"

"Maybe something soft," said Lionel. "Peanut butter and jelly would be good."

Harlen caught me at the table. "You and Lionel

talking to Floyd's granny?"

"She wanted a sandwich."

"She likes root beer, too," said Harlen.

I took the sandwich and the root beer back to Floyd's granny. Lionel and the old woman were laughing quietly. Lionel had tears in his eyes.

"Her boy," said Lionel, "was a real good storyteller. Always had a funny story to tell. He travelled all over the place and always came back with a good story. Sometimes we'd laugh so hard, it would hurt, and we would have to lie down. We were remembering one of his stories just now."

"I never knew him."

"Granny says you remind her of him. She says maybe she should adopt you. That boy of hers always had a good story."

"I'm sorry about her boy."

"Old women get like that, you know."

"Sure."

"Always worrying about the kids who don't have mothers."

"Sure."

"Fathers are important too," said Lionel, and he put his hands in his pockets and gestured with his chin towards Louise and South Wing.

Elvis and Joyce began herding the kids out of the river and over to the tables. They came wiggling along like a twist of eels all wrapped around each other.

Harlen nudged me. He had a sandwich in one hand, a soda in the other and another soda in his pocket. "This one's for you, Will," he said, handing me the half-empty can. "Been saving it.' He took the other can from his jeans and opened it. "Didn't know what kind of sandwich you like."

"Not hungry."

"How's the sun doing, Will? You watching the sun? Don't want to forget about that portrait."

"It's okay, Harlen. Lots of time."

"You going to be able to get everyone in?"

"Sure. Put Joyce and Elvis off to one side and line the kids up."

"What about the grandparents?"

"Well, we could set up a few of the lawn chairs in front."

"We got enough chairs?"

"Just the two sets of grandparents."

Joyce came over. "Will, soon as the kids get fed, we can take the picture."

"Whenever," I said. "How many you figure we'll have in the picture?"

"Are there too many?"

"No," I said. "Just wanted to know. You know, give me a chance to figure who should go where. Out here, I could take a picture of everyone."

"Okay," said Joyce, "that'll be real good."

"So how many you figure?"

"Everyone," said Joyce, and she walked back to the table.

"Boy," said Harlen. "That'll be some picture."

"Everyone?"

"You said you could do it, Will. Everybody's depending on you. You're the boss."

I could see that Harlen had another sandwich in his pocket. "Maybe you can help, Harlen."

"Sure, you're the boss."

"Any of those sandwiches left?" And I looked right at Harlen's pocket.

"Egg," said Harlen. "Not the kind you like."

"I love egg."

"Lots of onions in it. Not a good sandwich for a world-famous photographer to be eating."

My father died the week before my mother dressed James and me up in new blue wool pants and white shirts and hauled us down to the photo studio. That was the reason, and I told James.

"Dad died," I said, "and Mom wants to get a picture in case something happens to us."

The photographer kept telling us to smile, and James and me did our best. I don't guess Mom ever smiled. At least the portrait we got had her staring at the camera, her face set, her eyes flat.

It was hot that day, and on the way home James and me spent most of the time scratching and pulling at those pants. "Leave them pants be," Mom said. "They're new. Don't mess them up."

When we got home, she made us take the pants and shirts off. She put the pants in a box, and folded the shirts up real neat, fixed the pins and squeezed them back in the plastic bags. We never saw them again. The next day, which was a Sunday, my mother took us out to Smitty's for breakfast, and we got to eat waffles and sausages. Two days later, she came home and told us that she had lost her job at the Bay, that there had been some layoffs or something, but that she was going to start working at Petro-Can, only it was going to be at night.

We looked smart in those white shirts and blue wool pants, our hands on our mother's shoulders. The photograph stayed on the wall until the day we moved back to Medicine River.

"Okay," I said to Harlen, "we better get started. Let's get everyone over there by the river. Put the elders in front. Let them sit in the chairs."

"You're the boss, Will."

"Put the little kids in front on the sand. The bigger kids can stand around the grandparents, and we'll put most of the adults at the back."

Harlen ran around like a confused sheep-dog trying to coax and lead and push everyone into place.

"How's that, Will?" said Harlen.

The sun was beginning to drop. "That's great," I said. "Time to take some pictures."

"What about you, Will?" said Joyce.

"That's right," said Elvis.

"Something wrong?"

"Should have you in the picture, too," said Joyce.

"Someone's got to take the picture."

Through the lens, I could see Harlen bubbling out of the crowd. "Hey, Will. That's right. You can be in the picture, too. You can use that button thing. You know, set the button and run on over."

"That's okay, Harlen."

"Best you be in the picture, too," said Lionel.

As soon as Harlen explained, in detail, just what a time-delay device was, everyone insisted that I had to be in the picture, too. Floyd's granny even got up and moved her chair over, so I'd have a place to sit.

The first shots were easy. I set the timer, ran across the sand and sat down next to Floyd's granny. But with a large group like that, you can't take chances. Someone may have closed their eyes just as the picture was taken. Or one of the kids could have turned their back. Or someone might have gotten lost behind someone else.

Then, too, the group refused to stay in place. After every picture, the kids wandered off among their parents and relatives and friends, and the adults floated

back and forth, no one holding their positions. I had
to keep moving the camera as the group swayed from
one side to the other. Only the grandparents
remained in place as the ocean of relations flowed
around them.

I took twenty-four pictures. And each time I had to
set the camera, hit the shutter-delay button and run
like hell. After the fourteenth or fifteenth picture, I
tried to stay behind the camera, but Elvis wouldn't
hear of it.

"Come on, Will. This one's going to be the good
one."

I was red-faced and aglow with sweat by the time I
came to the end of the roll.

The pictures turned out good. There were four or
five where nearly everyone was facing the camera
and smiling. Harlen was in the studio when the photos came off the dryer.

"These are good, Will," he said. "Joyce is going to
be real pleased."

Harlen picked up another photo. "Hey, Will,
where'd you get this? That's James and you when
you were younger. Your mother, too."

"Had an old photo lying around. It was in pretty
bad shape. I fixed it up and made a new negative.
Thought I'd send a copy to James."

"Real different," said Harlen, and he held up a picture of Joyce's family and the copy I had made of the
portrait of Mom and James and me. "You and James
look like someone sprayed you up and down with
starch."

"That's the way they used to take pictures."

"Nobody smiling, huh?"

"I guess."

"Pictures of the family are good things to have."

"I guess."

"You know, Will, this is the first family portrait that Joyce Blue Horn has ever had. She told me that. She'll be real happy. Probably get a lot of new business once word gets around about what a good photographer you are."

"Don't know if I can run that fast again."

Harlen laughed. "Will, you're a card. Floyd's granny was impressed. Said you ran like the old-time men, fast, no noise."

"Floyd's granny must be deaf."

"Said you reminded her of her boy."

I worked late that night, got the portraits packaged up and ready to mail. When I got home, I tacked the picture of Mom and James and me up on the kitchen wall. Right next to it, I stuck a picture of all of us down at the river.

I was smiling in that picture, and you couldn't see the sweat. Floyd's granny was sitting in her lawn chair next to me looking right at the camera with the same flat expression that my mother had, as though she could see something farther on and out of sight.

chapter

sixteen

Harlen told Louise he thought she was formidable. Harlen liked words like that, not because they were big or important sounding, but because people didn't use them much, and there was the chance that they might get lost.

"Everyone watches too much television," Harlen said. "Good words are hard to find."

What Harlen meant was that Louise had corners which were hard to see around. Louise took it as a compliment.

"She's a strong woman, Will. Doris was like that."

"I like strong women."

"You know, Will, Doris could work all day and never get tired. Her father owned a farm up in Peace River. She could lift feed sacks, no trouble."

"Louise speaks her mind."

"That's right."

"Louise knows what she wants."

"That's right, too," Harlen said. "You got to admire Louise, even if she is formidable. She owns her own business. She owns her own car. She has a beautiful daughter. And she's done it all on her own."

"I own my own business, too."

"Sure you do, Will. Accountants just make more than photographers, that's all."

"And I own my own car."

"You bet. Pick-up truck is a handy thing to have. Especially the older ones. You know, you don't mind a few extra dents like you would with a new one. Course it's not a good family car."

"Louise doesn't own her own home."

"Neither do you, Will."

"That's right. Neither do you."

"That's right."

Monday evening, Louise called me. "Will," she said, "what are you doing tonight?"

The Raiders and the Redskins were playing at seven. Harlen was coming by at six-thirty with a large pizza from Tino's.

"Got a few things to get out of the way."

There was a pause, and then Louise said, "It's Monday, right. . . . I forgot, Will. Monday night football?"

I was glad she couldn't see me. "No . . . no . . . hey, I guess it is Monday. Forgot all about it. Who's playing?"

"You sure?"

"Sure. Just have to get these things out of the way, and I'm free."

"I don't want to bother you, really."

"No bother."

I could always get Harlen to videotape the game.

"I'm thinking of buying a house, Will, and I wanted to talk to you about it, first. I could use your help."

"Sure."

"Maybe around nine, after I get South Wing down?"

"Sure."

Harlen and the pizza arrived at a quarter to seven. I told him about Louise and the house.

"Hate to see you miss out on a good pizza."

"I don't have to go until nine."

"Going to miss the best part of the game."

"Raiders should beat them."

We ate the pizza and watched the game. The second half had just started. The Raiders were leading twenty-one to seven. I said something about the last play, when Harlen turned to me with his mouth all rolled up at the corners and his eyes full of bright stars.

"Hey!" he said. Just like that. And he sat up straight and slapped his legs. "Louise wants you to live with her. That's what she wants to talk about."

I shook my head. "You're leaping to conclusions."

"No . . . no. Listen, Will. It all makes sense."

"Harlen, she just wants my advice on houses. Wants me to take a few pictures."

Harlen waved his hand around and shook his head. "When was the last time Louise asked anyone for advice?"

"She asks me all the time."

"Sure," said Harlen, "that's right. When it comes to taking pictures or what to cook for dinner or what movie to see. Women like to do that. But the big things. . . . Did she ask anyone about having South Wing or becoming an accountant?"

"I don't know."

"See? This is her way of asking you to live with her and South Wing."

"You're leaping to conclusions."

"Come on," said Harlen, and he stood up. "We got to get you ready."

"It's just past eight."

"Just enough time. You got a clean shirt?"

"What's wrong with this one?"

"Got to look your best. That blue shirt with the little white stripes. Is it clean?"

"I don't need a clean shirt."

"You get in the shower, Will, and I'll find the shirt."

"Harlen, I've had a shower."

"You smell of pizza."

As I stood under the shower, I tried to remember exactly what Louise had said. I dried off and brushed my teeth. Harlen was just finishing up with the iron.

"Here, Will. That red tie's the one to wear. It's on the chair."

"I suppose you want me to wear my sports jacket, too?"

"Can't hurt. I polished your shoes for you. They were real scuffed. You only have so many chances."

"Harlen, I don't get this dressed up for work."

Harlen handed me my shirt. "Redskins scored a touchdown while you were in the shower, Will. Looks like a close game. I'll stick around in case you have any questions. Save you some of the pizza, too."

Louise was wearing a pair of old cut-offs and a University of Lethbridge sweatshirt.

"You been to a meeting or something?" she said.

"Something like that."

"You look great, Will. I must look like hell."

"No, you look great, too."

Louise wanted to buy a house. Now that South Wing was here, she said, it didn't seem right living in an apartment.

"South Wing should have a yard to play in, and the apartment is just too small. I'm thinking of something on the south side. Maybe one of those nice old homes with all the trees. What do you think?"

"Houses are nice," I said. "They're a lot of work, too. You know, taking care of the lawn and the garden, mowing the grass. Lots of things to buy for a house."

"I like doing those things."

"Big expense, a house."

"We need more room. You really look good, Will."

When Louise said *we*, she was talking about her and South Wing. I knew that. But I liked the sound of it, and I was glad I had worn the shirt and tie.

About six months after she moved her things out of my apartment, Susan called. I almost didn't recognize her voice at first.

"It's me, Will. Susan. How are you doing?"

It took me a minute to recover, and then I remember saying something like "How are you?" or "Good to hear from you" or "Hey, I was just thinking about you." Whatever it was, it was dumb, something to fill in the space, while I tried to find something clever.

"I was calling to see if you wanted to come by for dinner."

"Dinner?"

"You don't have to."

"No, that would be great. You okay?"

She said she couldn't be better, that she had a good job and a house. She and Ralph were doing their own divorce, and so far as it was possible, they had remained friends. "I'm in Pickering. I can give you directions."

"I don't have a car."

"I know. You can take the GO train and catch a cab."

"Sounds great."

"How about Saturday night?"

"Sounds great."

"Don't bring anything."

I could hear the pain in her voice. She needed me. She had needed me before, and I was sure she needed me again. But by the time I put down the phone, I wasn't at all sure I wanted Susan to need me.

Life is strange like that. When she left without a word, I was hurt at first. Then I was angry. Then I got lonely. Now I was angry again, and for the rest of that evening, I was sorry I had been so easy. Worse still, she hadn't given me her phone number. I tried calling information, but they didn't have a listing for her, and I guessed she was using her maiden name, which I didn't know.

I was stuck, I told myself. Besides, we could talk, and I could tell her how I felt. I didn't need to be needed the way Susan needed me, and the sooner I told her that, I told myself, the better I'd feel. There was no sense leading her on.

What Louise wanted me to do was to take pictures of the houses that she liked. Outside pictures, inside pictures, so she could keep track of the homes and compare them later on.

When I got back to my apartment, Harlen was watching a movie. The pizza box was empty.

"How'd the game go?"

"Great game, Will. Redskins beat them. Last-second field goal."

"Louise just wants me to go to the houses with her. Take some pictures. Give her advice."

Harlen smiled and got off the couch and shook my

hand. "You're a lucky man, Will."

The first house we went to on Saturday was a white two-storey with aluminum siding. There was a young fellow sitting at the kitchen table with a brief-case in front of him and a stack of what turned out to be something called "feature sheets". I was carrying South Wing.

"Hi, folks," he said. And he stuck out his hand. "I'm Bruce Klappe. Looking for a home, huh?"

Louise introduced herself, but before she could say much else, Bruce straightened his vest, smiled at me and said, "That's a pretty little girl, Mr. Heavyman. Got one myself. How old is yours?"

"He's not Mr. Heavyman," said Louise. "He's a good friend."

"Ah," said Bruce, "Mr. Heavyman couldn't make it? Well, if you like the house, and I think you will, we can set up a convenient time for him to see it, too. Is he working?"

"There isn't a Mr. Heavyman."

Bruce looked at South Wing, and he looked at me. "Sure," he said. "Lots of people are doing that these days." And he handed Louise a feature sheet. "House has plenty of room for three."

We spent the rest of the day and the next couple of weeks talking with realtors and looking at houses. I took pictures and gave advice.

"What did you think of that one, Will?"

"Seemed a little large."

"That was a nice one, wasn't it?"

"Seemed a little small."

We must have looked at every house for sale on the south side, and by the time we were done looking, Louise was no closer to buying one than when we had started.

"She's waiting for you to pick one, Will," Harlen told me. "You got to step in and be the man. You got to say, 'This is the one for us.' You got to be the man."

"She just hasn't found one she likes."

"Just waiting for you to say the word, Will."

Louise, according to Harlen, really didn't like living alone because she came from a large family. "That's why she had South Wing. She has eight brothers and sisters. You know the house that Floyd lives in?"

"The one on the lease road near the bridge?"

"That's it. That's where Louise grew up."

"Kind of small for nine kids."

"See?" said Harlen. "Louise likes a lot of people around."

"Maybe she likes the space."

"She's proud, Will. You see how she stands up straight. Granny Oldcrow says Louise is like the women who used to fight with the men. Real tough, those women. They could ride all day."

After all, Susan had left everyone. She had left Ralph. She had left her children. She had left me. And now that it suited her, she wanted me back. During the rest of the week, I found myself finding unflattering analogies and ironies with which to describe Susan. Most of them dealt with Horton the Elephant, a story my mother liked because the idea of an elephant sitting on an egg made her laugh. The others had to do with the nuclear power plant in Pickering.

I brought a bottle of wine with me, and as I sat on the train, I worked on exactly what I was going to say when she suggested that I stay overnight. I would say no, though I thought I might stay, if it got too late. I hadn't checked to see when the last train left. I might have to stay. But I could sleep in another bed or on the floor. Susan had her life, and I had mine.

It was a small house, and all the lights were on. Susan didn't answer the bell. A young girl in blue jeans and a maple leaf T-shirt opened the door. "Hi," she said, "I'm Meg. You must be Jerry."

"No," I said, "I'm Will."

"Sure," she said. "Of course. Come on in."

Behind her, gathered around a long table full of food, were about thirty people.

Louise called me Tuesday afternoon. "Will," she said, "I think I've found the house. I've got an appointment to see it at six o'clock. Can you come?"

The house was on Seventh Avenue. Louise's car was parked in front, and she was standing on the sidewalk talking to another woman. "Will," she said, as I got out of my truck, "this is Elizabeth Konsonlas. She's the realtor. What do you think?"

"Looks okay," I said to Louise.

"Great truck for moving furniture in," said Elizabeth. "I've got one just like it. Don't have to worry about the little dings."

The house was nice. There was a big kitchen with oak-and-glass cabinets. The living room looked out over a backyard filled with lilac bushes. There was a fireplace at one end and a built-in bookcase with glass doors at the other. The house had four bedrooms and three baths. The third bath was downstairs in the basement, and it had been converted into a darkroom.

"The woman who owns the house is an amateur photographer," Elizabeth explained. "She develops and prints her own photographs. I understand you're a photographer, too."

"He's a very good photographer," said Louise.

"I'll have to keep you in mind," said Elizabeth.

The darkroom was surprisingly complete. The woman had installed an expensive water-filter and temperature-control unit and had built a really nice redwood bench to hold the developing trays. There were overhead safe lights and a long square table for the enlarger. The toilet was covered by the table. "She uses the sink to wash the film," Elizabeth told Louise. "And that wire above the tub is for hanging the negatives."

It was a good-sized room. The window had been blacked out, and the door had seals all around.

"What do you think, Will?"

"She did a good job," I said. "My first darkroom was about half this size and not near as nice."

Louise slapped my shoulder. "Not the darkroom . . . the house."

Elizabeth smiled at me, and I smiled back. "I like the house, too."

Harlen was full of suggestions.

"You got to get moved in right away, Will. Women have a way of taking over. Man's got to mark out his territory or there won't be anything left. You give your notice yet?"

"I'm not moving in, Harlen."

"Have you talked to Louise?"

"No."

"Will, why do you think she bought a house with a darkroom? Why, she's probably been looking for a house with a darkroom for months."

"It just happened to be there."

"Four bedrooms, too?"

"She wanted a big house."

Harlen put his hands between his knees and

rocked forward. "A big house with a darkroom. Think about it, Will."

Louise bought the house, and two months later, Harlen and Floyd and Elwood and three of Louise's brothers and me drove our cars and trucks over to Louise's apartment, packed up her things, drove to the new house and helped move her in.

Harlen hadn't given up. As we carried in the stuffed chair, he said, "Where you want this, Will?" And, when Floyd and Elwood took the bed off the truck and asked Harlen where it should go, Harlen said, "You better ask Will."

Harlen even went downstairs to the darkroom and said, "Boy, looks like the kind of room a real professional could appreciate. Too bad it's going to waste." And he said it loud enough for the neighbours on both sides of Louise to hear.

We started moving at about noon and by five-thirty that evening, Louise and South Wing were in their new home.

Louise caught me as I was bringing in the last box. "Will," she said, "why don't you stay? I'll find a couple of pans and make us dinner. You can use the shower."

Louise gave Harlen thirty dollars. "Take the boys out for pizza or something. I really appreciate you guys helping me move."

I walked Harlen to his car. "Louise is just waiting for you to ask." He smiled and patted my shoulder. "Better do it before she gets those boxes unpacked."

Louise was able to find one pan. We discovered a package of hamburger that hadn't made it into the freezer. It was beginning to thaw, so Louise cooked it up and threw it on top of a pot of noodles with some butter and ketchup.

South Wing fell asleep between the boxes, and I set her crib up and put her in it. Louise wandered around the house, looking at the rooms. We tried to find the box with the toothpaste and the soap and the shampoo, and after a half an hour of looking, we gave up and fell into bed.

We made love that night, and afterwards, Louise rolled over and said, "Will, do you ever think about us?"

"Sure."

"You know what I mean."

"Sure."

"Will . . ." And she reached down and pinched me. "I'm serious. You ever think of us living together?"

"Sometimes."

"Well, what do you think?"

The blankets on the bed were heavy. I was beginning to sweat.

"I'm not saying we should," Louise propped herself up on one elbow. "It's just that sometimes it gets lonely with just South Wing."

"You've got me."

Louise curled up against me. "This is nice, Will," she said. "Don't mind me. It's just the new house."

There were another fifteen people in the kitchen. Susan was in an apron at the sink, talking with two other women.

"Will." And she turned off the water, shook her hands and gave me a hug. "I told you not to bring anything."

I didn't know anyone. Susan had her arms around my waist. "I'm sorry about what happened, Will. When all this calms down, we'll talk."

She took the bottle and put it on the drain board. "Jane, Alice, this is Will, the photographer I told you about. Will, this is Jane and this is Alice."

"Susan tells us you're Native, too," said Alice. "Kind of ironic, isn't it? I mean, being a photographer."

"What?"

"You know . . . the way Indians feel about photographs."

I got a glass of punch from the bowl in the middle of the table and looked around for a corner. Susan found me standing by a bookcase in the living room. "Come on," she said. "I'll give you a tour."

We started upstairs. "There's hardwood under the carpet upstairs and down. Alice says I should take the carpet up."

"Hardwood's nice."

"I've got to do the bathroom first, though. See what I mean?"

The bathroom was large. It had an old clawfoot tub and a pedestal sink. Someone had rigged a shower to the tub, but they hadn't done a very good job. The linoleum around the toilet was curling and starting to come up. There was a rather strong smell of urine.

"The family I bought the house from had three boys. God, but they must have all practised missing the toilet." Susan turned off the light and walked down the hall. "Come on. There are only two bedrooms, but they're both large. Did you ever meet Meg and Beth?"

Meg and Beth were sitting on a bed watching television. Meg looked up and smiled. "Hi, again," she said, and went back to watching the show. Beth was asleep.

"You've already met?"

"He was at the door. I thought he was Jerry."

"Jerry?" Susan looked at me and smiled. "This isn't Jerry, honey. This is Will."

"That's what he said."

"Why don't you turn that off and get ready for bed."

"It's almost over."

"When it's over, it's time for bed."

"I can't sleep with all that noise downstairs."

"Beth is sleeping just fine."

"Beth is boring."

The other bedroom was smaller. Susan closed the door behind us. "I'm going to fix this up, too, but the bathroom is first." She sat on the edge of the bed. "I'm sorry about the way I left, Will, but I needed to get away. It wasn't just Ralph. It was me. I kept giving my life away to people. To Ralph. To you. There was nothing left for me.

"You know what I've discovered? I don't really have to have someone. I can do everything myself. Men are used to that, but I never knew I could do it all by myself. Life, I mean."

I said I understood.

"That's what Ralph said, too. You're both sweet. There's something I wanted to tell you, and I didn't want to do it in a letter or over the phone."

I was feeling uncomfortable, standing there in Susan's bedroom, but I didn't want to sit down either.

"Things have changed, Will. I have a job, house, my two girls, and a new life. It's kind of exciting. You know what I mean?"

"Sure."

"So, that's what I had to say." Susan got up and took my arm. "I want you to be happy, Will. Come on, there's someone you should meet."

We went downstairs. If anything, there were more people now than before. Susan worked her way through the crowd to a grey-haired man in a blue suit.

"Let me guess," I said, extending my hand. "This is Jerry."

Susan shook her head and started to laugh. "No, Will. This is Ralph."

The next morning, Louise was up and in the shower before I had even rolled over for the first time. I lay there in bed listening to the water run. South Wing was moving. I could hear her beginning to cry. I found her standing in her crib with her arms stretched out and tears in her eyes. She wasn't awake yet, so I brought her back to bed with me.

Louise found us that way, South Wing rolled up like a sow bug next to me. "You guys . . . come on, I've got unpacking to do, and you have to go to work."

"Today's Sunday. I don't work on Sunday."

"What about the football games?"

"What games?"

I stayed in the shower as long as I could, and thought of ways to bring up the subject of living together. There was plenty of room, so we wouldn't get in each other's way. A darkroom at home would be nice. Maybe Harlen was right. Maybe Louise was just waiting for me to ask. Maybe she wasn't sure and was hoping that I would make the first move.

South Wing was in her chair, eating cereal. Louise had her head in a large box. "You want breakfast, Will?"

"Sure."

"Okay. You look in the big box in the corner."

"What for?"

"Breakfast."

We had graham crackers, cheese and tea. The kitchen looked like a trash bin. South Wing disappeared into the living room. We could hear her rattling around in the boxes.

"God," said Louise, "where will I begin?"

"Better start in the kitchen. You got to eat."

I stayed around and helped move some of the furniture and a few of the boxes. I couldn't think of a good way to bring the subject up. I left after lunch. Louise walked me to the door. "Why don't you come back tonight? Place will be in better order. Besides," she said, and she gave me a kiss, "moving makes me horny."

For the next week, I spent every night at Louise's new house. And every day, Harlen was at the studio offering advice.

"Take a few clothes over and leave them there.

"Do some of the repairs. Show her how handy you are.

"Ask her if it's okay to store some of your photographic equipment in her darkroom.

"Maybe walk her past Herron's jewellery, and see what she says."

I had to work Saturday morning, and when I got to Louise's a big white panel truck was just pulling away from the house. Louise was in the living room, lying on the couch. All the boxes were gone.

"What happened to all the boxes? I was beginning to like them."

"Will, I will never do this again. I think everything is finally away."

"This the end of sex?"

Louise got up and gave me a long hug. "As a matter of fact, it is. I've got a bladder infection. I've got some medication, but it's going to be cuddling for the next few days."

"Too much sex?"

"Too much sex."

"Come on," said Louise. "I want to show you something." And she headed into the basement.

"The plumbing people came by today," she said. "What do you think?"

The darkroom was gone. There were holes where the water pipes and the filter had been, and you could still see the line against the wall where the table had stood.

"I've got some people coming on Monday who are going to repair the tile, put down some new linoleum and do the drywall. I figured I could paint it myself."

Harlen was upset when I told him. First he was upset with me. Then he was upset with Louise. "You see what I mean, Will? Formidable. You just don't know what people like that are going to do. There's two bathrooms there already. What does she need a third one for?"

But I could see her point. I really could. And I wasn't upset at all. "You can always use another bathroom," I told Harlen. "She doesn't need a dark-room."

"It's symbolic, Will. Formidable people are always doing those things."

After a while, though, Harlen, who can always find a place where the sun shines, agreed that maybe we didn't need a darkroom after all, that having three bathrooms in the house would be better, especially if there were more children.

When Harlen gets like that, I just let him go.

I didn't talk to Ralph. He went with Susan on a tour of the house. Susan said I should mingle, that I should talk to Alice. I found a quiet corner instead and listened to other people's conversations for a while. Then I got my coat and left. I was half-way across the front yard when I remembered I was in Pickering.

"Nice night."

Alice was standing on the porch. She was just buttoning up her coat. "Susan said you might leave early and that you would probably need a ride."

"I thought I'd catch the train."

"Too late," said Alice. "The last one left an hour ago. Come on. I don't mind."

We got in Alice's car. She put on her seat-belt and started the engine.

"Where's the nuclear power plant?" I asked.

"You can't see it from here," said Alice. "You want to drive by it?"

"No."

"It's not out of the way. By the way, where do you live?"

I turned in my seat and looked back at the house. "Medicine River."

"Where the hell is that?"

"Just west of Toronto."

Alice put the car into gear. "I'll take you as far as Toronto," she laughed, "and from there you'll have to walk."

Louise got over her bladder infection. Harlen got over his disappointment. I got over four hundred dollars worth of filters, mixers and thermometers that Louise had asked the plumber to save for me. Even Harlen thought that that was nice.

Louise stayed in her new house, and I stayed in my apartment. Everything considered, it was probably just one of those times in life that we would all laugh about in the years to come.

seventeen

I liked to spend my Sundays watching sports on television. It didn't matter what sport. I enjoyed them all. I'd get up in the morning around ten and pour some cereal in a bowl and turn on the television. Cartoons were on for the first hour, and I'd eat and watch Coyote chase Road Runner or Elmer Fudd chase Bugs Bunny or Sylvester chase Tweety. Around eleven, a baseball game or a football game or a basketball game would come on, and I'd watch the Blue Jays chase the Yankees or the Vikings chase the Rams or the Bucks chase the Rockets.

It was a waste of a Sunday. I knew that. But it was relaxing, and to be honest, I enjoyed it.

Louise, on the other hand, spent her Sundays going to yard sales. She'd get the paper on Saturday and spend part of Saturday night marking all the ones that sounded interesting. She would even plan a route so that she could get from one sale to the next with the least amount of backtracking. There was a wonderful feeling of organization and efficiency to the lists she produced. But aside from the occasional toy or book, she seldom came back with anything.

My mother went to yard sales, too. There was hardly a Sunday went by that my mother wasn't off looking in a garage or a backyard, sifting through tables piled high with toasters and dishes and lava lamps and digging in boxes stuffed with old issues of *Reader's Digest*, paperback romances, clothing and car parts. She shopped with a vengeance, rifling the tables, quickly sorting the occasional find from the junk.

"Try this on," my mother would tell me. And if it didn't fit, if it was too small, she'd try it on James.

The clothes I grew up in had all belonged to other people. But it should be said that my mother was a careful shopper. Most of the clothes or shoes or jackets she brought home looked brand new.

"Maybe you'll take a dollar for this," she'd say about an item marked four-fifty.

"This has got a tear in it. Maybe you'll take fifty cents.

"Place down the street has one of these for two-fifty.

"My friend says Woolworth's got the same thing on special for five dollars. Brand new."

She continued to go to yard sales after I left for Toronto, and each Christmas, I'd receive a package with a shirt or a pair of pants or a tie. Each present was clean and pressed and folded as though it had just been taken out of the plastic wrapper.

Louise called me Saturday night.

"Will," she said, "what are you doing tomorrow morning?"

"Got some work to do."

"There's a big estate sale over on Ninth Avenue. You've been looking for a couch, haven't you?"

"For what?"

"They may even have a lamp, too."

"I don't need a couch."

"It won't take long. I could use your good judgement. You know, your artistic eye. We'll be done by noon."

The game I really wanted to see was the San Francisco Forty-Niners and the Dallas Cowboys. It didn't start until two.

"How about I pick you up early tomorrow?" Louise said.

"How early?"

"Nine o'clock?"

"Couldn't we go at ten?"

"Good stuff will be gone by then."

Harlen called half an hour later. "Hey, Will, ready for the big game?"

"Your television not working again?"

"Television's fine. Jumps a bit still. Thought you might like some company. You know, throw the ball around at half-time. I could bring chips and soda."

"I've got to go out with Louise tomorrow morning. Estate sale on Ninth Avenue."

"Hey," said Harlen. "That must be Mrs. Gedaman. She died a while back. You mind if I come?"

"Call Louise. She said nine o'clock."

My doorbell rang at seven o'clock. By the time I struggled out of bed, Harlen was already in the kitchen. "Hey, Will, where'd you put the coffee?"

Louise was standing in the front room with South Wing. "Can I use the bathroom, Will? South Wing needs to be changed."

"Never mind," said Harlen. "I found it."

Louise came out of the bathroom. "Take a quick shower, and I'll make you some breakfast. We've got to get going."

"What happened to nine o'clock?"

"Big estate sale like this, we need to be there early. All the good things get sold first. Harlen said we should get there before nine."

There was a cup of coffee and a bowl of cereal waiting for me on the back of the toilet when I stepped out of the shower.

"No need to shave, Will," shouted Harlen. "We'll meet you in the car."

My mother was like that. Every Sunday, she'd drag us out of bed at around seven-thirty, and we'd be out the door by eight-thirty. We didn't have a car, so we walked to the yard sales. My mother had short legs, but they moved relentlessly. She could walk for hours, and she never wasted a moment. Most times she could look in a garage or at a table and be able to tell with a glance if there was anything there that she wanted. James and me would hardly have a chance to look through the broken toys or the games before she'd give us a nod and head on down the street.

By the time we got to the estate sale, there were cars parked around the block. Couples were wandering along in front of the house, moving back and forth like sentries.

"See?" said Harlen. "Almost too late."

By eight-thirty, the people had stopped walking and were just standing there on the sidewalk. At a quarter to nine, the garage doors opened, and a short fellow in a red windbreaker came out and said, "Most of the stuff is in the garage, but there's some furniture and appliances in the house."

Louise and Harlen all but ran into the garage. South Wing and I stayed by the curb and let the stampede pass us by. "Come on, honey," I said to South Wing, and I took her hand. "Let's go in the house and see what's happening."

There wasn't much in the house. The guy in the red jacket was standing by the kitchen door.

"You have any couches for sale?"

"Afraid not," he said. "Most of the good stuff went to my brothers and sisters. There are a couple of beds left. You need any beds?"

"I've got a bed."

"My mother had a lot of antiques. You should have seen the place before we cleaned it up. There was stuff everywhere. She died last month. Took us three weeks just to organize it."

"I'm sorry about that."

"What?"

"Your mother."

"Oh, yeah."

"I know how you feel."

"Oh, yeah."

I was in Toronto when my mother died. I didn't even know she was sick. James didn't know, either. She kept things like that to herself. James came home from work and found her in bed. She was just feeling tired, she said. James took her to the hospital that evening.

"Will, Will, where you been? Hey, come on out here." Harlen was standing by the sliding glass door that led to the backyard. "You got to see what we found."

I picked up South Wing, and we followed Harlen.

"Look at this, Will. What do you think?"

It was a canoe. There was some wood piled up against it, and it was covered with dirt. Most of it was painted orange or pink, but you could see that there were other, darker colours underneath.

"What do you think?"

"A canoe?"

"Sure. Hey, I've been wanting to go canoeing. It would be fun. You know, you and me out on a river. Just like our grandparents used to do."

"The Blackfoot didn't use canoes."

"Sure they did. Some of the world's greatest canoeists."

The canoe was made out of wood and canvas, and it was in bad shape. The canvas had come loose in several places. One of the gunwales was cracked, and some of the ribs were broken.

"It's your money," I told Harlen.

"Not me," said Harlen. "You need to buy it. Get you out of the house on the weekends. You could use the exercise."

"I play basketball."

"Sure, but there's nothing like canoeing for the back and shoulders. Didn't you use to canoe back in Toronto?"

"Harlen, this thing is falling apart."

"Nothing we can't fix."

"I don't need a canoe, Harlen."

The guy in the red jacket came out. "That was my mother's canoe. You know, she was still using it until she fell and broke her hip. Give you a good price on it."

"Looks a little beat up," said Harlen.

"Give you a good price on it."

Harlen leaned up against my shoulder. "Offer him

fifty dollars, Will."

"I don't need a canoe." And I turned to Louise, who is always sensible in these matters. "I don't need a canoe."

Louise looked at the canoe and shrugged. "It might be fun."

We got my truck and came back to pick up the canoe. The guy in the red jacket helped us load it.

"Here," he said, "I found this in a box. You can have it. That's a good canoe. My mother really liked it."

"Look, Will," said Harlen. "It's a canoe book on the rivers around here. This is great. We can get the canoe fixed up and go canoeing next week."

James stayed with my mother in the hospital. The first day she was there, he tried to call, but it was a weekend, and I was off with friends. "You know what she worried about, Will? Each time I got to her room, she'd tell me to turn down the lights because they were wasting electricity. You know, like she used to tell us to do at home."

My mother talked a lot there in the hospital. James said she remembered all sorts of things that we had done. "She went on and on about that big black dog that used to chase us, until she gave us those squirt bottles filled with vinegar. You remember that dog? She even remembered about Henry and you and me and that dryer. And that trip to Lake Pokagon . . . you know, when we sank." James was with her each evening. "She talked about you a lot, Will."

The canoe sat in Harlen's backyard for a month. I didn't have any room for it at my place. We fixed the canvas and the ribs and put a few screws in the gunwales to keep it from cracking any more.

"We got to paint it, Will," Harlen told me. "Not sure I want to be seen in a pink canoe."

So we got some paint. Green. Dark green. Harlen had looked through some of the magazines at the Smoke Shop. "You get some that are yellow or blue, but the classy ones, Will, are all painted dark green."

The canoe looked pretty good. Louise and South Wing were there the day it was finished.

"You ever been canoeing?" she asked me.

One year, my mother saved up some money and took us to Lake Pokagon. There were some cabins you could rent, and we took some blankets and an old barbecue and some fruit and oil and salt and flour. We were going to rent a boat, my mother told us, and catch our own fish.

We wanted to rent a canoe, but my mother said a row-boat was safer. James and me got to row. My mother sat in the bow and gave directions. We were just beginning to row really good when we hit the rock.

We hit the rock hard, and it broke one of the planks in the boat. We sat there, the three of us, and the water began to pour in through the hole. We must have been a hundred yards from shore. James and me tried to paddle off the rock, but the boat was stuck and we were starting to sink. I looked at my mother.

"We going to die?" asked James.

"Next weekend," said Harlen, with a big grin on his face. "Next weekend, we go canoeing. I got the place all picked out."

The place was the upper part of the Medicine River where it cut through a long winding sandstone canyon. "'The first four miles,'" Harlen read aloud, "'are relatively easy with gentle and easily negotiated rapids. After you pass a farmhouse on the right, the river picks up speed and two- to three-foot standing waves are formed near the cliff face on the right. . . .' This sounds great, doesn't it?"

"Sounds a little dangerous," said Louise.

"Can't take you on the first trip, Louise," said Harlen. "Got to check it out and see if it's safe."

"Oh," said Louise, and she shook her head. "I feel better already."

"You can bring the lunch," said Harlen.

Harlen always has a plan, and most of the time, the plan gets changed or postponed or lost. The plan was for Louise and South Wing and Harlen and me to drive to the old Springvale bridge. We'd put the canoe in there, and Louise and South Wing could watch us as we took off downstream.

After we were out of sight, Louise was to drive down to the blue bridge just north of Reynolds and wait for us there. There was a small beach near the bridge, and Louise and South Wing could play in the water or something until we got there. Louise listened to the plan.

"So you guys want me to make you a lunch and be your taxi service?"

"Doing it for your own safety," said Harlen.

"I'll drop you off and pick you up," said Louise. "You can make your own lunch."

Sunday was a bright, sunny day. We took off at ten o'clock and, using Harlen's directions, were lost by eleven. We had to go back into Reynolds to try to find the right road.

"Never heard of that road," the attendant at the Reynolds Petro-Can told us. "Maybe you want the

Snake Road."

We tried three or four of the gravel roads. We saw a skunk and some ducks and lots of horses and cows. It was three o'clock before we stumbled on the bridge.

"Here it is," said Harlen.

"Thank God," said Louise.

It took another half an hour to get the canoe and the life vests and the paddles down to the river. Harlen looked at the book again. "First four miles are easy, Will. We can practise our strokes, before we get into the hard stuff."

Louise took South Wing by the hand. "We're going to go up on the bluff, honey, so we can watch the boys play with their boat."

"It's only a canoe trip," I said.

Louise stopped and smiled. South Wing had her arms around her mother's neck and was smiling at me. "Be careful," Louise said.

Harlen was bubbling with anticipation. "You get in the back, Will. The guy in the front should be more experienced. Has to call out all those critical turns, and watch out for the rocks."

So I got in the back, and Harlen got in the front. "Paddle left," Harlen shouted, and we were in the river. The first part was over a gravel bed, shallow and fast. I could see the bottom.

"Paddle right," Harlen shouted.

The river deepened, and the canoe rolled in the heavy waves. We swung past a tree that had fallen into the water, and Harlen guided the canoe around it.

I looked back and could see Louise waving to us.

"Paddle right," Harlen shouted. There was white water up ahead, but the waves didn't look very big. "White water," shouted Harlen. "Head left."

The canoe shot forward, and the waves that hadn't looked very big from a distance were suddenly hitting the bow. Everything happened quickly.

The first wave broke on the bow and poured in over us. The second followed the first.

"Bail!" shouted Harlen. "Bail! Will, bail!"

We didn't have anything to bail with, and it was already too late. The canoe lurched and twisted over on its side, and both Harlen and me were thrown into the river and swept away by the current. Harlen was behind me, and as I looked to find him, I was driven onto a rock, trapped there for a moment by the force of the water, and then snatched away again. Harlen was in the swifter current. As he shot by me, I could see his eyes staring through the spray, his mouth open.

"Will, Will," he shouted, above the thunder of the rapids.

"I'm here, I'm here." I tried to grab his life vest, but he was gone before I could reach him.

"Wiiiilllll," he shouted, as he plunged on into the next set of waves. "Damn, Will, if this isn't fun. Yahoooo!"

I floundered into smoother water, and my feet found the bottom. Louise was waving to me from the far bank. She was shouting something, but I couldn't hear what it was. South Wing ran back and forth on the bluff, alive with excitement.

Harlen washed ashore near a small island out of the current. He lay there in the water on his back, laughing, looking like a great yellow and orange garbage bag.

"Yahooooo!"

I stood in the shallow water, dripping and shivering, and watched the river cut its way past the sandstone cliffs. Harlen came splashing across the rocks like a retriever.

"Hey, Will, wasn't that great! What a ride!" He walked up on the bank, pulled his hair back, wrung out his hat and looked at the river. "Hey," he said, "where's the canoe?"

We found the canoe farther downstream, its nose buried in a sandbar, its green belly floating up in the sun. Both gunwales were broken and the canvas was ripped. We turned it over and emptied out the water.

"You know, Will," Harlen said. "We should have stayed to the right. Next time we stay to the right."

We dragged the canoe back up the river, stumbling and splashing and cursing and laughing. Harlen still had that book. It was soaking wet, the pages stuck together. "The first four miles," Harlen roared, "are relatively easy with gentle and easily negotiated rapids. . . ."

The sun dropped below the rim of the canyon, and the river was suddenly in deep shadows. The air cooled, and Harlen's teeth began to chatter.

My mother died on a Tuesday in the early evening. My clearest memory of her was that day the row-boat sank in Lake Pokagon. I remember my fear of sinking into that lake. James wouldn't let go of the side of the boat. I was sure we were going to die. And then my mother snorted as her short legs found the bottom. The lake wasn't deep at all, at least not there. It hardly came above James's chest, and it was warm. My mother shook her head. "Well, we ain't going to die today." And she laughed and told us to hold onto her hands.

As Harlen and I pulled the canoe along, I could feel

the large round stones under my feet, could hear the
hollow roll they made as they rocked beneath me,
and I thought about my mother and James and me,
laughing and walking through the mud and the
water to shore. James was with her when she died. I
should have been there, too.

The river swirled around us, sucking at our feet,
flashing at our legs as we went. Harlen began singing
a forty-niner, beating out the rhythm on the gunwales. And we brought the canoe back through the
dark water and into the light.

chapter

eighteen

David Plume was arrested on Saturday. I heard about it on Monday from Big John Yellow Rabbit when Big John came in to pick up his passport pictures. He heard it from Sam Belly who was in Cardston buying a bag of cookies and a jar of marshmallow whip at the Red Rooster. Sam didn't see it happen, but he saw the three police cars pull away from in front of the pizza parlour with their lights flashing. Sam Belly is almost as curious as Harlen, and as he walked up the street to see what was going on, he ran into Verna Green who had been in Paul's Pizza Time when the RCMP arrived and arrested David and three of his friends.

"Verna told Sam that the boys had just sat down to eat," Big John told me. "It was one of those specials Paul makes up with all the olives and tomatoes. Verna said the police made them leave the pizza there on the table. You'd think they'd let them eat the pizza. It's probably David's big mouth got him in trouble again."

Late Tuesday morning, Harlen came by the studio. "Will, you alive back there? I brought us some lunch." Which meant Harlen was going to stay for a while. Normally I didn't mind, but the Christmas season was busy, and I was behind.

"We got a problem."

Seasons had no effect on Harlen's problems.

"I've already had lunch, Harlen."

"Sausage," said Harlen, "from the Warsaw. The hot ones with the peppercorns."

The Warsaw's sausages were tasty, and they were hot, and the last time I made the mistake of eating one, I had stomach cramps the rest of the day and gas all night. But the main problem was the peppercorns. There were probably a dozen rock-hard, pellet-sized black peppercorns in each sausage, and part of the adventure of eating a Warsaw sausage was in guessing where the peppercorns were. It was like walking through a minefield with your mouth.

By the time I got to the front, Harlen had arranged himself a modest place setting on the coffee table and had just cut off a piece of sausage. "You know, Will, whenever I'm feeling queasy, I get a Warsaw sausage, and the next day, I feel fine. You sure you don't want one?"

I shook my head. "You want some coffee? Big John's already told me about David Plume."

"What about David Plume?"

"Didn't you come by to tell me that David Plume got himself arrested over in Cardston?"

"Arrested?" And Harlen stopped eating.

Harlen had come to tell me that Billie Camp was pregnant. Pete Good Shield, Billie's boyfriend and the father of the child, had come to Harlen to ask his help in breaking the news to Billie's parents.

"What did David get arrested for this time?"

"What about Billie and Pete?"

"No rush there. Billie's only two months along."

So I told Harlen what I knew. It wasn't much, and Harlen, not being one to take his information second-hand, finished my sausage, drank his coffee, told me to think of a good way to tell Billie's parents that they were going to be grandparents, and left.

In the meantime, Kevin Longbird, Gary Frank and Amos Morley were all released from jail. But the police didn't release David, and it didn't look like they were going to.

The *Medicine River Herald* carried the story. Ray Little Buffalo had been shot in the stomach. He was found in Chinook Park by the river. David had been arrested and held for questioning, but it was a back page story, and there weren't many details. For that, I had to wait for Harlen.

Harlen caught me at my apartment. He rang the doorbell once and then walked in. I didn't even bother to get out of my chair. "Fresh coffee in the kitchen," I said. "Help yourself."

"You read the newspaper, Will?" he said, as he rattled around for a cup.

"Every evening about this time."

"You read about Ray and David?"

"Almost made the front page."

"Did it say anything about David's jacket?" Harlen came out of the kitchen with a cup of coffee and the last of the fried chicken. "Hope you don't mind, Will. Real hungry. Been working hard."

"Got some leftover pizza, too."

"This is fine," said Harlen. "You remember that jacket that David always wears around?"

"You mean the red one?"

"When they found Ray," said Harlen, tearing a mouthful off the chicken leg, "he was wearing it."

"David's jacket?"

"Yep."

"That's crazy. David wouldn't let Ray wear his jacket. David wouldn't let *you* wear his jacket."

"Doesn't make any sense alright."

My mother had a favourite expression for all those times in life when things didn't make sense or couldn't be explained. "That's the way things are," she'd say. It wasn't an answer. It was more a way of managing the bad times. A lot of people like to blame those kinds of things on everything from luck to God. My mother would just shrug and get on with what she was doing. She'd use it when James and me asked those questions that kids will ask. "Why doesn't Dad come home?" "How come Henry got a bike for Christmas?" "How come the television doesn't ever work right?" She would just shrug and say, "That's the way things are."

"Just doesn't make any sense." Harlen finished his coffee and went back into the kitchen for another cup. "Where's that pizza, Will?"

About two months ago, David was in the American, just back from one of his trips. He was wearing the jacket, and he started bragging about Wounded Knee again. Ray had heard all the stories before, and he could have made allowances, but he didn't. "Hey," Ray said to David, "what does AIM mean? Friend of mine says it stands for Assholes in Moccasins."

David turned his back on Ray and said, so that everyone could hear, that he'd rather be an asshole

than an apple or a coward. Ray got out of his chair
and went over and stood at the bar next to David. "I
hear that most of those AIM peckers are ex-cons and
perverts."

Tony Balonca who was tending bar saw the fight
coming before it even started and called the police.
Ray and David were still staring each other down
when they arrived.

"Is this from Santucci's?" Harlen held up the last
bite of pizza.

"Heat it in the microwave."

"It's good cold."

"You figure it was David?"

Harlen finished the rest of the pizza. "David
wouldn't have given his jacket to Ray, that's for
sure."

David didn't give his jacket to Ray. By the time
Harlen dropped by the studio on Wednesday, he had
all the details. According to Amos Morley, who told
his mother who told Eddie Weaselhead down at the
centre who told Harlen, Ray and three of his friends
caught David behind the American Hotel and beat
him up. "Damn, Will," Harlen told me, "after they
beat him up, Ray took that jacket. Ray's a lot bigger
than David, and when he tried to put the jacket on,
you know, just to tease David, he ripped it."
According to Harlen, David jumped back up and
started swinging again, and Ray beat on him some
more. After it was over, David went into the
American to wash the blood off and then went to his
apartment and got his deer rifle. He found Ray down
by the river drinking and throwing rocks at the
empty bottles. Ray was still wearing the jacket.

"That jacket," said Harlen, "must have been real important to David; you know, like a woman or children."

"No jacket is worth killing someone for."

"What do you mean?"

"David. You know. Killing Ray like that."

Harlen shook his head. "David didn't kill anybody. You got it wrong, Will. I thought you knew."

"Knew what?"

"Well, you know that Ray beat up David and took his jacket?"

"Yeah."

"And you know that David got his rifle and went looking for Ray?"

"I know that, too."

"David found him and started shooting at him. But he missed. When he ran out of bullets, he went home."

"Who shot Ray?"

"Ray wasn't shot. The papers sort of got that mixed up. When David started shooting, Ray tried to get out of the way, but he slipped and fell on the bottle he had in his pocket. Cut his stomach pretty bad. At first, everybody thought Ray had been shot, but he was just cut and drunk."

"That was lucky."

"David never was much of a shot."

When James and me were kids, my mother bought us a ball. It was just one of those cheap, pink rubber ones. James really loved that ball, spent most of his time after school bouncing the ball and catching it. The ball was for the both of us, but I guess James came to think of it as his own. We were playing with it down by the river one day, and I threw it too far. I didn't mean to. It just went into the water and disappeared.

James ran along the bank looking for that ball, and

I guess, after a while, I laughed a bit. I didn't like losing it, but it was funny watching him run along the
shore looking for it in the dark water. James kept
looking, and when he finally came back up the bank,
there were tears in his eyes. He picked up a rock and
threw it at me as hard as he could, and then he ran all
the way home.

"A jacket," said Harlen, "is a poor substitute for
friends and family. I told David that."

"What'd he say?"

Harlen turned his head and looked at the pictures
on the wall. "He said he didn't have any friends."

About once a week, Louise would make dinner,
and I'd go over. It had gotten to be a habit. Louise
and I had gotten to be a habit, and all things considered, it was a good habit. When I got there Thursday
night, South Wing was waiting for me by the door.

"Weeb, Weeb, Weeb," she said and held out her
arms. "Weeb, Mummy, Weeb."

Louise was in the kitchen. I picked South Wing up
and spun her around.

"Pee-pee, pee-pee, Weeb."

Louise laughed. "You got here just in time. It's toilet training. You want a turn?"

South Wing was already climbing down my side.
"Pee-pee, Weeb, pee-pee."

"Dinner's not quite ready yet, anyway. She'd love
to show you her new toilet. Do you mind?"

"What do I do?"

Louise shook her head. "Men. Just watch her and
make sure she doesn't fall in."

"I can do that."

South Wing ran into the bathroom, and I followed.
There was a red plastic ladder contraption with a

toilet seat that fit over the regular seat. South Wing was already half-way up the ladder.

"Me," she said, and she sat on the toilet and rocked back and forth. "Me, me, me, me."

"Is this your new toilet seat?"

"Me."

"Can you go to the bathroom all by yourself?"

"Me."

"Maybe you should take your diaper off?"

"No!"

"How can you go to the bathroom with your diaper on?"

"Me."

I ran out of questions long before Louise called us for dinner.

"Did you show Uncle Will how you go to the bathroom?"

"Pee-pee, Mummy, pee-pee!"

"Did she do anything?"

"I don't think so."

"I don't suppose you looked."

"She didn't want to take her diaper off."

Louise laughed. "She just sat there, right?"

"Right."

"You know, Will, I paid thirty-five dollars for that thing."

"She sure says pee-pee well."

"Now if she'd only do it," Louise said. "Will's a hard name for kids to pronounce."

"Weeb's close enough," I said.

"Weeb," said South Wing.

After dinner, Louise did the dishes, and I got to give South Wing a bath.

"Will, could you put her sleeper on, too?"

"Sure, no trouble."

"That was awful about Ray, wasn't it, Will?"

"Crazy."

"All that over a jacket!"

James stopped looking for the ball after about fifteen minutes, but he stood down by the river for a long time. I finally shouted at him to come on up, that it was getting late. He didn't yell at me like I thought he would, and I almost said I was sorry about the ball, but I didn't. Instead, I told him to forget about the ball, and he leaned down and ran his hand over the gravel until he found a large stone.

"I just don't understand people doing things like that."

"It's the way things are."

Louise made some coffee, and we sat on the couch. Christmas was less than a week away, and I still hadn't got anything for South Wing. "What do you think South Wing would like for Christmas?"

"She'd like anything, Will. Maybe a doll."

"Okay, maybe I'll get her a doll."

"Sarah at the day home has a toy phone that she likes to play with, too. Anything'll be okay."

"Maybe I could stay over Christmas Eve. We could open presents or go for a walk or something."

"Or something, huh?" Louise smiled and shifted around on the couch. "That's what I wanted to talk to you about, Will. I've made some plans for Christmas."

"Your folks?"

"No."

"You going somewhere?"

"Yes."

"Do I keep guessing?"

Louise sighed and put down her coffee. "Will, South Wing and I are going to Edmonton for Christmas."

"What's in Edmonton?"

"Harold."

It's funny the things you forget. I'd completely forgotten about Harold. "You mean Harold . . . South Wing's . . ."

"That's right, Will, South Wing's father. You know, he calls maybe twice a month. He's even come down just to see her. I've always felt bad about the way I treated him. He's a nice guy. You'd like him."

"No, I wouldn't."

Louise laughed and shook her head. "Yes, you would, Will. He wants to see South Wing, and he wants his folks to see her, too. He's really very sweet, and she is his daughter. So, I said that I would. I'll only be gone four days. We can have Christmas when we get back."

"Does this mean we can't live together?" I laughed when I said it.

"It doesn't mean anything, Will. I don't love him, any more."

"I know," I said, still smiling. "He's South Wing's father. I understand, really."

"That's right," Louise said. "He is South Wing's father."

I stopped by Harlen's on the way home.

"Hey, Will," said Harlen, "glad you stopped by. Say, listen, my sister is having a big dinner at her place Christmas Eve. She said to invite you and Louise and South Wing. You know Howard Webster. He married Annie Whiteman. Real goofy guy. He's going to be there, too. Real good food. Norma's a good cook."

"Louise and South Wing are going up to Edmonton for Christmas."

"What's up there?"

I spent Christmas Eve alone in my apartment. It was no big deal. I'd done it before. I could have gone to the Lodge or the Pearl for dinner, or I could have gone out to the reserve with Harlen. Instead, I toasted up a cheese and tomato sandwich and opened a can of green beans and watched the news.

It wasn't the best Christmas I could remember. Louise and South Wing were in Edmonton with Harold. Harlen was at his sister's place in Standoff. David was in jail. Ray was in the hospital. I wondered how Susan was doing. James was in New Zealand or Australia or somewhere. I hadn't seen him since the funeral.

My mother would have said that that's the way things are, and she might have been right, but I lay in bed, anyway, hoping that James would call, so I could wish him a merry Christmas.

Early the next morning, Louise called to wish me a merry Christmas and to tell me that Harold had proposed, and that he had a ring and everything.

"It was kind of romantic, Will. He stood up in the middle of dinner, just like in the movies, and made this big proposal. Right in front of his folks."

"What'd you say?"

"Well, it was kind of flattering, too, and all I could really do was smile. Can you believe it, Will? During dinner. We talked after his folks went home."

"You're staying at his house?"

"You know, he really wants to marry me."

"And . . . ?"

"He's a nice guy, Will. But I don't want to get married. I told Harold I didn't want to get married. I hurt his feelings, Will. I didn't want to, but I did. We're going to drive back tomorrow."

"What about the ring?"

"Harold said he kept the receipt."

Being alone at Christmas had steeled me. I didn't feel sorry for Harold.

"Will," said Louise, and she said it in that warm way she has, "you know what I like about you? You understand me. Here, South Wing wants to say hello."

"Weeb," said South Wing, "Weeb."

James called just before noon. He was back in San Francisco again and was doing fine. He had a job with a commercial art company. It was a good-paying job, he said, and if things went right, he thought he'd be up in the summer. "I would have called last night, but I was out with a friend. We didn't get in until late."

We talked for a long time. I told him about David and Ray and the red jacket. We talked about being kids in Calgary, about Mom, and he told me I should come down and visit him in San Francisco.

After we got caught up, I asked him about the ball.

"Sure, I remember," he said. "You threw it in the river. I was really angry."

"I didn't do it on purpose. You threw a rock at me."

"That's right, but I missed."

"I just wanted to tell you that I was sorry."

"About the ball?"

"Yes."

James laughed. "Hell, Will."

"I just wanted to say I was sorry."

I put the coffee on and took the musical top out of the bag and tried it on the floor. It made a sweet, humming sound, the pitch changing as it spun in its

perfect circle: red, yellow, blue, green. The scissors
were in the drawer with the knives, and I spent some
time trying to wrap the top. In the end, it looked
awful. The bright blue paper was wrinkled and torn
and pieced together at angles with bits of tape. The
yellow ribbon was wound around the handle and
tied in a pathetic, lop-sided bow. But that was okay.
South Wing was going to love it.

I made lunch. The day had started out overcast, but
standing at the kitchen window, I could see that the
winter sun was out now and lying low on Medicine
River. Later that afternoon, I went for a long walk in
the snow.